Praise
of P

How to H

"Penny Warner's scintillating *How to Host a Killer Party* introduces an appealing heroine whose event skills include utilizing party favors in self-defense in a fun, fast-paced new series guaranteed to please."
—Carolyn Hart, Agatha, Anthony, and Macavity Award–winning author of *Dare to Die*

"Penny Warner blends humor and mayhem to create a unique mystery full of fun."
—Denise Swanson, national bestselling author of *Murder of a Wedding Belle*

"Penny Warner dishes up a rare treat, sparkling with wicked and witty San Francisco characters, plus some real tips on hosting a killer party."
—Rhys Bowen, award-winning author of the Royal Flush and Molly Murphy mysteries

"There's a cozy little party going on between these covers. Don't miss Penny Warner's new series."
—Elaine Viets, author of *Half-Price Homicide*

"Fast, fun, and fizzy as a champagne cocktail! The winning and witty Presley Parker can plan a perfect party—but after her A-list event becomes an invitation to murder, her next plan must be to save her own life."
—Hank Phillippi Ryan, Agatha Award–winning author of *Drive Time*

"A festive romp complete with chocolate, champagne, and murder. Really, it doesn't get much better than this!"
—Joanna Campbell Slan, Agatha Award–nominated author of *Paper, Scissors, Death*

"I love how Penny mixes crime with confetti and crudite."
—Patty Sachs, PartyPlansPlus.com

"The books dish up a banquet of mayhem."
—*The Oakland Tribune* (CA)

continued . . .

"With a promising progression of peculiar plots, and a plethora of party-planning pointers, *How to Host a Killer Party* looks to be a pleasant prospect for cozy-mystery lovers."　　—Fresh Fiction

"Fans will enjoy this fun amateur-sleuth mystery starring a charming party planner who fears her business will go bankrupt if she wears stripes."　　—The Merry Genre Go Round Reviews

"This delightful cozy is filled with suspense, mystery, and a touch of romance. The wonderfully different, eclectic characters are delightful, as well as party-planning tips included at the beginning of each chapter."　　—Reader to Reader Reviews

"[V]ery readable . . . it's no wonder Mrs. Warner is a bestselling author."　　—Once Upon a Romance Reviews

"Warner keeps . . . the reader guessing."　　—Gumshoe

Praise for Penny Warner's
Connor Westphal Mystery Series

Dead Body Language

"Delicious, with a fun, irreverent protagonist."
　　　　　　　　　　　　　　　　—*Publishers Weekly*

"A sprightly, full-fledged heroine, small-town conniptions, frequent humor, and clever plotting."　　—*Library Journal*

"The novel is enlivened by some nice twists, an unexpected villain, a harrowing mortuary scene, its Gold Country locale, and fascinating perspective on a little-known subculture."
　　　　　　　　　　　　　　　　—*San Francisco Chronicle*

"What a great addition to the ranks of amateur sleuths."
　　　　　　　　　　　　—Diane Mott Davidson, *New York Times*
　　　　　　　　　　　　bestselling author of *Fatally Flaky*

HOW TO CRASH A
Killer Bash

A Party-Planning Mystery

PENNY WARNER

AN OBSIDIAN MYSTERY

OBSIDIAN
Published by New American Library, a division of
Penguin Group (USA) Inc., 375 Hudson Street,
New York, New York 10014, USA
Penguin Group (Canada), 90 Eglinton Avenue East, Suite 700, Toronto,
Ontario M4P 2Y3, Canada (a division of Pearson Penguin Canada Inc.)
Penguin Books Ltd., 80 Strand, London WC2R 0RL, England
Penguin Ireland, 25 St. Stephen's Green, Dublin 2,
Ireland (a division of Penguin Books Ltd.)
Penguin Group (Australia), 250 Camberwell Road, Camberwell, Victoria 3124,
Australia (a division of Pearson Australia Group Pty. Ltd.)
Penguin Books India Pvt. Ltd., 11 Community Centre, Panchsheel Park,
New Delhi - 110 017, India
Penguin Group (NZ), 67 Apollo Drive, Rosedale, North Shore 0632,
New Zealand (a division of Pearson New Zealand Ltd.)
Penguin Books (South Africa) (Pty.) Ltd., 24 Sturdee Avenue,
Rosebank, Johannesburg 2196, South Africa

Penguin Books Ltd., Registered Offices:
80 Strand, London WC2R 0RL, England

First published by Obsidian, an imprint of New American Library,
a division of Penguin Group (USA) Inc.

First Printing, August 2010
10 9 8 7 6 5 4 3 2 1

Copyright © Penny Warner, 2010
All rights reserved

OBSIDIAN and logo are trademarks of Penguin Group (USA) Inc.

Printed in the United States of America

Without limiting the rights under copyright reserved above, no part of this publica-
tion may be reproduced, stored in or introduced into a retrieval system, or transmit-
ted, in any form, or by any means (electronic, mechanical, photocopying, recording,
or otherwise), without the prior written permission of both the copyright owner and
the above publisher of this book.

PUBLISHER'S NOTE
This is a work of fiction. Names, characters, places, and incidents either are the
product of the author's imagination or are used fictitiously, and any resemblance to
actual persons, living or dead, business establishments, events, or locales is entirely
coincidental.
    The publisher does not have any control over and does not assume any responsibil-
ity for author or third-party Web sites or their content.

If you purchased this book without a cover you should be aware that this book is
stolen property. It was reported as "unsold and destroyed" to the publisher and neither the author nor the publisher has received any payment for this "stripped book."

The scanning, uploading, and distribution of this book via the Internet or via any
other means without the permission of the publisher is illegal and punishable by law.
Please purchase only authorized electronic editions, and do not participate in or encourage electronic piracy of copyrighted materials. Your support of the author's
rights is appreciated.

To my husband, Tom, who helps me clean up crime scenes. To my kids, Matt and Sue, Rebecca and Mike, who love to party. And to my mother, a continual inspiration in all things.

ACKNOWLEDGMENTS

Many thanks to everyone who helped with this book: To my talented writers' group: Colleen Casey, Janet Finsilver, Staci McLaughlin, Ann Parker, and Carole Price. To Mirian (sic) Saez, Director of Treasure Island Operations, and Marianne Thompson, Treasure Island Development Authority. To Geoff W. E. Pike, my computer guru. To those who prefer to remain nameless: Security Guards at the de Young Museum, and on Treasure Island, Police Officers at the San Francisco Hall of Justice, and Members of the Treasure Island Yacht Club. And to my incredible agents, Andrea Hurst and Amberly Finarelli, and my amazing, insightful editor, Sandra Harding, at Obsidian Books

"Hear no evil, speak no evil—and you'll never be invited to a party."

—Oscar Wilde

Chapter 1

PARTY PLANNING TIP #1

When planning a Murder Mystery Party, make sure you don't use real weapons as props. They may be too tempting for some of the guests.

The murder weapon lay on a black velvet cloth, traces of blood so deeply embedded in the carved hilt that centuries of wear hadn't eroded the terror it could still induce in the viewer.

At least it looked like blood.

In the dimly lit room, the ivory-and-jade dagger glowed an eerie greenish hue. I was dying to touch this exquisite artifact, which had been used countless times on helpless, horrified victims.

I reached for it. My fingers collided with the cold protective Plexiglas case.

Too bad it's locked up, I thought. The real dagger would make the perfect weapon for the murder mystery play I'd be hosting the next evening at San Francisco's world-renowned de Young Museum. Instead we would have to make do with a Styrofoam prop from the museum's art restoration department.

I set my vente latte on the top of the case and pulled out my iPhone to take a picture. Glancing at the security camera high on the wall, I noticed that the motion-sensing light was yellow. Alone in the room after hours, I was being watched—and probably filmed.

A footfall creaked behind me.

My heart skipped a beat.

I snatched the latte from the top of the case.

A hand clamped down hard on my shoulder, and I nearly dropped my coffee.

I whirled around, raising the only weapon I had besides lukewarm coffee—a "Killer Parties" promotional pen. At a moment's notice I was ready to stab—or at least heavily mark up—the shadowy figure. He stepped into the glow of a spotlight that illuminated the case.

"There's no food or drink allowed in here, ma'am," the uniformed security guard said.

I lowered my killer pen and caught my breath.

"You scared the crap out of me!"

The guard raised an eyebrow. Apparently he meant to scare the crap out of me.

"Ma'am, you're also not supposed to be in here after hours."

I raised my latte in apology. "Sorry. I just wanted to take another look at the dagger."

"I'm afraid the museum is closed to the public tonight."

"Oh, I'm not the public. I'm Presley Parker, the event planner for the mystery play tomorrow night. I have permission from Mary Lee Miller to be here." That was stretching the truth a bit. I had permission to be in the museum for the rehearsal, not necessarily to have free run of the place.

The security guard held up his flashlight and shone it on my face.

"Oh yes, I recognize you. You've been here several times lately, haven't you?"

"Yep. Trying to get ready for the big fund-raiser." I tried to sound casual.

"Sorry about sneaking up on you. Didn't mean to scare you. I know this place can get kind of creepy when there's no one around." He looked me up and down. I must have appeared suspicious, wearing an old-fashioned button-down jacket and loose-fitting khaki pants, not to mention the leather boots. He eyed the badge pinned on my lapel.

I looked down at my outfit. "This is my costume," I explained. "Tonight's our dress rehearsal, and I'm going as Kate Warne, the first female Pinkerton detective."

The guard surveyed the room—probably making sure I hadn't stolen anything—then looked back at me. "So what are you doing up here? Isn't that event taking place on the main floor?"

"Uh, I just wanted to see the dagger once more, to make sure the art department copied it accurately. After all, I can't have six of the world's most famous fictional detectives trying to murder the museum curator with a rubber knife, can I?" I gave a nervous laugh.

He didn't crack a smile.

"And you are . . . ?" I reached out my hand.

Stone-faced, the guard shook it. "Sam Wo. Head of security."

I took a moment to study—and diagnose—him, a habit I'd formed while teaching abnormal psychology at San Francisco State University. He was Asian, in his sixties, and shorter than me by several inches. His hand was small, dry, and ringless; I noticed a contrasting tan line around his wedding ring finger. He wore black faux-leather loafers, the discount variety from Target or Walmart popular with underpaid service employees. From his impeccable uniform and well-worn but polished shoes, I guessed he had a touch of OCD—obsessive-compulsive disorder—a trait well matched to this particular detail-oriented job.

"I wish Ms. Miller would tell me when people are going to be running around the museum after closing." Eyeing me again, he added, "So you're the one who's putting on this mystery thing?"

"That would be me. And I'd better get back to the rehearsal. Make sure no real murders are being committed. Although I suppose if that happened, you guys could figure out whodunit pretty quickly." I nodded at the nearest camera, watching us.

"True. This wouldn't be the best place to kill someone. The cameras are motion-triggered—that's how I knew you were here. Just be careful about touching the cases. You could set off an alarm."

My eyes widened. "Really? Are the alarms that sensitive?"

"Sure. Especially the ones with priceless pieces inside, like that Dogon statue over there." He gestured toward a nearby case.

I glanced at the piece he was referring to and grimaced.

The grotesque three-foot statue looked to be carved out of wood. Shaped like a human body, the figure had long pendulous breasts that hung nearly to the waistline. But that wasn't the disturbing part. Dangling from just under the waist—and nearly reaching the feet—was an equally pendulous penis.

The guard broke into a grin, showing a mouthful of crooked teeth. "Nah, I'm just messing with you. We don't have alarmed exhibits here. That's an East Coast thing. But I love to tease the schoolkids when they come. They couldn't care less about the art. All they want to know is whether anything's ever been stolen and if we have alarms."

"You're quite the kidder, Sam Wo," I said, forcing a friendly laugh. A little surprised at the low-level security, I glanced back at the case holding the ceremonial dagger. "Seriously, has there ever been a theft?"

"No, ma'am. Surprising, perhaps, since we have more than twenty-five thousand works of art from around the world. Top names, too—Homer, Cassatt, Frank Lloyd Wright. But we still manage to keep an eye on things."

I scanned the room filled with incredible artifacts from Oceania, Mayan, African, and Andean cultures. "So you've never had a problem?"

"Not on my watch. At least, not with thefts. This is a friendly museum, a museum for the people, not like some of those hoity-toity ones back east. The biggest problem we have are the transients who come to the Friday-night open house for the wine parties and end up drunk and lying on the marble floor." Sam Wo chuckled. His stiff official manner had softened, replaced by an easy manner and a contagious laugh. Being in charge of these irreplaceable objects insured for more than $90 million would have made me nervous, but Sam Wo appeared relaxed.

"What about fakes?" I said, lowering my voice to sound conspiratorial. "I mean, does the museum have any art scandals I could include in the script?"

"You mean like questions of provenance?"

I made a face. Museum-speak was a whole new language for me.

His face lit up. I had a feeling he got pretty bored on the job and loved the opportunity to share his authority and expertise with the public.

"Provenance means where the objects come from and whether they're authentic."

"That's a concern in this day and age?" I asked.

"Yes, ma'am. Some museums take a 'don't ask, don't tell' attitude. But not the de Young. Our curator only works with reputable dealers."

I sensed his feeling of pride about the objects that surrounded him.

"There are museums that don't?" I took a sip of my now-cold latte. It was my third today, but I needed regular doses to help control my ADHD—attention deficit hyperactivity disorder. It was either triple the caffeine or go back to Ritalin, which pretty much turned me into a zombie. Old psychology secret: While caffeine is a stimulant for most people, for those of us with ADHD, it does the opposite and calms us down.

Sam Wo shone his flashlight around the room while he talked, as if it were habit. "I guess you didn't hear about the Getty or the Met scandals. They made the news a few years ago. There were questions about how they acquired some pieces."

"You mean they had fakes?" I stole another glance at the encased dagger, wondering how one could tell a replica from an authentic piece. I'd been impressed with how much the Styrofoam stage dagger looked like the real thing, right down to the dried-blood effect.

"More like they were 'taken without permission,'" he said, making finger quotes. He stepped over to another display and shone his flashlight inside the case. "See these ceramic bowls and whatnot? They're authentic. We have the documentation to prove their provenance. But similar ones were recently acquired illegally at another museum."

Surprised, I asked, "How does that happen?"

"Some museums aren't as careful as the de Young. They'll deal with the black market."

"Where does the black market get them?"

Sam tucked his thumbs into his black leather belt. "Professional thieves usually steal them from the country of origin and sell them to questionable curators who think art should be 'shared with the world for the greater good.' But if you think about it, it's like taking pieces of the Statue of Liberty and displaying them at, say, a museum in Egypt."

I saw his point. Not only was I unaware that this kind of looting occurred, I was impressed that a security guard knew so much about art. More than I did, anyway. My walls tended to display classic posters for movies like *The Maltese Falcon*, and my "display cases," aka table- and desktops, showcased party props and event catalogs. I guessed Sam Wo had absorbed a lot just by osmosis.

"There's a lot of competition between museums to build a world-class collection," he added. "And the de Young—"

His words were suddenly cut off by the echoing click of razor-sharp heels and the yapping of a small dog coming from down a shadowed hall. As if he recognized the sounds, Sam Wo jerked to attention, pulled down the front of his jacket, and adjusted his hat.

Mary Lee Miller stepped into the dim light. The woman who'd hired me to produce a murder mystery at the museum was the de Young's major fund-raiser and philanthropist. She was a petite blond woman in her fifties, trying to look under forty. Tonight she wore a pink Chanel suit and matching stiletto heels that would have made killer weapons. Peeking out of her pink Coach bag was a teeth-baring, pink-ribboned purse-pooch. A pit bull wrapped in a poodle's clothing? The metaphor fit both the dog and the woman.

"Oh God, Sam. Do hush!" Mary Lee said to the security guard. She waved him away with a whisk of her manicured hand. Sam nodded, tipped his hat to both of us, and shuffled off into the darkness, waving his flashlight from side to side like a blind man with a cane.

"Sam's a character. The older he gets, the more he talks. We only keep him around because his father was my father's gardener." Mary Lee patted her poodle with a diamond-riddled hand. "No doubt he was telling you one of his exaggerated stories? I do believe he's a frustrated Indiana Jones."

I smiled. "Well, a museum can always use a little mystery."

Mary Lee Miller raised a perfectly designed eyebrow.

"Yes, but it can't afford a real scandal. See that Dogon figure over there?"

Oh God, not that piece again.

"Superb, isn't it? We paid over one million dollars for this truly incredible piece. The de Young would rather have one great object than a hundred ordinary ones. We strive to make sure our museum is *not* your dowager grandmother's provincial museum. It's contemporary, user-friendly, and with my name on it, it has to be the best. Believe me, I have the scars to prove it."

She was referring to the controversy that had dogged the museum since she first took on the job of major money-raiser a decade ago. Everyone in the San Francisco Bay Area knew about the frequent arguments over everything from the architecture and location to the financing and environmental impact. But somehow Mary Lee Miller had managed to overcome these obstacles and raise more than $200 million worth of funding in the process.

"Blockbuster art brings in millions of visitors—that's a fact. And we now rival the Met, the Louvre, and the British Museum with our collection. Plus the art-related trinkets we sell in the gift shop make great mementos for tourists. When the Tut exhibit was here, we made more money selling Tut shirts and bags than we did on admission."

Remembering what Sam Wo had said, I asked, "Is it difficult making sure all the objects are legitimate?"

"Absolutely not," she snapped, petting her purse pooch vigorously. He . . . she . . . it panted in response. "We trust our dealers implicitly. When we acquire something like the Dogon statue, we make sure it has a reliable provenance."

I nodded my understanding, but she continued as if I were a schoolchild on a field trip.

"Provenance, Presley, is the documentation of an object's origin and ownership."

I tried to ignore her condescending tone, but it irritated me. "Sam said there's still a black market for things like the Dogon statue?"

Her eyes narrowed. I knew I'd offended her as soon as the words "black market" tumbled out of my mouth. It was like saying "plastic surgery" to a trophy wife.

"Certainly there are still looters, smugglers, unethical dealers, and desperate collectors who will turn a blind eye to the origins of some art," Mary Lee said. "Not to mention the occasional forgery. But our staff is top-notch, impeccable. I personally recommended Christine Lampe, who was hired as our curator. And that's why this fund-raiser is so important. If it's got my name on it, it's sure to bring in hundreds of thousands of dollars we need for the new wing and collection. And it has to be perfect."

Her mini-speech reminded me how pompous Mary Lee really was. When she hired me for this gig, she insisted she be given full credit for the fund-raiser. I'd agreed, as long as a percentage of the money went to the Autism Foundation. My friend and part-time assistant, Delicia, had a sister with the disorder, and I wanted to do something to help stem the puzzling rise in cases.

"Now, shall we return to the main court, Chou-Chou?" Mary Lee said to her dog in a nauseating baby voice. The dog licked her fingers as if they were covered in gravy.

She spoke to me in a normal voice. "Do I have to remind you, Presley, that I hired you to do an event, not wander around the museum unescorted? The rehearsal is not going well, and you won't see a dime for your company or your charity if this event isn't perfect." Her face tightened.

I stole a last glance at the bloodstained ceremonial dagger, safe in its plastic case. Good thing it was inaccessible, I thought, or I might have "borrowed" it to use on Mary Lee. Instead, I followed her down the stairs, her stilettos tapping out a strident beat as she led the way. Her threats had been repeated so many times over the past couple of weeks that they no longer struck terror in my heart like they had initially. Still, I wasn't above the occasional dagger-in-the-back fantasy.

But before I could picture shoving the blade between her pink shoulders, I heard a scream echoing up from the stairwell ahead.

A scream so loud, it could have shattered Plexiglas.

Chapter 2

PARTY PLANNING TIP #2

Ask your guests to come to your Murder Mystery Party dressed as their favorite sleuths. Then give them clues to costuming, so you don't end up with a bunch of lame Scooby-Doos.

Keeping up with Mary Lee's swift step wasn't easy—the woman had the energy of a cheerleader on crack—but the scream momentarily stopped her in her tracks. She glanced back at me, her heavily lined eyes underscoring her look of horror.

After that momentary pause, the heels began clacking double time. I picked up the pace and followed her tap dance down the stairs to the first floor. Moving past the main court, she headed for the adjacent mural room, then froze, squeezing her purse-pooch in a stranglehold. Standing next to her, I saw her inhale sharply at the scene in front of us. She covered her glossy pink mouth with glossy pink fingernails.

"Oh my God!" she whispered between fingers.

Lying in the middle of the marble floor was the lifeless body of a woman, and my friend and part-time coworker, Delicia Jackson, one of the actors in the play, was kneeling by her side.

The woman's legs were twisted at an impossible—and indiscreet—angle, her arms akimbo. Blond curly hair masked her face. Her pink polyester skirt was hiked up high enough to reveal a matching pink thong.

But it was the hilt of a dagger jutting from the woman's back that held both Mary Lee's and my attention. A circle of blood surrounded the ornate handle.

Delicia gave another bone-chilling scream that echoed throughout the main court, causing the hairs on my unshaved legs to stand at attention. Delicia bent down in her vintage floral frock and chunky black heels, circa 1940s Nancy Drew, and hesitantly touched the pool of blood with her fingertip. Recoiling in horror, she cried, "Oh. My. God. She's totally dead!"

Dee glanced up and spotted Mary Lee staring at her.

She licked her bloody finger.

Then she grinned.

Mary Lee, still frozen to the spot, finally released her death grip on her little dog Toto—or whatever. Before she could sic the little pooch on Delicia, I shouldered past her and called out, "Stop tape."

My videographer and fellow office worker, Berkeley Wong, lowered his video camera, a look of exasperation on his youthful face. Costumed as Kutesy Millstone, the Alphabet Detective, he wore a simple black dress that fit him perfectly. He finished the look with a "Santa Teresa" baseball hat covering his normally spiky hair. The only accessories that didn't fit his role were the purple Chuck Ts on his feet.

I moved closer to the body, then said, "Delicia, you sound more like Miley Cyrus than Nancy Prude."

Acting as if she was offended, Delicia stuck out her tongue at me. But then, Dee was almost always acting. She'd had bit parts in every local production from *Beach Blanket Babylon* to *Teatro ZinZanni*, but her dream was to be on Broadway.

Berk shuffled over, giggling. "Presley's right, dude. You're not a Disney tween—you're the World Famous Valley Girl Detective. Try it like this." He put a hand on his waist, stuck out his hip, and spoke in a falsetto. " 'Oh. My. God! She's *like* totally dead!' "

"And, Dee," I added, "try not to lick the blood off your finger during the real performance tomorrow night."

"Good *God*!" came a screeching voice behind me. "What are you people *doing*?"

Remembering Mary Lee, the constant thorn in my balloon, I turned around to explain the crime scene to her. While Botox kept her from frowning, it didn't prevent her face from turning the color of her pink outfit.

"It's okay, Mary Lee. They're just rehearsing."

I turned to Delicia and whispered, "Better leave out the scream until showtime." I rolled my eyes toward Mary Lee.

Delicia grimaced, displaying teeth tinged pink from licking the fake blood. "Where did you get this stuff?" She spat. "Tastes like cherry cough syrup. Yuck."

I glanced down at the weapons strewn about the "deceased" mannequin. All the red herrings were there— various artifacts copied from authentic museum pieces that doubled as murder weapons. The dagger, a nearly perfect replica of the one encased upstairs, protruded from the mannequin's back, supported by a hunk of clay hidden under the "victim's" pink polyester blouse.

"Berk, can you do a sweep of the crime scene so we can—" I started to say.

The shrill voice behind me cut me off. "Excuse me. But is that supposed to be *me*?" The sound of clicking heels and yapping dog started up again as Mary Lee closed the gap between us.

"Well, yes, but—"

"Because I have *no* intention of lying on the floor in my Chanel suit. Especially not like that!" She indicated the obscene way in which the corpse was lying—the hitched-up skirt and glimpse of pink thong—another one of Delicia's many pranks to further irritate the woman in charge.

Mary Lee, thinking it was the starring role, had insisted on playing the soon-to-be-deceased museum curator California de Young. Once she realized she only had a few lines before her "death," she'd promptly glammed up her meager role with expensive designer clothes, heavily insured jewelry, and movie-star makeup. I could hardly argue with her, since she was running the show, so to speak. I just hoped she'd play dead for most of the evening.

"Don't worry, Mary Lee," I said, biting my tongue before I said something more that I'd regret. I knew if I opened my piehole and spewed every time Mary Lee annoyed me, I'd be left with a mouthful of mincemeat and no job. A small price to pay, I thought momentarily, then remembered I needed the money, after being downsized from my college teaching job.

After taking a deep breath, I explained the logistics of the play and her role once again. "We'll have a nice cashmere throw on the floor so you don't get your clothes dirty. And you won't have to stay there long. We'll replace you with the mannequin."

Mary Lee stomped closer to the corpse for a better look, brushing past Delicia as if she wasn't there. Sticking out her razor-sharp Manolo toe, she gave the mannequin's torso a little kick.

"That doesn't look anything like me. Where did you get that *hideous* plus-sized outfit—Walmart? I'm a size one, for God's sake. Those shoes are a disgrace. I wouldn't be caught dead in those thrift-store knockoffs. And that wig—it looks like someone combed it with the dagger. My hair doesn't look anything like that. Not at *my* salon's prices. Is this supposed to be some kind of a joke?"

While Mary Lee ranted, Delicia had risen like a ghost from her kneeling position, the bloody dagger in hand. Slowly drifting back, she slipped behind Mary Lee, raised the phony knife, and brought it down to within millimeters of Mary Lee's back.

Repeatedly.

The "Eee—eee—eee" from the *Psycho* shower scene screeched in my brain. Good thing that dagger was made of Styrofoam. This was supposed to be a make-believe murder.

While the weapon might not have been real, the murderous expression on Delicia's face looked authentic. I didn't blame her for her lethal thoughts. Delicia and Mary Lee had been at odds since the first rehearsal a couple of weeks ago. I had a feeling that was when Mary Lee began to suspect there was something going on between her son, Corbin, and Dee.

According to Delicia, the young man had been coerced by his strong-willed mother into playing the part of Sam Slayed, Hard-Boiled Gumshoe. An aspiring artist and son from Mary Lee's first marriage to Jason Cosetti, Corbin had been raised with a silver paintbrush in his hand. He'd reluctantly agreed to participate in the museum fund-raiser in exchange for some help from his influential mother in getting a sponsor for his own art show.

In spite of her sharp tongue and pit-bull personality, I felt for Mary Lee. Her relationship with her son seemed to be the only real human connection she had—and she apparently felt threatened by Dee.

No wonder. Petite, curvy, with long dark hair, Delicia was a natural flirt. More than one man who'd crossed her path had fallen for her. But unlike other romantic adventures she'd had, this time she seemed truly interested in the scruffily attractive urban-chic artist, in spite of the fact that at twenty-five, he was five years her junior.

Once Mary Lee realized what was going on between her prized son and a "common out-of-work actress," she had shown her dislike and disapproval of Delicia every chance she got, often referring to her as "the help," "that little girl," and "what's-her-name." Naturally, this did not bode well for the overly dramatic Dee.

At the moment, Mary Lee stood hands on hips, shaking her head at her "deceased" doppelgänger. Behind her back, Delicia quietly picked up another bogus weapon—a bow and arrow—and pretended to shoot it through Mary Lee's head. By the time Delicia lifted the fake statuette and mimed clobbering Mary Lee, it was all Berkeley and I could do not to laugh. Good thing Mary Lee was oblivious to the pantomimes behind her back.

Pressing my lips together, I glared at Delicia and shook my head sharply, hoping she'd get the hint and knock off the theatrics.

Mary Lee caught me out signaling Dee and said, "What's going on?"

I shrugged like a student caught passing notes in class. "Nothing . . . I . . . we—"

Mary Lee spotted the thickly beaded mock necklace Delicia had just retrieved from the floor—perfect for strangulation.

"I was just cleaning up . . . ," Delicia began, looking as innocent as Jack the Ripper.

"That's it!" Mary Lee screeched, startling all of us. She turned to me, but kept her eyes on Delicia. "I've had it. I want her out of here. Now!"

Before I could defend Dee, a voice called out from across the court.

"Mother!"

Mary Lee whirled around, her face twisted with rage. Corbin Cosetti strode into the room, wearing a trench coat and snap-brim fedora, à la Sam Spade. He looked better in the costume than in his usual torn-and-paint-splattered shirt and jeans, and I could see how Dee might be attracted to him. With dark hair and eyes, he was a quite a contrast to his fair mother.

"This is none of your business, Corbin," Mary Lee hissed. "Please don't interfere." She turned back to me and pointed to Delicia. "That woman has done nothing but disrupt the play, distract the others, disrespect my authority, and . . . and . . ." she sputtered.

Poor woman. Her controlling attachment to her son was threatening to ruin the fund-raiser. I had to do something to ease the tension. But before I could reassure her, Delicia stepped forward—and into Mary Lee's face. She looked dumbfounded at Mary Lee's outburst and accusations.

"What are you talking about, lady?"

"Don't act innocent with me, missy," Mary Lee said. "I know your game. And I refuse to have you ruin this important event!"

"Listen, lady," Dee said. "I don't work for you. I work for Presley. And you and I both know what this is really about. You're not worried about your stupid-ass fund-raiser. You're trying to control your twenty-five-year-old son!"

Before Delicia could do something stupid with the fake knife she still held in her hand, Corbin moved in between the two women and pushed them apart. At nearly six feet, he towered over them.

"Knock it off! Both of you!" He turned to Mary Lee. "Good God, Mother. Dee's right. Stop interfering in my life! I'll see whomever I want, when I want, and you have nothing to say about it."

He spun around to Delicia, who was gripping the knife handle so hard, her knuckles were white. "And you. For God's sake, stop baiting her. You know how she is."

I frowned at the mini-drama playing out in front of me. This was way better than the little murder mystery I'd prepared. Unfortunately, while there might not be the sudden appearance of a dead body, there would certainly be a dead career if I didn't take charge of this imploding situation.

I looked at Delicia. "Dee? What's this all about?"

She shrugged like a pouty teenager.

I turned to Mary Lee's son. "Corbin?"

He continued to glare at his mother.

"Mary Lee?" I finally said.

She snarled. "This tramp you've hired is trying to get her hands on my money."

"What?" I said, almost laughing.

"Oh, don't be so naive. I know her type. She's digging her hooks into Corbin to get at my money. She might be fooling you, Corbin, but she doesn't fool me. And I should know, since it's happened to me more than once."

"Mother!" Corbin shouted. "That's crazy. Dee's . . ." He looked at Delicia. "She's just a friend."

Delicia flashed Corbin a daggered look. Translation: "Oh really, mama's boy?"

Corbin quickly backtracked. "I mean, sure, we've gone out a few times. But your accusations are ridiculous! You've got to stop trying to control my life. You asked me to do this play—and I agreed, only because you said you'd find someone to show my work. But that doesn't mean you can run my life."

"Don't you see, Corbin?" Mary Lee pleaded. "She's nothing but a common *actress*! And a lousy one at that. She's only acting like she cares about you. Just like the others, she's after the money. How can you be so blind?"

Corbin crossed his arms. "If she leaves, I leave. And you'll be without two key characters the night before your play. Good luck finding replacements at this late date."

I pulled Mary Lee aside, not unaware of Dee's piercing eyes. "He's right, Mary Lee," I said. "We can't afford to lose anyone at this point. Look, the event will be over tomorrow night, and it's going to be a real moneymaker. You don't want anything to go wrong now, after all the work you've done." My voice turned to a whisper. "I'm sure this 'thing' will take care of itself once the play is over."

Mary Lee pulled away from me and turned to the dozen cast members staring at her. Locking her jaw, she spun around and stomped away, her clicking heels like knife points on the marble floor.

"Bee-otch," Dee said under her breath. "I should have stabbed, clubbed, and garroted her when I had the chance." I shot a look at her. Berkeley stifled a grin, while Corbin just shook his head as he watched his mother walk away. I caught a glimpse of Sam Wo, the security guard I'd been speaking with upstairs, standing in the doorway. He lifted his hat at me sympathetically and disappeared into another room.

As soon as Mary Lee left the room, the cast visibly relaxed. Me included.

"Take five, everyone," I said, and plopped myself down on a nearby bench in the main court to think about my next move. This was another fine mess I'd gotten myself into.

I'd originally wanted to hire only my own actors to play the roles of suspects. But Mary Lee had gone ahead and given the part of Sam Slayed to her son, without my knowledge. Next she offered the de Young's real museum curator, Christine Lampe, the part of Agatha Mistry, Cozy Snoop. Christine had done a great job using makeup and costuming to age herself from fiftysomething to well over seventy, playing the part of the tea-sipping sleuth.

She'd also promised Dan Tannacito, Christine's assist-

ant—who preferred the title "exhibit developer"—the role of
Pipe-Smoking Sherlock Bones. I found Dan at over six feet,
with his romance-novel good looks, broad shoulders, and
highlighted blond hair, almost too perfect for the part. It was
hard to believe he had a thirteen-year-old daughter. He must
have had her while he was still a teenager.

I'd filled out the rest of the cast with my office mates, who
worked in the same barracks/office building on Treasure Island. This man-made strip of landfill had once been home to
the 1939 Golden Gate Expo and the U.S. Navy; now it was
where I lived and worked. Besides Delicia Jackson, who'd
begged to play the role of Nancy Prude, Valley Girl Detective, I'd asked videographer Berkeley Wong to play the role
of Kutesy Millstone, Biker Sleuth—which he chose to do in
drag. Treasure Island security guard Raj Reddy, a wannabe
Bollywood star, rounded out the cast of suspects as Hercules
Parrot, Blustery Belgian Detective.

After the major roles were cast, I let my mother play a bit
part as an assistant crime scene tech. She had insisted on
being included when she heard about the event, claiming her
decades-old stint as an afternoon-TV-movie hostess gave her
serious acting chops. Since she was in the early stages of
Alzheimer's, I'd asked Brad Matthews, a crime scene cleaner
who shared office space in my building, to supervise her. I'd
only recently learned his cleaning job involved more than
just soap and water and a cute jumpsuit.

Like most murder mysteries, things are never as simple as
they appear—even in real life.

Thanks to the publicity I'd garnered hosting the San
Francisco mayor's ill-fated "surprise wedding" on Alcatraz,
my event-planning business, Killer Parties, was getting more

requests for events than I could manage. Living in a low-priced condo on TI enabled me to use most of my profits for my mother's care. I'd raised a lot of money for Alzheimer's research, and hoped I'd do the same for autism. But the behind-the-scenes catfights and real drama I could do without. Unfortunately it was all part of the event-planning business. Our motto, after "The customer is always right," is "Whatever can go wrong, will."

"Okay, people, break's over!" I clapped my hands to gather everyone's attention. Time for another panic-filled pep talk. "We only have twenty-four hours before showtime!"

After some brief directions, I got them started on another rehearsal in the main court, sans blood and screams. Meanwhile, I returned to the adjacent mural room to check out the crime scene and the mannequin that lay on the cold marble floor, outlined with masking tape. Each of the weapons, artfully copied from real artifacts, was in position around the outline, and the Styrofoam knife had been replaced in the back of the body, along with fresh "blood."

Back in the main court, I reviewed the decorations, props, and clues. I'd placed framed, poster-sized "mug shots"—front and side views—of all the suspects in the play. Black and white balloons almost obscured the twenty-foot-high ceiling, each tied with a black ribbon. Attached to the ends of the ribbons were small tchotchkes related to the mystery theme—magnifying glasses, flashlights, handcuffs (the size of cat-cuffs), and tiny replicas of Clue weapons I'd found on eBay. Mystery novels had been arranged as centerpieces for the tables, with mocked-up covers emblazoned with titles like *Blood All Over the Place* and *Death by Cuisinart*. Drinks and appetizers would be served in glasses and on plates embossed "Murder at the Museum," while a pianist would play the theme song from *Murder, She Wrote* in the background.

I took a deep breath, wishing I could open a bottle of champagne and chug a few liters. With only twenty-four hours before the curtain lifted, so to speak, I was down to the proverbial wire. Now, if I could keep behind-the-scenes drama to a minimum, I just might make it through the mystery party without a major mishap.

As if.

Chapter 3

PARTY PLANNING TIP # 3

When the amateur sleuths arrive at your Murder Mystery Party, offer them extra props to use as accessories, such as a magnifying glass, flashlight, pair of gloves, or Groucho glasses.

"Welcome to Murder at the Museum," I announced on the dot of seven to the two hundred plus guests attending the de Young fund-raiser. As requested on the dossier-style invitation, these well-paying attendees had dressed as their favorite sleuths to solve the impending murder of museum curator California de Young, aka Mary Lee Miller.

Fortunately, rehearsals had gone well after Mary Lee stopped harassing the cast, allowing me precious time to finish decorating the main court and the mural room. With help from my staff, I finished decorating by adding centerpieces of bloodred roses, along with miniature replicas of the murder weapons. By the time San Francisco's high society royalty trickled into the main court, I was confident the party would be off the hook.

Delicia, dressed as Nancy Prude, and I, in my Kate Warne, First Female Pinkerton Detective outfit, stood at the sidelines as attendees entered, trying to guess who was who.

"Not another Nancy Drew!" Dee whispered after we'd ticked off half a dozen copies of the young sleuth. "Jeez, girls, get a clue. Don't they know that's *my* role?"

"Don't worry about it. Having extra Nancy Drews just creates more red herrings to distract the amateur sleuths. Besides, you have the best costume—very authentic."

It was true. Dee as Drew looked as if she'd stepped out of a River Heights boutique. She had on the same flowery, mid-calf frock she'd worn at the dress rehearsal, along with a blue felt cloche hat. She'd stayed away from the contemporary image of Nancy Drew, the one from the recent movie who dressed in smart plaids and sassy pins. Dee kept it old school, Nancy circa late 1930s and early 1940s, from the top of her titian wig down to the seamed hose and ankle-wrapped platform peekaboos. Her red fingernails matched her glossy toenails, and the vintage beaded handbag dangling from her wrist would have made the perfect place to store stolen diamonds or state secrets.

While there were plenty of Nancy Drew replicas, I didn't see a single guest competing for my character, Kate Warne, credited as the first female Pinkerton detective back in 1856. I'd been a fan of Kate's ever since I discovered her while reading about the Pinkertons on Crimelibrary.com, especially when I found out how she'd gotten the job in a time when "lady detectives" were almost unheard of. According to legend, when she'd applied, Allen Pinkerton had mistaken her for a clerical worker, not a detective.

Typical.

Warne had to argue to get the position, reminding Pinkerton that women could be "most useful worming out secrets in places which would be impossible for a male detective," such as "befriending the wives and girlfriends of suspected criminals and gaining their confidence."

Smart woman.

She'd also argued that women "have an eye for detail and are excellent observers."

Kate Warne was my kind of role model. For my costume, I copied her look from the only photo I could find—baggy khaki pants, a short button-down jacket, bolero-style hat, well-worn boots, and the famous badge featuring an eye in the center encircled with the Pinkerton slogan—"The eye that never sleeps." It wasn't the most flattering outfit, but as the event planner, I preferred to remain in the shadows.

The main court filled quickly with a variety of popular detectives, especially those who practiced their trades in the noir city of San Francisco, like Hammett's Sam Spade, Marcia Muller's Sharon McCone, and her partner, Bill Pronzini's Nameless. (One attendee wore a nametag that said "Nameless," while another's nametag was simply blank.) There were Charlie Chan permutations, a couple of Continental Ops, and one man came as Sister Carol Anne O'Marie's nun detective, Sister Mary Helen—only sporting a disconcerting beard.

Berk joined us for the guessing game, and we raced to identify the rest of the sleuths as they sifted in. Magnum PI wore a Hawaiian shirt and fake caterpillar mustache. Columbo swaggered in with his fake cigar, his tattered overcoat dragging behind. Bond held a shaken martini and wore a classic suit. Jessica Fletcher wore a picture of a typewriter around her neck. Scooby-Doo looked, well, like a dog in a rented costume. There was no way to tell if it was a man or a woman. And there were way too many Sherlock Holmeses.

Berk won the game, of course. He was just too pop savvy. He beat us to Jake Gittes from *Chinatown* (bandaged nose), Adrian Monk (who kept straightening people's clothes), and Precious Ramotswe (an African-American woman in a colorful dress and head wrap).

Eventually Dee and Berk moved into the crowd, mingling and passing out "Killer Parties" pens and "Police Reports." On the back of the reports I'd printed a list of slang terms which guests could translate to win a prize—like "bean-shooter" (gun), "bracelets" (handcuffs), "caboose" (jail), "Chicago overcoat" (coffin), and "chin music" (punch on the jaw). At least it would keep them occupied until the play began.

My mother looked stunning in a long red silk dress and a black wig, in spite of the fact that she'd come as Mata Hari— a spy rather than a detective. Hopefully no one would really notice, especially after she covered her outfit with the crime scene assistant's coat. The tight dress outlined her full figure nicely, and her face still had the classic bone structure that had translated so well on her old afternoon TV show.

I was quite proud of her. I just hoped she wouldn't become confused and give anything away—like tonight's killer.

By seven thirty, all of the suspects were accounted for— except Brad. He wasn't supposed to make an entrance as a CSI tech until after the crime occurred, but so far he hadn't checked in, and I hadn't seen any sign of him. He knew how important this event was for me, and his absence irritated me.

The only glitch so far had been a brief altercation between Mary Lee and a man I didn't recognize. Apparently he'd tried to crash the party, dressed in a Sherlock Holmes outfit, but had been turned away by a security guard. When he'd demanded to see Mary Lee, they'd had a heated argument, and he finally left. Unfortunately, I learned this from Dee, who relished telling me about the scene in a told-you-so tone.

At least Mary Lee was leaving Delicia alone—for the time being.

"Where's Corbin?" I asked, glancing around the crowd. "He was here earlier."

Delicia nodded toward a shadowy corner. There sat the young artist, staring into his drink and ignoring the people around him.

"Is he all right?" I asked her.

She shrugged, downed her own drink, and disappeared into the mass of gumshoes, dicks, flatfoots, shamuses, and ops, all having a criminally good time.

I sipped my drink and checked my watch.

Where the hell was Brad?

Showtime, I said to myself, and finished my drink. I stepped up on a bench and tried to get the attention of the crowd, well lubed by champagne. Everyone ignored me, happily chatting and drinking and nibbling on fancy appetizers. I signaled Sam Wo to flash the overhead lights. When most of the conversations had quieted, I lifted the portable microphone.

"Thanks for coming tonight to support the de Young Museum. I'm Presley Parker, aka Kate Warne, Pinkerton's first female detective, here to welcome you to de Young's Murder at the Museum.

"As you know, our museum curator, California de Young"—I gestured to Mary Lee, who gave a queenly wave—"asked you here tonight to help raise money for a new exhibit at the museum, an interactive, simulated archaeological dig. She hopes this cutting-edge technology will bring people to what was once a stuffy world of antiquities."

The crowd clapped politely.

I continued. "Tonight California de Young has invited six of the world's greatest detectives here to solve a baffling mystery. However, in the event these great minds are unable to solve this difficult task, you amateur sleuths will assist us by searching for clues and using your little gray cells to ferret out the truth. But first, let me introduce our professional detectives."

During the brief applause, I glanced at my cast to make sure they were ready for their debuts. I presented them one at a time, allowing each to make his or her own character introductions. Corbin Cosetti stepped up first, wearing the traditional trench coat, fedora, and some real stubble for his character, Sam Slayed.

"Hey, schweetheart," he began. To my surprise, his Bogie accent was right on target—and the guy could act. I didn't know he had it in him.

Christine Lampe was up next. She moved into the spotlight wearing a ruffled white blouse, long wool skirt, ratty shawl, thick, droopy stockings, and old-fashioned nursing shoes. She completed her Agatha Mistry look by twisting her hair into a bun and adding wire-rimmed glasses. When she spoke, she used a high-pitched, nails-on-the-blackboard English accent.

"Yoo-hoo, everyone . . ."

When she finished her humorous introduction and the laughs died down, her assistant Dan Tannacito took center stage. He was dressed to kill in a tweed cape/coat, deer-stalker cap, and black boots. In one hand he held a curvy meerschaum pipe, and in the other a giant magnifying glass.

"Good evening. My name is Sherlock Holmes . . ."

He nailed the stuffy English accent, reminiscent of Basil Rathbone's Holmes—and the women in the room instantly fell in love with him.

Dan lifted his hat to the adoring crowd, then made room for Delicia, who stepped up in her role of Nancy Prude. She spoke with a perfect Valley Girl accent, a jarring—and hi-larious—contrast to her vintage outfit. She wowed the crowd with her over-the-top portrayal of the beloved girl sleuth.

Totally.

It was a hard act to follow, but Treasure Island security guard Raj Reddy nervously moved to the microphone. As Hercules Parrot, he'd padded his belly, waxed his fake mus-tache, put on high-water pants, and slicked back his hair. His combination French/Indian accent only made him funnier.

"*Bonjour, mes amies.* I am being Hercules Parrot, ze fa-mous Belgian detective . . ."

But Berkeley Wong's take on Kutesy Millstone, the tough-gal detective, brought down the house. Dressed in drag in a classic black dress, Berk had removed the cap he'd worn earlier and replaced it with a sweatband around his forehead, then spiked his hair into a porcupine do and added tats featuring menacing knives, swords, and guns.

"Yo, Millstone here . . . ," he/she began.

He had me laughing out loud.

As the detectives took a group bow for their introductions, the audience cheered riotously. When the roar died down, Mary Lee made her grand entrance onto the platform, in the guise of California de Young. Refusing to wear a costume of the stereotypical stuffy museum curator, she'd opted for her trademark look. She was dressed to match her mannequin double, in yet another pink Chanel suit with matching Choo shoes and Coach handbag. She'd even dyed her purse pooch pink to coordinate with her outfit. Her makeup was expertly, albeit overly, done, and her blond curls formed an incongruous halo around her head. She grinned at her benefactors as she took over the microphone and began to read her lines.

"Welcome, everyone! I'm California de Young, the museum curator. I'm hoping to make our museum the best in the world, but as you know, state-of-the-art costs money, so we'll be doubling your annual donation requests after tonight."

The crowd laughed at the financial joke. As for Mary Lee, she was having the time of her life. After all, she was the star.

She went on. "You're here tonight to solve the 'Mystery at the de Young Museum,' and compete with six of the world's best mystery detectives." The crowd gave an appreciative round of applause as the sleuths took another bow behind her.

"Each of the masterminds will receive a weapon to defend themselves in case something happens during the evening." Mary Lee continued to read her script as she handed out various replicated antiquities/weapons to the suspects—the dagger, the bow and arrow, the beaded necklace, and so on.

She wrapped up her speech and announced a twenty-minute break, encouraging the amateur sleuths to question the suspects, hunt for hidden clues, and down more champagne. After waving at the crowd like a queen acknowledging her loyal subjects, she stepped off the stage to collect accolades from the guests.

Twenty minutes later, I rounded up the suspects—all but Mary Lee, whom I hoped had taken her place on the floor in the mural room for the crime scene. She was to stay there and await the discovery of her "dead body" during the second act. I glanced around and saw no sign of her. Good.

Meanwhile, Brad had finally arrived. He was chatting with Sam Wo in a far corner, and looked very official—not to mention hot—in his white Crime Scene Cleaners jumpsuit.

About time, I thought, still annoyed.

At my signal to Sam, the lights in the room flickered on and off, gathering the attention of the guests for Act II. The lights went out again, this time for nearly thirty seconds, alerting Delicia to scream from the mural room.

Her scream was bloodcurdling. She'd been practicing.

When the lights came on again, the crowd looked half amused, half puzzled.

"A scream!" Christine called out as Agatha Mistry.

"Coming from in there," Dan's Holmes said as he pointed toward the mural room.

The crowd buzzed as they moved toward the doors of the waiting crime scene. I couldn't wait to see their reactions when they found Delicia hunched over the body of the recently "murdered" California de Young.

But before Dan could open the doors to let in the amateur sleuths, they burst open.

Delicia stood at the entrance to the room, her face flushed.

This wasn't in the script. Was she ad-libbing again?

Before I could shoot her a questioning look, she held up her trembling hand. It was covered in fake blood.

I looked down at Dee's flowered Nancy Prude dress. It too was stained red.

Half the crowd gasped; the other half giggled.

Brad appeared behind me, having elbowed his way through the crowd instead of being summoned. The whole second act appeared to be falling apart right in front of my eyes.

Mary Lee was definitely going to kill me now.

Brad stepped up to Delicia, took her arm, and gently lowered her upraised hand. Pulling out his cell phone from his pocket, he commanded, "Presley, get everyone back."

He took hold of Dee's wrist and led her back into the mural room.

"Presley!" he said, shaking me from my trance. None of this was in the script.

"What? We're supposed to go into the crime scene room and—"

Brad reached out, grabbed my arm, pulled me into the room, and closed the door.

Delicia stood frozen to her spot. Fake blood mixed with mascara was smeared on her face from wiping away her tears. What had that witch said to Dee that would make her so upset? I looked from Delicia to Brad, searching for answers.

"Brad, what's going on? What did Mary Lee do to Delicia?"

Brad nodded toward Mary Lee, who lay facedown a few feet away.

I stepped over. "Mary Lee?"

The fake dagger in her back was encircled with fake blood.

She wasn't moving.

I glanced back at Brad, the hairs on the back of my neck raised like a porcupine's quills.

"Mary Lee really has been stabbed," he said gravely. "She's dead. Seriously."

Chapter 4

PARTY PLANNING TIP #4

Choose a theme-within-a-theme for your Murder Mystery Party, such as a "Noir Soiree," a "Cozy Conundrum," or "Case of the Hardy Boys vs. Nancy Drew."

"We need an ambulance . . ." Brad was talking on his cell phone, but I went on asking questions, a wave of heat rushing through me.

"What . . . what do you mean, dead? She can't be . . . There must be some mistake . . . ," I stammered, not comprehending what had just happened. My murder mystery was supposed to be fiction, not real life. Following the heat wave, a cold sweat broke out over my body. I shivered.

Brad covered the mouthpiece. "Parker!" he commanded. Then he lowered his voice and spoke to me slowly, as if I were a child. "Get. Those. People. Away. From. Here. Now."

I nodded, zombielike, hoping the feeling would return to my wobbling legs.

"But don't let them leave!" he added.

"What about Delicia?" I looked at my friend across the room. Tears streamed down her flushed, mascara-streaked cheeks.

Brad moved over to her and wrapped his free arm around her. "I've got her. Go!"

With a last glance at the bloodied body lying on the floor, I slipped out of the room to face the puzzled crowd gathered near the doorway. Granted they were supposed to be puzzled, but not like this. What now? I didn't relish canceling the event, but obviously the fictional murder mystery couldn't continue, not with a real murder mystery in the second act.

I stepped up on a nearby granite sculpture, no doubt a priceless piece of art, even though it just looked like a big rock. Waving my hands at the murmuring crowd, I shouted, "May I have your attention, please?" I repeated the words several times until the raucous noise quieted to simmering whispers.

"Thank you." I took a big breath and ad-libbed my lines. "Thank you all for coming tonight and . . . uh . . . supporting the museum. Unfortunately, there's been . . . an accident, and I'm going to have to ask you to return to the main court."

People glanced at each other, clearly puzzled. A man channeling Charlie Chan yelled, "It's a clue!" Several others giggled at his outburst.

"No, seriously!" I said, trying to be heard over the excited conversations. "I need you to—"

Before I could finish, half a dozen uniformed San Francisco police officers flooded into the room, hands on their sidearms, ready to draw their weapons.

"Awesome!" a young Dick Tracy called out. I recognized Ed Kaufman from the mayor's office.

"Real cops!" a Perry Mason look-alike shouted. Rodney Worth from the Board of Supervisors.

"Hey, they do look real!" yelled Judy Wheeler, well-known philanthropist, dressed as another Nancy Drew.

The police spread out, surrounding the crowd, weapons ready, waiting for orders. From behind them stepped a tall, good-looking man with slicked-back hair, an Italian suit, and black wing tips.

My nemesis, San Francisco Police Department homicide detective Luke Melvin.

He moved forward, spotted me standing on top of the big expensive rock. He covered his mouth with a hand and shook his head.

Uh-oh.

Meanwhile the crowd watched the action, mesmerized. Apparently they believed the police invasion was part of the script.

Corbin Cosetti, still wearing a London Fog overcoat, shouldered his way through the mass of people. He glanced at the police surrounding the crowd, then frowned at me, clearly confused at this latest turn of events. He—aside from the other cast members—was the only one who knew we had veered far from the original story. And he also knew who was in the next room—his mother. He started for the door and was blocked by a uniformed officer.

"Excuse me, but I'm going in there!" Corbin shouted loud enough to be heard by nearly everyone in the room. The crowd hushed, eyes wide. I heard the scratch of pencil on the mini-notebooks we had provided.

Detective Melvin, who'd reached the door to the crime scene room about the same time as Corbin, recognized Mary Lee's son. "Hold on, son. You don't want to go in there—"

Corbin forced his way around the detective, causing a uniformed officer to raise his weapon. Detective Melvin held up a hand to stop the cop as Corbin ducked inside. Melvin mumbled something to the officer, then followed Corbin into the crime scene room. All eyes stared at the door, anticipating the next scene.

Seconds later I heard an agonized "No!" from inside the room.

Corbin.

My skin broke out in goose bumps at the heartrending sound.

Detective Melvin reappeared at the door, alone. He motioned for an officer to enter, said something to him, then headed for the rock, where I still stood frozen to the spot. Offering a hand, he helped me down, then stepped up and took my place.

"Ladies and gentlemen, could I have your attention? I'm Detective Luke Melvin from the San Francisco Police Department." He flashed his badge.

A woman dressed in something "tart-noir" said, "He looks too cute to be a real cop. They should have got someone who looked like Bogey to play the part. That guy should be on *Male Runway Models*."

Her partner, apparently Magnum PI in a Hawaiian shirt, replied, "You know, I think I've seen him somewhere. In a commercial or something."

The crowd gradually quieted, waiting to hear the detective give his lines.

"I'm afraid the party's over," Melvin announced.

Everyone looked puzzled for a moment.

"There's been a homicide . . ."

The crowd broke into mirthful murmurs and nodding heads.

"I'm afraid Ms. Miller, your host tonight for the de Young Museum fund-raiser, has been . . . killed."

A few exaggerated gasps. A few inadvertent chuckles.

"You mean California de Young, don't you, Officer?" a Dick Tracy shouted.

They still didn't get it.

"No," Melvin continued. "I mean Mary Lee Miller. She's . . . been stabbed. I'm going to have to ask you not to leave the premises until one of my officers has taken your statements. They'll escort you into the adjoining auditorium, where you'll be sequestered until we can interview each of you."

Chuckles turned to grumbles.

"What?"

"You're kidding."

"What's going on?"

"We'll get to you as quickly as we can," he continued. "Please, just—"

The door to the crime scene room opened. All eyes left the detective and focused on the door. Corbin Cosetti staggered out, head down. In his hand, he held his mother's yapping dog. Its pink-dyed fur was spattered with blood.

"Mother . . . ," Corbin stammered, his face pulled back in a pained grimace. "She's . . . dead. Someone murdered my mother."

That's when the serious screaming began.

*   *   *

While surprises can be great fun at a party, this wasn't the kind I had in mind. The surprise was supposed to be the revelation of the "killer," followed by the anticipated gasps of delight from the amateur sleuths. What now pounded against my eardrums were screams of terror.

Luckily my cast took direction well, even off script. Along with the San Francisco police officers, they helped herd the large, nearly hysterical group into the large auditorium to await their turn to be questioned. I cooled my heels while the cops began interviewing guests. The VIPs were released sooner than you could say "Where's my lawyer?" while the rest talked on cell phones or to each other, anxious to be set free.

It was nearly an hour before I was called into a small classroom where Detective Melvin, ever the party pooper, waited for me.

"Ms. Parker, we meet again," the detective said, after I'd been escorted into one of the museum's educational classrooms. He sat behind a desk, his manicured hands folded, his silk tie perfectly aligned. While the room lacked the hot lights of a police station interrogation room, the Mayan murals depicting human sacrifices did nothing to put me at ease.

"So . . . you wanted to see me?" I said innocently, avoiding meeting the detective's eyes. I fiddled with the buttons on my costume.

When I finally glanced up, he smiled. Sort of.

"Look, Detective Melvin. I don't know what I can tell you. Everything was going fine until—" I broke off.

"Until your 'victim' became real." He sat back in his

chair, hands behind his head, and gestured for me to sit. I took the front-and-center chair and reluctantly sat down.

"So tell me what happened," Melvin said.

"I have no idea. We were about to herd the guests into the mural room—the crime scene room—for the second act when suddenly Dee came out . . . her hands all bloody. I thought it was fake blood . . ." I shook my head. Poor Dee. What she must be going through now.

Melvin sat up and placed his hands flat on the desk. "Let's back up a little. The rehearsal last night. I heard there was a confrontation between Ms. Jackson and Ms. Miller."

I smushed my lips together before answering. Nearly everyone at the rehearsal had heard Dee's idle threats. Who had blabbed? "Where did you hear that?"

He ignored my question. "What happened at the rehearsal?" He eyed me, as if he knew something I didn't and was trying to trap me. But I knew Detective Melvin better than he thought, having "worked" with him on a previous case involving the death of one of my party guests. Although good at his job, he was quick to jump to conclusions. And he overcompensated—that was clear from his intricately embroidered wing tips. I knew from teaching abnormal psychology that this was a classic sign of narcissistic personality disorder.

"Sounds like you already know," I said, crossing my arms.

"I want to hear it from you."

I glanced at one of the murals on the wall. Four scantily clad men held down a bleeding victim on some kind of round altar. One of the men gripped a dagger in one hand and the victim's heart in the other. I shuddered. Was Detective Melvin about to cut out my heart and have it with a little Chianti?

"Okay, sure, there was a little tension between Dee and Mary Lee at the rehearsal. That always happens during rehearsals. They're stressful. But we worked it out."

He flipped a page of his notebook and scanned the chicken scratch that was supposed to be his handwriting. "According to my *source*, Ms. Jackson actually threatened to kill Ms. Miller last night." He read from his notes: "'Bee-otch, I should have stabbed her when I had the chance.'" He glanced up, eyes narrowed on her. "Is that about right?"

I leaned forward. "She didn't mean she would really have done it! It's just something she said, you know, like we all do during times of stress. You know, like, 'I'm going to kill that paper boy if he doesn't stop throwing my newspaper in the sprinkler.'" I sat back in my chair, wondering who had felt the need to repeat Delicia's meaningless threat.

Detective Melvin glanced back at his notes. "According to my *source*, Ms. Jackson picked up several weapons—a knife, gun, and rope, to be exact—and enacted Mary Lee's virtual death behind her back." He looked up at me for my reaction. He got what he wanted.

I sat openmouthed, unable to speak. My only thought was: Who was this so-called *source*? Was someone out to get Delicia?

"I assume from your silence that this is correct? Do you want to tell me why Ms. Jackson might have wanted Ms. Miller dead?"

"She didn't!" I said and stood up to leave. This was getting Dee nowhere.

The detective pushed another button. "I understand your

friend was having an affair with Corbin Cosetti, Mary Lee Miller's son. And Miller wanted him to break it off."

I glared down at him. "So? Delicia wouldn't kill her for that. Ridiculous."

"Not really. If she were to marry Miller's son, she'd find herself among the city's wealthy elite, wouldn't she?"

I could feel the color rise in my face in fury. "Look, Detective. As a former abnormal psychology instructor, I don't use this term loosely, but you're nuts. Once again you're jumping to conclusions, based on hearsay."

"Actually, we have motive, opportunity, and means." He ticked off his fingers as he listed his "evidence." "Motive: Jackson had threatened to kill Miller for trying to end her relationship with Corbin. Opportunity: She was in the room alone with the victim—and all those weapons. Means: When we find the real weapon, no doubt hidden somewhere in that room, I'm pretty sure it will have her bloody fingerprints all over it. Not exactly hearsay."

I thought for a moment. The Styrofoam copy of the dagger obviously couldn't have killed Mary Lee. It wasn't strong enough or sharp enough.

"So you don't have a weapon?"

"Not yet. But we'll find it. With all the security, no one can get in or out of the museum without something like that being discovered. Like I said, it's most likely in that room. My officers are searching for it now."

I felt another wave of heat rise up from my toes. This wasn't happening. My friend and coworker was not a murderer. But if I'd written this as a play, even an amateur sleuth would convict her on this damning evidence.

"How do you know she was alone in there? All of my actors entered the room at some point to place their weapons. Any one of them could have done it."

I stopped abruptly. What was I saying! That Raj or Berkeley could have murdered Mary Lee Miller? Not a chance. That left one of the museum staff, or even Corbin . . .

"The room is only accessible from two points," the detective said. "From the front, where the guests were to enter. And from a side door where the suspects supposedly made their covert entrances."

"Yes, that's right," I said. "Once Delicia entered—she was supposed to be the last suspect to drop off her weapon—she was to discover the dead body and then scream to alert the guests, cueing the second act. But"—I was thinking out loud here, visualizing the possible scene—"when she discovered Mary Lee had really been stabbed . . . she must have freaked out . . . and screamed for real."

"That doesn't explain why that side door was locked. Which it was, according to the security guard."

That stopped me for a second. While Detective Melvin drummed his fingers on the desk, I tried to come up with an explanation.

"Inside or outside?"

The detective stopped drumming and frowned.

"Was it locked from the inside or the outside?"

"Inside."

Uh-oh. That would make it look like Dee locked it after she entered.

Detective Melvin waited.

"Look," I said, leaning in. I felt like a passionate prosecutor trying to convince a skeptical jury. "Anyone could have locked that door after Dee entered—to make it look like she was the last person in there. They could have reached in and locked it without her knowing. And that means anyone could have come in there and stabbed Mary Lee—*before* Dee even went in there."

Detective Melvin blinked. I could see the wheels turning and thought I had him. Then he said, "But the killer stabbed her with something sharp, then replaced the weapon with the Styrofoam knife. Delicia Jackson was the last one in that room. And her hands were covered in blood."

Chapter 5

PARTY PLANNING TIP #5

When it's time to reveal the killer at your Murder Mystery Party, have him or her confess. Otherwise you may hear a number of inappropriate accusations hurled at several of your other guests.

After Detective Melvin dismissed me, I found Brad just leaving the crime scene room. He'd just ducked under the yellow police tape in the entryway that the police had used to cordon off the area.

I ran up to him. "Brad!"

"Not now, Presley," he said abruptly, brushing past me.

I backed up, taken by surprise at his change in mood. What the hell was up with him?

I raised my hands in a gesture of surrender. "Okay. Could you at least get me in there to see Delicia? I'm sure she's upset and needs a friend."

Brad glanced back at the police officer standing guard, hands folded across his crotch. He stepped over, said something to the cop, then returned. "He'll let you in to see her. But don't do anything—"

"Stupid," I said, finishing his sentence. "That's what you were going to say, right?" I glared at him.

"Not now, Presley," he said, and took off across the vast, empty room.

I looked at the officer, wondering briefly what a crime scene cleaner could say to an officer that would get me inside. Heading over, I smiled sweetly at him, then ducked under the tape before he could change his mind.

Delicia sat in a folding chair, near where a small table had been brought in. She was shaking her head and mumbling to herself as I approached her. She jerked her head up the moment she saw me. I expected her to stand up and hug me. Instead, she stiffened and returned her gaze to the table.

Something was seriously wrong.

"Delicia, are you all right?" I pulled out another folding chair next to her, sat down, and put my hand on her shoulder.

She shook it off. "What do you think is wrong?" she snapped and pulled off her titian wig.

This was not the Delicia I knew and loved.

"It's going to be okay, Dee. They'll find out who did this and—"

Her head whipped around to face me, her tearstained face filled with hurt and rage. "Don't you get it? They think I did it! I was in that room with her, alone. And I have her blood on me."

"That's just circumstantial—"

She cut me off. "They know about my relationship with Corbin."

"That doesn't mean you—"

"And *someone* conveniently overheard me say I wanted to kill her and told the cops!"

I had a feeling the word "someone" was meant for me.

"No, Dee. I didn't tell Detective Melvin that. I didn't tell him anything that would incriminate you. I know you didn't do it."

She said nothing as more tears welled in her eyes.

"Besides," I continued, "the knife you handled was made out of Styrofoam. There's no way it could have killed her."

She blinked back the tears. "He said I switched the knives, that I used the real one to kill her and then hid it somewhere and replaced it with the fake one."

"But why would you do that?"

"Good question—although that hasn't stopped Melvin."

"It doesn't make sense. You had no reason—"

She interrupted me again. "You were the only one who heard me say that about Mary Lee. It was just an expression, but you had to tell him, didn't you?"

"Tell me what?"

Startled, I whirled around in my seat. Detective Melvin and an African-American female officer stood at the door. I hadn't heard them come in.

Delicia shot a look at me.

Melvin's face tightened.

I turned back to Delicia. "I didn't say anything, Dee, I swear."

"Well, *somebody* told him I threatened her," Delicia hissed. "And you were the only one close enough to hear me."

I was about to argue that there were several others mill-

ing around when Detective Melvin strode into the room,
shadowed by the young officer. He nodded to the officer, and
on cue, she pulled out a small card and began reading: "You
have the right to remain silent . . ."

A sudden buzzing in my ears kept me from hearing the
rest. I grabbed Delicia's hand and felt her trembling, just before she jerked her hand away.

"Don't say anything," I said. "I'll find you a lawyer."

I turned to Detective Melvin and pleaded, "You can't be
serious! She didn't do anything!"

He ignored me as he waited for the cop to finish her
speech. Where the hell was Brad? Maybe he could talk some
sense into his by-the-book Melvin. After all, they were
friends, weren't they?

When the female cop finished her not-yet-memorized
recitation, she pulled out handcuffs.

"Seriously! You're *not* going to take her out in handcuffs!"
My voice reached a fevered pitch. Delicia, on the other hand,
said nothing—in words, that is. Her face told another story
as tears streamed down her smeared face.

I stood up. "Delicia, don't worry. I'll take care of this. I'm
coming with you."

Delicia shook her head. "No, thanks, Pres. You've done
enough." She stood and wiped away tears with the shoulder
of her Nancy Drew costume. But her eyes filled again as the
cop handcuffed her.

My eyes brimmed too, as I watched the young officer lead
her out of the room like a common criminal. My chest ached
with the pain I felt for her. I stood there a moment, a combination of dumbfounded and enraged at what I had just witnessed, before turning to Melvin.

"How can you arrest her? You know her! She works with me. She has an office in my building. She wouldn't hurt anyone. This is crazy!" I practically screamed the words at him. Surely anyone left in the museum heard me. But Detective Melvin acted as if I hadn't said a word.

I started for the entryway.

"Actually," Melvin said, "I need to ask you a few more questions, Ms. Parker. Have a seat." He indicated one of the folding chairs.

I crossed my arms in a show of resistance. "No, thank you, Detective. I'm busy. I have to figure out a way to get my innocent friend out of jail for a crime she didn't commit."

"I'm afraid there's a little matter in your statement I need to review."

"Oh, what's that? You haven't paid much attention to anything I've said so far."

"It's what you didn't say that interests me." His piercing eyes narrowed, as if he were trying to see through me.

"What do you mean? I told you everything I know. There's nothing left to say."

"You can tell me what she did with the weapon."

Speechless, my mouth dropped open.

"I thought I could trust you to tell me the truth, Ms. Parker," the detective said. "After the last time—that incident with the mayor, remember? Keeping things from me didn't help you much then. If you do the same this time—if you're helping her cover up this crime in any way—I'll charge you with aiding and abetting."

"This is total bullshit, and you know it."

"Did you or did you not overhear Ms. Jackson say she wanted to kill Ms. Miller?"

I dropped my arms in exasperation. "She didn't mean it!"

"But you *did* hear her say something to that effect."

I stonewalled him. It's no use arguing with a narcissist who thinks he's always right.

His jaw tightened. "Thank you, Ms. Parker. I'll be in touch." He flipped his notebook shut, stuffed it inside a pocket, and ducked out of the room.

Oh my God. Melvin thought I was helping Delicia conceal some kind of evidence. Meanwhile, Delicia thought I'd ratted her out. Now neither one of them trusted me.

But the biggest issue here was the fact that my friend Delicia was headed for jail on suspicion of murdering Mary Lee Miller.

Un-frigging-believable.

I dropped into a chair, a gazillion questions about the murder competing in my head with a gazillion to-dos regarding the party. Cleanup on aisle de Young . . .

I mentally went over the questions popping to mind like balloons.

Question: Who wanted Mary Lee dead? According to her popularity rating around the museum, quite a few people.

Question: Who had the opportunity to enter the crime scene room and kill her? With all the replica weapons left behind, it seemed as if all my costumed suspects had become real suspects.

Question: Mary Lee had been stabbed with—what? The Styrofoam knife certainly hadn't done the job.

Question: How was I going to clear Delicia of murder when I had no clue what had really happened?

Answer: Use my party planning guide. The simple form,

borrowed from my mother's bestselling handbook, *How to Host a Killer Party*, had actually helped me figure out who had killed the guest of honor at my last big event.

I pulled a reprinted sheet from my bag and jotted down what I knew in the spaces provided, substituting crime details for party info.

Step 1. Start with a Theme

Party Plan—What's the occasion? Murder Mystery Party at the museum.

Investigation—What's the crime? Real murder, real mystery.

Step 2. The Guest of Honor

Party Plan—Who is the GOH? Mary Lee Miller.

Investigation—What was the Victim hiding? No clue.

Step 3. Timing Is Key

Party Plan—Plan the party from start to finish.

Investigation—Note the events before and after crime.

Step 4. Location, Location

Party Plan—Set the stage.

Investigation—Check out the crime scene, the mural room at the museum. Two ways in and out, second door locked.

Step 5. Greet the Guests

Party Plan—Welcome the attendees.

Investigation—Interview the guest lists/suspects. Anyone else?

Step 6. The Element of Surprise

Party Plan—Expect the unexpected.

Investigation—No shit, Sherlock.

I looked over the list and added a few more party/crime details.

> *Decorations & ambience, aka weapons & clues.* Faux artifacts and real weapons, plus Dee's fingerprints on the Styrofoam dagger. What became of the real dagger?

> *Games & activities, aka What really happened?* Suspects entered the crime scene through the side room during the break so they wouldn't be spotted by the guests, then set down their faux weapons and left. Last person to enter was the killer?

> *Refreshments, aka drugs.* Champagne—anything else?

> *Favors & mementos, aka Who took away the most from the party?* Check cell phone snapshots and videotape of guests.

Not much there—at least not enough to start a party. I

folded the paper, stuffed it back into my purse, and headed out of the room to look for Brad. Most of the guests were gone, finished with their interrogations by the officers. A few of the cast members were downing the remaining champagne. I located my mother, who was chatting—flirting—with one of the security guards. Upon closer look, I recognized Sam Wo from our encounter upstairs the day before. He stood close to her, laughing and talking. I wondered if he was truly amused at her stories, or was he hoping to find a wealthy dowager at a charity event? Little did he know, she hadn't a cent to her name.

Someone tapped me on the shoulder. I spun around.

"A little jumpy, aren't you?" Brad said.

"Where have you been? I've been looking all over for you."

He shrugged. "Around. Where've *you* been?"

"Your friend has arrested Delicia!" I said, ignoring his question.

Brad glanced away, as if he couldn't meet my eyes. He was keeping something from me.

"Brad . . . what do you know?" I demanded.

He stared down at his well-worn New Balance Zips—the ones he wore for work. "Nothing, really."

"Brad!"

"Look, I haven't had a chance to talk with Melvin yet. But it doesn't look good. They have a pretty strong case. Has she got a lawyer?"

"I'm sure she doesn't. She hasn't needed one—until now. I need to find her a good one."

"I know someone. Let me handle it."

"Did you find anything in the crime scene room?"

Brad's pocket began playing the "Clean Up" song from that purple dinosaur TV show. I stared at him as he withdrew his phone.

"Yeah?" he said; then his eyes widened. He turned around and stepped away, out of my range of hearing.

Suddenly feeling chilly in the vast grand room of the museum, surrounded by symbols of murder and mystery, I hugged myself. Mary Lee Miller was dead. Delicia was in jail for murder. And Brad seemed distant. What was up with him?

Deciding not to wait, I headed over to the table that held mostly empty bottles of champagne to check on Mom and drag her away from another future ex-husband. After chugging the dregs of a less-than-cold glass of bubbly, I put my tipsy mother to work gathering party paraphernalia while my hired staff packed up the big stuff.

It was past midnight by the time the two of us headed down to the underground parking lot to my red MINI Cooper, both exhausted from the long and trying evening. It would be an expensive night, not only in materials but also emotionally.

Driving past the Golden Gate Park panhandle toward my mom's care facility, I half listened to her excited talk about the party and the "new man in her life," while I tried to come up with plausible suspects for Mary Lee's murder. By the time I reached her place off Van Ness Avenue, I couldn't wait to get back to my condo on Treasure Island and collapse.

"Thanks again for helping out with the play, Mom," I said, walking her inside the facility. A security guard had let us in after recognizing my mother. "Hope you're not too upset about . . . you know . . . the incident . . ." With early-stage Alzheimer's, my mother seemed cognizant most of the time, but I never knew when she left reality for another dimension.

"Oh, you mean the murder! That was quite exciting! I never liked Mary Lee Miller anyway. She was too . . . bossy. I had a dog like hers once. Lhasa-poodle mix. I named her Pumpkin, remember? Anyway, I'm not at all surprised. Sam said she wasn't terribly popular around the museum."

"Mom!" I said, stunned at her response.

"Oh, not that she deserved to be stabbed to death, but I doubt very many will be saddened by her loss. Of course, the museum is going to need a new person to take over fundraising. Maybe I could step in. I've had a lot of experience raising money over the years for good causes—the Union Square Pigeon Shelter. The Pier 39 Seal Birth Control Project. And don't forget my Save the Historic Tenderloin campaign."

At the late hour, the lobby was empty, aside from the guard. I signed her in and gave her a hug.

"We'll see, Mother. I'll call you soon, okay."

She headed for the elevator to her room, then looked back and said, "Let me know if there's anything I can do to help free your friend Delinda."

"It's Delicia. And I will, Mom."

"I could have a thousand 'Free Delinda' T-shirts ready by tomorrow, you know. I've got connections."

I thanked her again, blew her a kiss, and headed out, hoping my mother didn't do anything more than toss out wild ideas. I wouldn't put it past her to get involved in her own creative way. If the number of times I've picked her up from SFPD was any indication, I'd have my hands full.

I got in my MINI, turned on the ignition, and sat there for a moment, thinking. What was that my mother had said as we'd driven back to her place: "I never liked Mary Lee Miller . . ."

Nah. She couldn't have.

But it was the mention of her dog Pumpkin that left me wondering where Mary Lee's little dog Chou-Chou was. The last I'd seen it, it was with Corbin. Had he taken it home? I recalled from one of the rehearsals that he hadn't cared much for the pooch. Was he transferring his feelings to the dog?

Or did he have other plans for little Chou-Chou?

The drive from the city onto Treasure Island reminds me of sailing on ocean whitecaps into a glassy lake. I could feel the tension of the evening melt as I took the sharp exit ramp, down twisty Macalla Road to the flatlands. As I drove past the tall palm trees, the Art Deco World's Fair building, and the deserted navy barracks, I felt my shoulders relax and my breathing slow. I glanced back at the city I'd left behind, now a showcase of blinking lights, then headed for my neighborhood, where I rented a renovated condo that had once been military housing.

Pulling my MINI into the carport, I gathered as many party props as I could hold, grabbed my purse with the only finger I had left, and walked to the door. Juggling arms full of party crap, I inserted my key into the lock, opened the door, and tripped over Thursby, lying in wait for me. Cairo and Fatman meowed and ran for their lives.

"Darn cats," I whispered as Thursby fled the downpour of props. While I managed to stay upright, everything else went flying, including my knockoff Dooney & Bourke purse. After I cleared a path to the kitchenette, I made myself a cup of pomegranate tea and sank into the couch. Too wired to sleep, I began making a list of anyone who might have wanted to see Mary Lee Miller with a dagger in her back.

Other than Delicia, I came up empty. This was going to take a little more investigating if I hoped to find anyone else who had a motive. It had to be someone at the party— someone who knew Mary Lee was alone in the mural room, waiting for Act II. That left me with a handful of viable suspects, many of them my coworkers. Not to mention my own mother.

Great. All I had to do was figure out which one it was.

With little or no help from Detective Melvin or the San Francisco Police Department.

Or Brad?

My cell phone rang, playing the tune from "Halloween." I looked at the caller ID.

Unknown.

I said, "Hello?"

No answer.

The perfect ending to a perfect night.

Chapter 6

PARTY PLANNING TIP #6

*Low lights and flickering candles offer a nice atmo-
sphere for your Murder Mystery Party. Just try not to
burn down the party venue. Guests dislike going
home with singed eyebrows and soot-covered costumes.*

Morning comes earlier to Treasure Island than it does to the
rest of the San Francisco Bay Area. I'm sure of it. Surrounded by water, the island catches the first rays of sun re-
flecting off the bay, which spill directly into my bedroom
window.

Sunday morning I awakened to blinding light, in spite of
the mini-blinds, plus the prickly massage of cats kneading
my legs. Throwing off the covers before the cats could draw
blood, I sat up in my Tweety Bird tank top and matching
elastic shorts that served as pajamas, rubbed the sleep out of
my head, and made tracks for the tiny bathroom to take a
much-needed shower.

As the warm water rained down on me, visions of last

night's disaster popped into view. The murder. The police. The arrest of Delicia. I rinsed off quickly, dried myself hard enough to cause rug burns, and dressed in fresh black jeans and a T-shirt that read, "I don't have a short attention span. I just . . . Oh look, a chicken . . ." A latte would help control my ADHD, and hopefully channel it into something more akin to multitasking on speed.

I headed for my small kitchen to feed Thursby, Cairo, and Fatman gourmet cat food. After rinsing a cinnamon raisin bagel down my throat with a large latte, I grabbed my purse and roller blades and drove to the office a few blocks away. When I needed a physical and mental break, skating the path around the island helped clear my head better than Adderall any day.

There was only one other car in the lot when I arrived— Delicia's tiny yellow Smart Car. I'd given her a ride to the museum last night—she hated driving in the city—so she'd left her car behind. I tried the door handle—locked.

I walked up the rickety steps of the barracks office to the paint-peeling door and slipped my key in the lock. The large front office served as a waiting room for the several small businesses in the building. It sported an old gray metal desk left behind by the navy, a garage-sale sofa with a fake-fur slipcover, and a disconnected landline phone that was just for show. When we needed to impress important clients, we took turns posing as the office secretary.

This was actually my second office building. The first had burned down a few weeks earlier, and we'd moved to an identical one next door. I had the first office beyond the entry room, on the right. The office directly opposite me had recently been rented by Brad Matthews, who owned a crime scene cleaning business, but I suspected that was only a part-time job. What he did at other times was still a mystery. I'd recently learned he had connections with the police department, the mayor's office, and high-level companies who seemed to hire him for more than just cleaning up bodily messes.

Yeah, he was hot. And he'd helped me out a few times. I couldn't put my finger on it, but I didn't fully trust the guy.

I sat down in my office swivel chair, pulled out the party form from my purse, and added it to the top of my cluttered desk. According to my notes, I had over two hundred suspects for the murder of Mary Lee Miller.

That narrowed it down.

I switched on my laptop and skimmed the thirty-plus e-mails waiting for me. Most of them related to upcoming parties, with demands like "Could you make all the balloons blue—it's my son's favorite color!!" and "I'm allergic to shellfish, so NO crab or shrimp!!!"

Ignoring the ones that weren't pressing, i.e. all of them, I typed in Mary Lee Miller's name. Brad had told me to "study the victim," which he said he'd learned from cleaning up after a few homicides.

Several hundred links popped up for the name Mary Lee Miller. Great. Reading all the entries would take most of the day—time I didn't feel I had. After weeding out the Mary Lee Millers that had no connection to the museum and skimming the rest—ADHD makes me good at skimming—all I learned was how much money Mary Lee had made for the de Young and what an incredible philanthropist she was. I scanned more articles, quoting her "vision" for the museum, her "love of art and artifacts," her charitable fund-raising parties, and her pleasure at having a future wing of the museum named after her.

The woman was a saint, at least in the museum community.

Who'd want to kill someone like that?

I kept searching for something unusual, something more—or less—than sainthood. It wasn't until I discovered a news article written several years ago for a small newspaper that I found any kind of dirt. The interview had been with Jason Cosetti, Mary Lee's first ex-husband and father of her son, Corbin.

"When she left me, she took everything," Jason was quoted saying, "including our son. I never saw a dime of the money we earned the year we were together. She may have made a fortune for her museum, but the only other person who got anything from her was her lawyer. And he didn't have to live with her to get it."

Apparently Jason wasn't a fan. I wondered what their relationship status was today.

I had just added his name to my notes when someone tapped me on the shoulder, startling me. I spun around to find a giant marshmallow man standing behind me. I slapped my chest in relief.

"You've got to stop sneaking up on me," I said to Brad, who looked like an alien, if not a marshmallow man, in his white Crime Scene Cleaners jumpsuit.

"I didn't sneak up on you. You were so engrossed in whatever you're doing, I guess you didn't hear me come in." He pulled open a folding chair and sat opposite me. "Find out anything?" He nodded toward the computer screen.

Still miffed at being ignored last night, I shrugged non-committally.

"I haven't known you long, Presley, but I do know you're not going to let up on this thing with Mary Lee. So what have you found?"

I turned to the screen. "Well, as a matter of fact, I'm following your advice."

"What's that—leave it to the police?"

"No, *cherchez la victime*—look at the victim. I've been Googling Mary Lee Miller."

He nodded. "I should learn to keep my mouth shut. So did you find anything?"

"That she was a saint—at least to the museum crowd. And that her ex-husband might disagree. They were divorced soon after Corbin was born. She was making more money than he was, so he asked for spousal support. Didn't get it. She even took their son, claiming Jason was away too much and unavailable to share custody." I looked at Brad. "Think he's still holding a grudge after all these years?"

"Anything's possible, but that's a long time to bottle up revenge. Any chance Jason was at the party?"

"Not sure," I said. "He wasn't on the guest list, but I suppose he could have sneaked in, wearing a costume like everyone else."

We heard the front door to the office building creak open and then slam shut. I expected to see one of the other business tenants—Berkeley or Raj or Rocco. Anyone but the person who entered the hallway: Detective Melvin.

As usual he was dressed impeccably, not a slicked-back hair out of place. He'd brought along a burly officer in uniform who stayed quiet in the detective's shadow.

"Oh shit," I said under my breath. "Now what?" Ever since the detective and I butted heads over another murder case a few weeks ago, we'd been civil to each other, but it had been an effort.

Brad, on the other hand, greeted him like an old friend. He stood up, and they shook hands and briefly discussed their last golf game. I never quite understood Brad's relationship with the *GQ*-style cop.

Detective Melvin finally acknowledged me and nodded curtly. "Ms. Parker."

"I think you can call me Presley, Detective, after all we've been through."

He ignored my comment and glanced over at Delicia's tiny office next to mine. The walls that connected our offices were made of wood on the bottom half and glass on the top. I watched the detective stretch his neck and do a superficial scan.

"Have you found the killer yet?" I asked, getting to the point.

He gave me a condescending smile and said nothing.

I pressed him. What did I have to lose? "So what are you doing here, Detective? You know Delicia didn't kill Mary Lee, and neither did my other office mates, even though they also played parts at last night's event. Shouldn't you be looking for her murderer instead of peeking into people's office windows?"

Letting his eyes pass coolly over me, Detective Melvin headed to Delicia's office.

I stood up. "Wait a minute. What are you doing?"

Melvin slipped his hand into his suit jacket and pulled out a paper that was becoming all too familiar to me: a search warrant. Several weeks ago he'd brought one to search my own office.

I crossed my arms and called after him, "You're wasting your time, Detective. You're not going to find anything incriminating in there, like the murder weapon."

He tried the door handle, then felt along the top of the door frame, obviously searching for a key. Finding nothing, he turned to me. "Any chance you've got a key to this office, Ms. Parker?"

"Nope," I lied. Delicia had a habit of locking herself out of her office, so we'd made duplicates and exchanged them soon after we'd moved in.

Brad raised an eyebrow at me. I raised one right back at him.

Melvin signaled for the burly officer, who stepped over to Dee's door and pulled out a key.

"How did you get her key?" I asked.

Brad leaned over to me and whispered, "It's not her key."

I watched as the cop began to twist the key inside the lock.

"What's he doing, then?" I whispered back.

"It's called 'bumping' or 'rapping' a lock. Works pretty well, especially with older cylinder locks. Not everyone can do it. Takes practice."

Brad narrated the action as the big guy continued working. "In a bump key—some call it a nine-nine-nine key—all the cuts are as deep as they can be. It fits the lock, even though the cuts are different."

A key like that would be handy to have. "Where did he get it?"

Brad smiled. "Well, you can't just go to your local locksmith and ask him to make you one. I suppose you could always file it down yourself."

"How do you know all this stuff?"

"Let's just say I was a weird kid," he said. "So anyway, you insert the key, then pull it out one click. Then you jiggle it while you tap on the back end."

The officer did exactly what Brad said. After inserting the key, he pulled it back a fraction of an inch. He continued pushing and pulling on the key, then struck the end of it with his nightstick. With a last turn, the door opened.

"Oh my God," I said, stunned at having witnessed a professional break-in.

"You want the physics behind it?" Brad asked.

"No, thanks. If I need to break into an office, I'll check Wikipedia."

"Good, because I didn't do so well in that class. Has something to do with the energy from the strike transferring from the key to the tumblers, causing them to jump."

"In other words, breaking and entering," I said.

The officer stepped aside, allowing Detective Melvin to enter Dee's office. Once inside, he began riffling through papers, opening drawers, and scanning the scattered messages that lay on her disaster of a desk. As an often-out-of-work actress, Dee usually had her desk cluttered with résumés, head shots, and messages from her agent.

Brad and I watched through the doorway as Melvin sat down in Dee's chair and switched on her notebook computer. The detective's large fingers had difficulty working the small keyboard, and he repeatedly had to backspace and retype commands. After several minutes of punching keys, he frowned and closed the cover.

I wondered if he'd found anything significant. Or incriminating.

Unfortunately, I didn't get a chance to find out. He unplugged the computer, gathered up the cord, and carried it out of the office. The burly officer followed him down the hall, without locking the door behind him.

"Can he do that?" I asked Brad. "Just take her computer like that?"

"With a warrant he can do just about anything."

"Why do you want her computer?" I called to the detective as I followed him toward the reception area.

"Sorry. That's confidential."

"But—"

He stopped and turned to me. "But what, Ms. Parker?"

I glared at him, then spun around and returned to my office to pout. I heard him call out "Later" to Brad, just before the front door closed.

"Humph," I fumed.

I was certain that Detective Melvin, rather than trying to find the real killer, was building his case against Delicia. What had he found on her laptop? Something like "I'm going to kill Mary Lee Miller" written in a giant red letters using a fancy Gothic font?

I hoped not. But Delicia had a flare for the dramatic. That's what made her such a good actress. And now, no doubt, a good suspect. I had to talk to her and find out if there was anything Melvin might have found on her computer.

Only problem was, she might not be speaking to me at the

present. Mainly because she blamed me for ratting her out to the cops.

Until I could get to the jail, I'd spend every minute I had trying to work up a viable list of suspects. Top of my list was Mary Lee's embittered ex-husband, Jason Cosetti.

All I had to do was find him.

I returned to Delicia's unlocked office to rummage through anything Detective Melvin had left behind. The first thing I wanted to check was her cell phone, but it was nowhere in sight. Impounded? I'd hoped to find a phone number for Corbin in order to track down his father. The only contact I had for him was e-mail—too slow.

I glanced around the desk. No Rolodex. No address book. Not even a sticky note with a recently dialed phone number on it. With all the cell phone apps, no one wrote on paper anymore.

I was about to return to my own office when I noticed a yellow piece of paper stuck to the bottom of my shoe. I lifted my foot. A sticky note. It must have fluttered to the floor during the detective's whirlwind visit, and I'd stepped on it. I snatched it off and found a phone number.

I pulled out my cell phone and dialed it.

"North Beach Pizza . . . ," an accented voice said. Sounded like he said "pizzer" instead of "pizza."

I hung up.

Finding Corbin's number like that would have been way too easy.

But it gave me an idea.

I pulled open her top drawer. Jackpot. It was filled with a

sticky collage of yellow notes, all with phone numbers on them. And a few with names.

I tried the top five and reached a movie theater, a Chinese takeout restaurant, a hair salon, and a clothing boutique before I heard a familiar voice

"Yeah?"

"Corbin?" I asked.

"Yeah?"

"This is Presley Parker."

"Yeah?"

Not the response I expected.

"I'm . . . so sorry about your mother."

"Yeah."

"Uh, I wondered if I could talk with you. About Delicia."

A moment of silence, then, "Yeah, I guess. She all right?" His voice was flat and unemotional. A sign of depression, no doubt.

"I don't know. That's why I want to talk with you. I think we can help her. Would you be willing to meet me?"

"Where?"

I mentioned the Bittersweet Café on Fillmore. The place was like a crack house for my two addictions—coffee and chocolate. Might as well get a fix while interrogating the dead woman's son. We agreed to meet in an hour. I thanked him, he said, "Yeah," and we hung up. I hoped he'd be a little more talkative once I filled him up with caffeine.

I closed my laptop and gathered my purse, suspect list, and cell phone. I'd barely made it into the hall before Brad called, "Hey, where're you going?"

"NYOB," I called back, showing off my latest texting vocab word.

Brad laughed at my attempt to sound hip. "Dyslexic, aren't you? It's NOYB."

I turned around and made a face at him.

"So . . . ," he said.

"So what?"

"So where are you going?"

"I thought I made that clear."

He sidled up to me—close, really close—causing me to blush. He slowly reached out a hand and touched the front of my shirt. I couldn't breathe. Pulling his hand back, he held a black cat hair in his fingers. Thursby. I felt my entire body heat up like a live volcano.

"Listen, I'd be glad to help," he said, brushing the hair from his fingers. He glanced over my shirt as he talked. Looking for more cat hairs? Or something else? "I've got connections, you know. I uncover a lot of dirt in my business."

"Literally," I said, referring to his crime scene cleaning business.

He laughed. Apparently I was becoming his main source of entertainment. I sighed. "Okay, but I don't want anything I tell you to go to your BFF Melvin." His close relationship with the detective could be a serious problem this time.

He shook his head and crossed his heart. "Your secrets are safe with me. We crime scene cleaners are like doctors. What happens in Presley's World, stays in Presley's World."

"All right. I'm going to see Corbin Cosetti."

"Mary Lee's spoiled son? Delicia's secret lover?"

"First of all, how do you know he's spoiled? And secondly, how did you know they were secret lovers?"

"Because he does whatever mommy tells him to get what he wants. And everyone knew about Corbin and Delicia. You think he killed his mother?"

"No! Of course not. But he may know someone who had a reason to kill her. Like his father . . ."

"Hmm," Brad said, pondering my statement. "So, you want company?"

"I . . ." Standing so close to him was making me nervous. I was tempted to take him along, but he was too distracting, and I needed to think.

"Maybe next time. I think he'll open up to me more if it's just the two of us." I took a step back and looked him over in his white jumpsuit. "Besides, don't you have a crime scene you need to clean up?"

"I'm between jobs right now," he said, shrugging. "Finished the museum late last night. But if you want to do this yourself, go for it."

He glanced back at my office. I followed his gaze. Through his eyes, with killer party props strewn around from last night's murder mystery event, the place must have looked like a violent death had recently occurred there. I wondered if a crime scene cleaner would help.

Brad reached into his pocket, pulled out a small roll of yellow plastic tape, stretched a piece across my door, and stuck a thumbtack in both ends. The words on the tape read: "Crime Scene—Do Not Enter."

"LOL," I said, and left the building.

Chapter 7

PARTY PLANNING TIP #7

For those guests playing suspects at your Murder Mystery Party, remind them to stay in character, even if something unexpected happens. Otherwise, the other guests may become confused, irate, or even violent.

I pondered my reservations about Brad Matthews as I drove to the Bittersweet Café in the Fillmore near lower Pacific Heights. Brad was a nice guy, attractive and sexy as hell, and had seemed sincere when he offered to help me. But he had lied to me in the past, and I couldn't get beyond my mistrust of him. Something lurked beneath that tight white jumpsuit—and I didn't mean just his hot body.

Thoughts of said body distracted me, and I missed the turn on Fillmore. The trouble with San Francisco streets is, there are too many one-ways and no-left-turns and not enough through streets. Not to mention the lack of parking. After circling around, I found a space between a big black Cadillac and a big white Lexus—both parked over their lines. Luckily the MINI just fit. Of course, if I'd had Delicia's Smart Car, I wouldn't have tapped both the front and rear bumpers pulling in.

I entered the narrow, high-ceilinged café, decorated in shabby chic, with distressed tables, mismatched chairs, and wall-sized art. I found Corbin at one of two window tables. He was hunched over an espresso, his hair disheveled—on purpose?—and his clothes splotchy—was that paint? He didn't look up when I entered, so I stepped over to the counter, ordered a double latte with a shot of chocolate, and watched him texting on his cell phone while I waited for my drink. I retrieved my drink and sat down opposite him in a wooden chair.

He looked up, touched his cell phone screen one last time, and slipped the BlackBerry into his pocket. "Hey," he said in a gravelly voice.

"How're you doing, Corbin?" I asked, searching his face. His eyes were red, but I couldn't tell if that was from crying over the loss of his mother, allergies, or some kind of drug use. The smell of chocolate brownies wafting through the café would disguise any telltale aroma of marijuana. There was no sign of Mary Lee's little dog.

He ran his fingers through his wild hair. "Okay. You know. Kinda hard to believe she's really gone. She was such a . . ."

I wait for him to finish, then suggested, "Strong person?"

He shrugged. "Yeah. Whatever."

I took a sip of my chocolate-rich latte while he stared into his tiny cup, still full of espresso.

"Thanks for meeting me, Corbin. I know it's a hard time

for you, but I'd like to do what I can to help Delicia. You knew her. You know she didn't have anything to do with your mother's death, but the police seem convinced by the circumstantial evidence. And they aren't doing much to find the real killer. I thought maybe you could help."

I wasn't sure he was listening as he continued to stare into his cup. Then he raised his head and said, "How?" He shuffled his feet under the table, and one foot bumped into mine. He stretched his lanky legs out to the side. I glanced down at his shoes. They were frayed, laceless, and paint-spattered Doc Martens athletic shoes. I guessed Corbin couldn't care less about brand names. His mother had probably supplied the black designer shoes. Or perhaps the starving-artist look was affected.

I tried again.

"Corbin, a lot of people went into that crime scene room last night. I can vouch for my office mates, Raj and Berk. They had no reason to harm Mary Lee. But I don't know Christine Lampe or Dan Tannacito that well. I thought you might give me some insight into the museum staff. Can you think of any reason they might want your mother . . . out of the picture?" Bad choice of words, but I found it difficult to discuss this with him.

Two girls entered the café, dressed in glittery BeBe tees and tight jeans, with rhinestones decorating their derrieres. Corbin followed them with his eyes, then took a sip of his drink. Was he thinking about something? Avoiding my question? Or just interested in the two girls?

He set the cup down and met my eyes. "Actually, there were lots of people who didn't like my mother. I mean, everyone acted as if they liked her, but she could be really abrasive and controlling. I'm not saying it was enough to make someone want to kill her, but still . . ." He glanced again at the girls as he took another sip.

When he didn't continue, I asked, "Did you get along with your mother, Corbin?"

He smiled, but there was no joy in his eyes.

"Sure. As well as any kid with a mother who—" He stopped. The smile faded, and his handsome face clouded over. "Wait a minute. You don't think *I* had anything to do with my own mother's death, do you? Is that why you're here?" His voice rose as he spoke, anger building quickly.

"No, no, of course not," I said hastily. "I'm just trying to get a sense of her." Perhaps it was time to change the subject. "Tell me about your father, Jason. Did he get along well with your mother after the divorce?"

Corbin visibly relaxed.

"They got along fine, you know, for divorced parents."

"I read somewhere that it was quite a bitter divorce. Your father resented the fact that he didn't get anything in the settlement. And he was upset that your mother got full custody of you."

Corbin drummed his fingers on the small wooden table. Was he bored? Anxious? Or just ADHD like me?

"That was like years ago," he finally said. "Lately they'd been talking more. He had some ideas about fund-raising that he'd been pitching to Mother. In the past few years he'd gotten good at charming old ladies out of their money to fund his art-finding treks."

"Really?" I leaned forward. "They were getting along pretty well?"

"Yeah. He was finally getting his act together." Corbin's eyes brightened.

"What do you mean?"

"Oh, you know. When I was a kid, I used to hear people talking about them. They said Mother only married him because she thought he was going to be a great artist. And that he only married her for her family inheritance. They called him her trophy hubby behind her back. But he got nothing in the divorce, thanks to a prenup. And after a couple of bad reviews, he quit painting and started dealing in art and artifacts. Thought there was more money in it."

"How did he do?"

"Not so well. After a kind of shady deal he tried to make with MoMA, none of the museums would trust him. Including the de Young. Word spreads fast in the art world. He was always looking for ways to make money."

"Not all of them legit, I gather."

Corbin glanced at the two girls, who had taken the other table window.

"Do you think he might have . . ." My question trailed off.

He jerked his attention back to me. "What, *kill* her? No way. Like I said, they were getting along better lately, talking and stuff. No, no way would he kill her. He didn't have any reason to, after all these years."

"Corbin, I'd like to talk to him. Can you tell me how I can contact him?"

"He's houseboat-sitting right now. At the marina. You could try him there, although it's tough to catch him. He's gone a lot."

I took down the location of the boat and Jason's cell number. Before I'd talked to Corbin, I thought Jason was a real possibility as a suspect in Mary Lee's death. But after hearing he and Mary Lee were friendly again, his motive had vanished like city fog in the afternoon.

Still, maybe he continued to harbor a lot of resentment from the past. And he could easily have been at the party. Could he have smuggled in a knife, sneaked into the crime scene room where Mary Lee was waiting, and killed her? Sure, except he didn't seem to have a motive. At least, not an obvious one.

I filed the thought away for future consideration and moved on.

"Is there anything you can tell me about Christine, the museum curator? Or her assistant, Dan?"

Corbin took a deep, sorrowful breath and let it out slowly. "Not really. Mother and Chris were tight years ago, when I was a kid. They went to the same college, up in Oregon. Chris was my godmother, and Mother got her the job at the de Young. But they had some kind of falling-out recently. When I asked about her, Mother just shook her head and changed the subject. My mother didn't confide in me much."

A falling-out? Motive?

"What about Dan Tannacito? Did he have anything against your mother? Any deep, dark secrets?"

"Ha. He's a joke," Corbin said, looking disgusted, as if he smelled something bad in the air. "But that's no secret around the museum. Calls himself an 'exhibit developer,' but he's just another assistant. A wannabe curator who thinks he's Indiana Jones. Recently he'd been hanging around

Mother a lot, no doubt trying to get her to fire Chris so he could take over her job. At least, that was the gossip. He's a total phony."

Whoa. That was harsh. Did Corbin have a grudge against Dan for some hidden reason?

"Was there anyone else who might have been at the party who might have . . ." I couldn't finish my sentence.

"Murdered her?" Corbin sat up, cupped his espresso in both hands, and downed the dregs in one swallow. Setting the cup down, he ventured, "How about everyone?"

My eyebrows shot up.

"Seriously," Corbin continued. "It could have been anyone. Like I said, a lot of people acted as if they liked her. But she didn't have many true friends. And those she did have didn't seem to last long."

Corbin squirmed in his chair. It was time to wrap this up.

"Corbin, are you planning to see or talk to Delicia?"

He looked down at his empty cup. "Nah. I don't think it's a good idea. Not until all this is . . . over."

I felt the muscles in my neck tighten. "You don't believe she did it, do you?"

He didn't meet my eyes. Instead, he shifted, then pulled out his cell phone and began checking his messages. I got the hint and collected my purse.

Did he really think Delicia might have killed his mother?

Clearing Dee wasn't going to be easy without Corbin in her corner.

I stood up, thanked him, and offered my hand. He shook it limply.

"Oh. One last thing," I added. "Where's your mom's little dog?"

Corbin kept his eyes on his cell phone as he said, "I have no clue."

I drove the short distance to the marina near Fort Mason, hoping somehow to catch Jason Cosetti. He hadn't answered his cell phone, but I figured, since I was in the neighborhood, it was worth a try. Corbin had warned me that I wouldn't be able to get past the locked gate at the pier—and he was right. As soon as I found the East Harbor, aka "Gashouse Cove," I parked the MINI, got out, and located G-4, where the No. 90 boat slip was moored. Unable to get inside without a key, I stood on the dock for a few minutes waiting for someone to exit the gate so I could sneak in, while watching the colorful sailboats, kites, and tourists enjoying the unseasonably warm November day. Warm for San Francisco, that is, where weather usually ranges from overcast to fog to cloudy.

After a few minutes, a guy in white shorts and a blue-and-white-striped shirt appeared from within a nearby boat and stepped onto the dock.

But instead of coming my way, he began fiddling with some ropes.

"Excuse me!" I called and waved.

He looked up, squinting. "Yes?"

Now what? I couldn't tell him I'd forgotten my key. These people all knew each other. I tried another tack. "I came to see a friend of mine, but can't seem to get him on his cell. Could you let me in so I can check on him?"

"What's his name?" the man called.

"Uh, Jason Cosetti."

"Never heard of him. You must have the wrong dock."

Nuts! Of course he hadn't heard of Jason Cosetti. Jason was boat-sitting for some other guy—and I didn't know the boat owner's name.

"Actually, I think he's staying on the boat and keeping an eye on it for a friend."

The man looked down at his ropes and shook his head.

"Nope. Not here. No one's allowed to live on their boats in the harbor. Most you can stay is seventy-two hours." With that he leaped back onto his boat deck and disappeared inside.

Well, that trick didn't work. And I had more questions than answers.

So was Jason living on the boat illegally?

Or was Corbin lying to me about where his father was staying?

I checked the time—a little after ten—and figured I'd go on over to the de Young Museum to see if I could find out anything new. Two other names kept rearing their ugly heads—Christine Lampe and Dan Tannacito. Maybe they could shed some light on Mary Lee's untimely death. Both were personable people, at least superficially. But I'd barely gotten to know them in the short time they'd served as suspects in my murder mystery play. After Corbin had filled me in on their "backstories," I was intrigued.

Maybe they'd open up their secrets to me, a simple, non-threatening party planner. Event planner, I corrected myself.

I parked in the lot and headed for the museum. In spite of last night's murder, the place was open to the public, although I guessed the crime scene room had been cordoned off. After opening my purse to the guard at the door, I walked to the mural room. Instead of a "Do Not Cross" police tape across the door, a discreet sign read "Temporarily Closed to the Public."

I moved on to the front desk, showed my membership card to the docent, and lied, "I have an appointment with Christine Lampe."

The nice thing about docents, besides the fact that they donate their time and knowledge to the public, is that they're usually kindly older volunteers who work part-time and don't really get involved with administrative staff. I hoped my air of authority would allow me access upstairs.

The elderly woman paused for a moment and frowned, clearly befuddled. Then looked up the curator's office number on a plastic chart. "It's on the fourth floor, but you can't get there without a passkey. She'll have to come get you. I'll dial her extension."

I placed my hand on her wrist to stop her. "Oh, no, that's not necessary." I patted my purse. "I have a passkey. Thanks."

I turned and headed for the elevators. I didn't want Christine to know I was coming, preferring to take her by surprise, but I had to figure out a way to get up to the fourth floor.

I got on the elevator and spotted the button for the fourth floor. Underneath the buttons was a metal box with a blinking light. Apparently I needed to swipe a passkey to access the administrative upper floors. I rode to the seventh floor—the tower—and got off. Ignoring the breathtaking view from the panoramic windows, I walked over to a staircase on the other side of the room and well hidden from the gift kiosk. Strung across the entrance was a rope with the sign: "No admittance."

If I could just get past that rope . . .

"Excuse me, ma'am, but you're not allowed in there," came a voice from behind me.

I spun around, startled, until I recognized the security guard from the other night, Sam Wo.

"Sam! Hi, it's me, Presley Parker, from the party . . ."

He stared at me blankly.

"The event planner? For the mystery fund-raiser?" I reminded him.

Sam broke into a grin and nodded vigorously. "Yes, yes, I remember you. And your delightful mother." The smile abruptly faded. "Terrible thing, what happened to Ms. Miller. Terrible."

I nodded, commiserating. "Yes, actually that's why I'm here. I'm trying to find out who might have had a reason to kill her."

Sam raised his eyebrows. "I thought the police had arrested someone."

"That's just it. Delicia is my friend, and I know she didn't have anything to do with it. I want to help clear her."

"She didn't do it?" he said, lifting his cap to scratch his head.

"No, no way. And I need to talk to Christine Lampe and Dan Tannacito, but I don't want them to know I'm coming. Can you get me onto the fourth floor?"

He glanced around to see if we'd been overheard, then lowered his voice. "Oh no, Ms. Parker. I could get into trouble—"

"Please, Sam. I'm sure, as the head of security at the de

Young, you want to find out who really killed Mary Lee—
Ms. Miller—don't you?"

Sam glanced around again for eavesdroppers. "Yes," he
whispered, "but I don't want to lose my job. I've already lost
too much."

I frowned. "What do you mean? Because of the murder?"

"No, no. My retirement—it's gone. All my savings. Then
my wife left me. I lost my home. So you see, I can't afford to
lose this job."

I felt a sudden empathy for this man I hardly knew. I
reached out and touched his arm. "Sam, what happened?"

"I made some stupid investments," he said, shaking his
head.

"I'm sorry, Sam. That's terrible." I thought for a moment.
"Listen, if you help me, I'll do my best to make sure you
keep your job and get credit for your part in helping me find
the real killer. Maybe even get a raise."

Just how I was going to do that was a mystery to me.

"I really can't. Things are tense around here, and I feel
some responsibility for Ms. Miller's death. After all, it happened on my watch."

"I understand. I swear I won't mention you, except to say
you helped me find the killer when the time comes."

The deep line in his brow softened. I was getting to him.
I had one more ace up my sleeve.

"I know my mother will be impressed that you're trying
to help. She's been talking a lot about you."

His face lit up. "She has?"

Great. Now I was offering up my dear mother as a sort of
bribe. What kind of daughter was I?

Stealing another glance around, he said, "Okay, but make

it fast. This staircase leads to the floors below. There are cameras, so give me five minutes to get to the security office and take over the watch. You'll still be recorded on tape, but if there's no reason to review them, you should be okay."

"Thanks, Sam. I won't forget this. Nor will my mother."

Sam tipped his hat. "Ms. Parker, please be careful. If your friend didn't kill Ms. Miller, then someone else did. Perhaps someone from the museum."

Those were my thoughts exactly.

Chapter 8

PARTY PLANNING TIP #8

Tell the suspects at your Murder Mystery Party to exaggerate freely, and improvise whatever adds to their characters. Then suggest they add a little of their own personalities for authenticity.

Staring out at the view of the city, I waited the required five minutes before running down the stairs. When I reached the fourth floor, I yanked open the door and began looking for Christine's office.

"Presley!" a voice called from behind. "What are you doing here?"

I turned around to find Dan leaning out of his office doorway. "Oh hi, Dan," I said. "Uh, I was on my way to see Christine." I tapped my watch, implying that I had an appointment.

He stepped out into the hall, a wide grin on his chiseled face. He looked relaxed and casual, in spite of his perfectly pressed tailored suit and swank, stylish Rockports—the hybrid kind that combined cozy with cool. These shoes said he cared about his appearance, but his personal comfort came first.

His cheery face quickly turned sober. "You're here about Mary Lee? What a loss. She did so much for this museum, for the city. She'll be missed." He sounded sincere, but his body language told another story. In his hand he held a pen that he never stopped flicking.

"Come in, come in." He waved me over and gestured for me to enter his office. "I want you to meet my daughter."

Reluctantly I backed up and peered in the doorway. I spotted a teenage girl sitting behind Dan's desk, listening to music on her iPod. I waved at her.

"Come in, come in," he repeated, more insistently.

I glanced at my watch. "I'm going to be late for my appointment."

"I don't think she's there," Dan said. "Her office is right next door, but she hasn't been there much. I have a feeling she's taking Mary Lee's death pretty hard. Is there anything I can do for you?"

"Oh, uh—"

"Please." He gestured to a wooden chair opposite his desk. "Sit down. I'm sure this has been hard on you too, what with ruining your party and all. How are you doing?" Again, the voice sounded sincere, but the flicking pen was disconcerting.

"I'm okay," I said. "I'm more concerned about my friend Delicia. I guess you heard she's been arrested." I glanced at Dan's daughter, who was tapping her foot in rhythm to a beat. No doubt she hadn't heard a word we'd said. Her hot

pink hair was swept up like porcupine quills, defying grav-
ity, and was the only color in her ensemble aside from black.
Her lips were black, her nails were black, her eye makeup
was black, and her T-shirt, sporting the word "Evil" in the
shape of a skull, was black.

Dan caught me looking at her and turned to her. "Presley,
this is Stephanie, my daughter. Stephanie," he said loudly to
compete with the music. "Say hello to Ms. Parker."

She rolled her eyes at him, then glared at me.

"She prefers to be called Vampira," Dan said quietly.
"She's going through a Goth phase. Last year it was pop star.
The year before that was Harriet the Spy. She's quite creative." Then louder, to her, "Aren't you, Snuffaly?" She either ignored him or didn't hear him through the music. He
lowered his voice again. "Snuffaly—that's what she used to
call herself when she was little and just learning to talk.
Stephanie came out Snuffaly. Isn't that cute?"

Stephanie hoisted herself out of the swivel chair as if she
bore the weight of the world on her black-clad shoulders.
Thin, maybe anorexic, she shuffled toward her father and
held out her hand. I caught a glimpse of her torn leggings
and lace-up boots—black, of course.

"I'm going to the café."

Dan reached into his wallet and pulled out a twenty. "I'll
meet you down there in a few minutes. Save me a seat,
Snuffy."

Snuffy left without a good-bye, thank-you, or even a
whatever.

"She's been having a tough time lately. Doesn't like me
dating, even though I've been divorced from her mother for
a couple of years now. She probably thinks she's going to

lose me, but of course, that's not going to happen. Still, it's not easy, for either of us."

I had a feeling there were a lot of women interested in the tall, well-built man with highlighted blond curls. I had to stop myself from picturing him in his Calvins.

I was about to head out too when Dan walked over and closed the door to his office. "Listen, Presley, can we talk?"

Surprised, I stopped and turned around.

"About Mary Lee's death? Do you know something, Dan?"

"Oh no, nothing like that. Snuff is turning fourteen in a couple of weeks, and I want to surprise her with a party. Do you think you could put together something fun for her? I'd really appreciate it."

Good heavens. He wanted to talk about a party? Now?

"Oh, I don't think—"

"I know it's short notice, but I'd pay you well."

"I can't even—"

"It would mean a lot."

"But I have to—"

"I've already got the site reserved. I just need you to flesh out the details." He got out his checkbook, leaned over the desk, and began filling in the lines. When he handed it to me, I did a double take. Whoa. How did a museum assistant have this kind of money to blow on a kid's party?

He grinned, revealing ice white veneers. "I've invested well in antiquities, and they've paid off recently. I want to spend on my daughter. So, do we have a deal?"

Recovering quickly from the shock of seeing the amount, I slipped the check in my purse. "What kind of theme—"

"She's really into vampires and horror movies and stuff

like that. Can you come up with something freaky? Maybe
with bloodsuckers and zombies and whatnot?"

I swallowed. That was a new one. "I guess so. Where's
the venue? You said you'd reserved a place."

"The Wax Museum, down by Fisherman's Wharf. They
do private parties and they have this big room with all the
characters from the great horror films—*Frankenstein*,
Dracula, *The Wolfman*. Remember them? Plus some of the
popular ones today—Jason, Michael, Freddy. It's perfect!"

Perfect.

"I'll call you for details," I said, reaching for the door-
knob. I paused. "Dan, do you know anyone who might have
wanted Mary Lee dead?"

His eyebrows shot up. "I thought they had the killer. That
girl who played Nancy Drew—what's her name?"

"Delicia. No, she didn't do it. That's why I'm here. I'm
trying to find out who really killed Mary Lee. Do you know
anyone who could have had a reason to do it?"

He rubbed a manicured hand on his sharp jaw, almost as
if he was trying to appear thoughtful. How did a guy like
this make it all the way to "museum exhibitor," or whatever
he called himself?

"Hmmm," he finally said. "Mary Lee did step on a few
toes in her Manolos on her climb up the social and financial
ladder. I know she and her son clashed a lot. I used to hear
them arguing in her office down the hall when I passed
by."

Passed by? I wondered. Or eavesdropped?

"And Christine had a problem with her recently, although
I don't know why. I think they used to be good friends, but
something must have happened."

He hadn't overheard what it was, even though his office was next door to Christine's?

"Then there was the staff," he continued. "They talked about her behind her back. You know how they can be."

Goodness. Sounded like Dan spent more time keeping track of Mary Lee than he did of the exhibits.

"Oh, and that sleazy ex-husband of hers. He'd been dropping by a lot."

Great. The list of suspects was increasing exponentially.

"But that's about it. So you really don't think that Nancy Drew gal did it? Remember that big fight they had during the dress rehearsal."

"No, she didn't do it," I said firmly. "But thanks for—"

He cut me off. "Say, I just had an idea!"

More, I thought. Now who? The docents?

"Why don't we make it a Nancy Drew theme at the Wax Museum! Snuff could play Nancy, and all her friends could try to figure out who was turning people into wax figures—like that Paris Hilton movie!"

"You mean *House of Wax*. The original was with Vincent Price," I said. "I'll see what I can do." I opened the door before he could come up with another twist to the party theme and pulled out my business card. "Would you give this to Christine when you see her, and ask her to call me?"

Dan palmed the card. "Will do. And let me know what you need from me for the party. I'll text Snuff's friends and let them know it's a surprise. She'll be blown away!"

I nodded. What had I gotten myself into? Hey, it was his money—and he apparently had a lot of it. I got into the elevator, pushed the button for the ground floor, and pulled out the check, rereading the amount.

So Dan Tannacito had recently come into some money?

Had he won the lottery? Won big at a casino? Inherited from a rich—now deceased—relative?

Hmmm.

Lunchtime, my stomach said. I'd only had a latte and bagel for breakfast and needed some real food. I called my mother before pulling away from the museum to see if she was up for a roast beef dip from Tommy's Joynt. It was her favorite place and right around the corner from her assisted-living facility.

On the drive over, my cell phone rang three times. All three calls were "Caller unknown." I answered the first one—illegally, now that talking on a cell phone while driving is not allowed in California. No one was on the other end. After the third time, I shut off the phone. I didn't have time for silly crank calls.

When I arrived to pick up Mother, she was dressed in her San Francisco best, right down to the white gloves and pill-box hat. Mom was old-school when it came to being out and about in the city, a tradition passed on to her by her mother, a San Francisco native.

Her grandparents, Bryson and Lanneau Parker, had immigrated from England and started their own business—a flower stand on the corner of Powell and Sutter streets back in the 1950s. More curbside stands followed, in Union Square, on Market, at Gumps, even at the Naval Exchange at the Treasure Island Navy Base, all offering nosegays, corsages, and bouquets. Through Bryson and Lanneau's hard work and determination, the business blossomed into a brick-and-mortar florist and flourished, until flower shops had nearly become a thing of the past, thanks to flower boutiques in big-box stores and supermarkets. Luckily San Francisco is old-school, and you can still find stands around the city. But none of them are Parkers.

In their day, these unique and colorful kiosks captured faithful customers from local society. Delivering flowers to gala events had inspired my mother to nurture her own café life. I, on the other hand, was in the party business only because I'd lost my job teaching abnormal psychology at San Francisco State University and couldn't think of anything else I was qualified to do. When I hit upon combining hosting events with raising money for charities, I settled in somewhat comfortably, albeit naively.

I had a feeling this latest murder would do nothing to enhance my career.

I parked the MINI in a tight spot along the street and entered the care facility using my key. Mother was waiting for me in the lobby.

"Mom! You look beautiful."

And she did.

In spite of her age and her encroaching Alzheimer's, she'd kept her Katy Keene cheekbones, her Veronica Lodge hair, and her Wonder Woman legs. Not only was she queen of the comic-book heroines, she was my real-life superhero.

She wrapped me in her arms in welcome. "Hello, sweetheart. Do you like the shoes?" She stepped back and pointed the toe of her alligator pumps.

"I love them! Where did you get them?"

"The Haight, of course. They have so many wonderful vintage stores. These are hard to come by, you know. I was lucky to find them."

The stores in the Haight-Ashbury were also lucky. They

had benefited from many of my mother's discards over the years, remnants from her partying days.

We headed for Tommy's Joynt on the corner, placed our orders for drippy roast beef dip sandwiches with the meat carvers behind the sneezeproof glass, and sat at our usual table under the stairs. From this vantage point, my mother could see everyone who entered, as well as all the memorabilia tacked to the walls. I checked to see if her signed photograph was still in its prime location—under the neon "Miller's" beer sign. Although I couldn't read the words from where I sat, I had them memorized: "Veronica Parker—Your 'Afternoon Delight' Movie Hostess." That had been her slogan during her five-year stint as a local TV personality.

"So have they caught the real killer yet?" my mother asked as we waited for our sandwiches to arrive.

"So you agree with me. Delicia didn't do it."

"Of course she didn't. She's one of your best friends. Best friends don't murder people."

"Finally! Someone who believes me."

"Have you seen her?"

I shook my head while sipping my overly creamed coffee, nearly spilling it down the front of my T-shirt. My attempt to turn black coffee into a latte hadn't worked. "I've been putting it off—I'm not sure she wants to see me. Thought I could do more good trying to find out what really happened. But I want to get her a lawyer as soon as possible."

"Maybe I can help," she said, eyeing the sandwiches that had just arrived. I was so hungry, I planned to wolf mine down as quickly as possible. "I know plenty of attorneys in this town," Mother continued. "Slept with half of them."

"Mother!"

"Sorry, dear. Anyway, I'll call Mel and see if he can take the case."

I blinked, my sandwich halfway to my mouth. "Mel? You mean Melvin Belli?"

"Of course. We were very close at one time." She actually fluttered her eyelashes.

"Mom," I said, gently placing a hand on her bracelet-covered arm. "Melvin Belli died several years ago."

She looked confused for a moment, a look I was becoming familiar with. "Oh dear. Poor man. Did somebody shoot him?"

"No, Mom. Natural causes."

"Oh good, because a lot of people wanted to shoot him at one time or another. Never mind. I know other attorneys. I hear Bob Arns is good. And Sheldon Siegel. I'll call them."

"Actually, I think Brad has someone in mind. But thanks anyway."

We chatted between bites of roast beef au jus, mostly about the plethora of activities at my mother's center—her scrapbook class, bridge group, yoga workouts, Sudoku tournaments. We didn't return to the topic of Mary Lee's murder until the food was gone.

I had an idea.

"Mom, how would you like to go with me to the jail? I want to visit Dee." I had checked online to find out visiting hours, and although I hadn't planned to go so soon, the thought of bringing my mother along gave me the confidence I needed to face Dee.

"Oh goodness, I'm not dressed for jail. But a field trip would be nice. I get so bored in the hotel." Hotel is what she called her care home.

I smiled. "I'd love your company."

That settled, we downed our coffees and headed for the San Francisco County Jail. As I drove, listening with half an ear to my mother's chatter, I plotted out what I would say to Dee when I saw her.

That is, if she would even speak to me.

Chapter 9

PARTY PLANNING TIP #9

Hire extra help for your Murder Mystery Party. You'll need assistance when serving refreshments, keeping suspects from overimbibing, and cleaning up any unexpected blood. You might even have your attorney stand by.

The San Francisco County Jail doesn't look like a jail. It looks more like a modern apartment building, only with frosted windows and bars instead of curtains and blinds. A Pulitzer Prize–winning architecture critic, Allan Temko, once called the place "a stunning victory for architectural freedom over bureaucratic stupidity."

Gotta love that.

However, for most of us locals, the jail is a strong reminder not to break the law. Unfortunately, not everyone heeds the warning. There are nearly sixty thousand men and women incarcerated in the eight jails operated by San Francisco County.

And now my friend Delicia was one of them.

I'd read up on the jail at their Internet site, and after making a few phone calls, I'd discovered that Delicia would have been brought to the "intake and release" center on Seventh. She would be held in one of nineteen "holding tanks," along with three hundred other prisoners.

I shuddered to think of her in there.

I also learned they'd fingerprint her and issue her a new orange outfit and colored plastic wristband with her name and jail number. Then she'd be allowed to make a phone call and arrange to see a public defender if she didn't have an attorney. After twenty-four hours she'd be moved to more permanent housing where the female prisoners were kept— County Jail 8 on Seventh Street.

Permanent housing.

A chill ran down my back.

I parked the MINI as close to the jail as I could, hoping to deter any car thieves lurking about the run-down area. The jail is located adjacent to the Hall of Justice, referred to as "850 Bryant." The Internet site calls it "a national model for program-oriented prisoner rehabilitation."

I also learned that I could visit on the weekend for twenty minutes. Luckily, today was Sunday. Plus I had to bring an ID, I would be subject to search, and I couldn't be under the influence of any drugs.

Did caffeine count?

Furthermore, I would not be admitted if I wore gang-related clothing or extreme hairstyles. I hoped my bobbed hair would allow me in. There was no way I could hide a file in there. But my mother could have secreted away a chain saw in her puffy, heavily sprayed, swept-up style.

The worst part was, I wouldn't be able to bring Dee any personal items or even hug her.

Mother and I stood in line for several minutes before being metal-detected, purse-scrutinized, and identity-checked. We shuffled into the general waiting room, which was barred, locked, and sparsely decorated with metal picnic tables and warning signs: "No physical contact," "Do not leave children unattended," "No one under eighteen without accompaniment," "All visitors subject to search at any time." The dingy walls looked as if they'd been repainted many times, thick with paint and lumpy drips.

"They could really use a decorator in here," my mother whispered as we sat down at an empty table. We watched the eclectic crowd of visitors chat while they waited their turn to see their loved ones, clients, or pimps. While Mother watched their faces, I checked their shoes. The loved ones usually sported well-worn loafers, oversized athletic shoes, or bling-trimmed flip-flops. The lawyers wore black Italian shoes. And the pimps had on everything from bejeweled cowboy boots to red patent-leather platforms.

It wasn't long before my mother struck up a conversation with a haggard-looking woman at the next table. While she talked the woman's ear off, I spent the waiting time diagnosing personality disorders according to shoe style. I had just diagnosed a woman in Gladiator sandals as possibly narcissist when a pair of men's New Balance Zips appeared in front of me.

I looked up.

Brad.

"What are you doing here?" we both said simultaneously.

Behind him stood a thin young man, maybe late twenties, with perfectly trimmed and combed dark hair, black-rimmed glasses, and an off-the-rack black suit that looked slightly askew on his ramrod-straight posture. He held a ragged brown briefcase in front of him with both hands, as if he planned to use it as armor. His shoes, brown lace-up Dockers, matched his briefcase rather than his suit.

"I asked you first," Brad said, channeling a second grader.

"Did not!" I replied, channeling a first grader. I couldn't keep myself from grinning. It was good to see him.

He sat down next to me in defeat. The other man remained standing, picking at an invisible piece of lint on his jacket sleeve.

"I told you I would get Delicia a good lawyer." He nodded to the man, who sneaked a glance at me, then forced a brief, tight smile. "Presley, this is Andrew. He owes me a favor. Don't you, Andrew?" Brad gently punched the man's shoulder.

The man nodded curtly and released his grip from his briefcase to shake my hand. His hand was damp and cold and bony. "Pleased to meet you," he said, not meeting my eyes.

"You too, Andrew," I said. "Thanks for doing this."

Andrew took a step back and returned to his lint removal preoccupation. His behavior was a little odd, but that didn't mean he wasn't a good lawyer. I appreciated Brad's attempts to help.

I turned to him, tempted to kiss him, but touched his arm instead. "I . . . don't know what to say . . . except thanks."

"No problem. You're here to see her too, I take it?"

"Trying," I said. "If she'll see me. She thinks I ratted her out to the cops, so she may refuse my visit."

"Did you?"

"Of course not!" I snapped. "But someone did. That's what I want to explain to her. And I want to let her know I'm trying to get her out of here."

"Tell you what." Brad rested his hand on my knee, sending a jolt through my body. I hope it didn't show. "Let me go in first. I'll introduce her to Andrew, explain things, including what you just told me. Then you go in. I'm sure she'll believe you. You guys are good friends. This isn't going to change that in the long run."

I nodded. I didn't want him to take his hand away from my leg, but if he kept it there another second, we might have to get a room. I wondered where they held the conjugal visits around here.

"Good idea. So you'll tell her it wasn't me?"

He squeezed my leg, then removed his hand. "Promise."

The jailer called my name, apparently on the list before Brad's, but I explained that I wanted him to go first. Brad headed inside to the inmate/visitor meeting room, with the lawyer at his heels like a loyal, albeit nervous, puppy.

Judging from first impressions, I wasn't sure this was the right attorney for Delicia. There was something about Andrew that bothered me. But if Brad knew him and vouched for him, then I could only trust his judgment. When things got serious, Brad had never let me down, in spite of our petty conflicts.

Fifteen minutes later Brad and Andrew reappeared. By then my mother had recipes for beer-can chicken and Coca-Cola cake from the woman she'd been chatting with, and I had a sore butt from sitting on the cold, hard bench. I jumped up to greet him. I was anxious to hear what he'd learned, and to see her.

"How did it go?"

"Good. Andrew's going to represent her. They hit it off immediately. We went over a few things, and then I told her you were here to visit her."

"How did she react?"

"She made a face, but after I explained things, she started crying. I think she really wants to see you."

Tears welled in my eyes. "Okay, thanks. Would you mind staying with my mother while I go in there? I'm afraid she might organize a revolution or lead a breakout while I'm gone."

"Sure. She'll be safe with me."

On my way inside, I told my mom I'd be back in a few minutes and thanked Andrew for seeing Dee. He stood stiffly, again clutching his briefcase to his chest with both hands. He nodded, but again didn't meet my eyes. With a sense of trepidation, both for hiring Andrew and seeing Delicia, I hurried off to see my incarcerated friend.

The meeting room was a twin to the waiting room—same heavy paint, same cold tables, same signs on the walls and doors. The only difference was that this room was less crowded, yet at every table sat a woman in prison orange, along with her family, friends, or attorneys. Some of the women were weeping, while others looked either depressed or angry as they chatted with their visitors. Only a few smiled.

Delicia sat at a far table, looking down at her folded hands. I couldn't read her expression; her face appeared uncharacteristically blank for such an animated woman. She looked up as I approached and broke out into a smile tempered by tears. I wanted so much to reach out and hug her, then remembered the warnings of no contact. I hugged her with my own teary eyes and sat down opposite her.

"You look beautiful!" I said. "Even in orange!"

She laughed self-consciously and smoothed her hands over her baggy top. Her nail polish was chipped, which was also unlike her. "I don't know. You think it makes me look fat?"

We both laughed. The tears rimming my eyes broke free and ran down my face. "Dee, I just wanted to tell you . . . I didn't tell the police anything they didn't already know."

She nodded and began picking at her polish again. "Brad told me. I'm sorry I said those things. It . . . it just took me by surprise. The knife. The body. The blood. And then to be arrested. It all seemed so surreal. And now jail . . ." She glanced around at her surroundings.

I patted the table, as if I were patting her hand. "I know. It's unbelievable, for sure. But no one thinks you had anything to do with it."

"No one but the cops, you mean," Dee said bitterly. "And I'd still like to find out who blabbed that off-the-cuff remark I made about wishing Mary Lee was dead. *Someone* told Melvin what I said—which was a joke, people!" A bit of her dramatic nature was beginning to shine through as she spoke.

"We all believe that. Brad and I are working hard to find out who really killed Mary Lee and get you out of here. He even hired that attorney for you."

"That was nice of him, although I *still* don't know why I even need a lawyer—or why I'm here. This is all so *crazy*."

I spent the next few minutes catching her up on the latest news; then, realizing time was running out, I asked, "Dee, do you have any idea who might have wanted Mary Lee dead? Her ex-husband? Someone on her staff? Her son, maybe?"

Dee shook her head. "No. Corbin's too much of a mama's boy to commit murder, even if she deserved it."

I shushed her and glanced around. "Hey, talk like that is what got you here."

She bit her lip, then said, "Anyway, I don't think he did it. I haven't seen him yet, but I'll talk to him if he comes to visit and see if he has any ideas."

I looked down at the graffitied table, marred by permanent markers, and thought for a moment. Based on my conversation with Corbin, I had a strong suspicion he wouldn't be coming by to visit, but I didn't have the heart to tell her. Did she still have feelings for him?

"Is there anyone you can think of who could have gone into that room and stabbed her before you found her?" I asked.

"Besides the whole cast?" she said sarcastically. "Seriously, not Raj or Berk—they had no reason to kill Mary Lee. But that museum curator—Christine? She's kind of weird. I think she and Dan Whatshisname are hot for each other. They were always shooting these looks at each other. At least, when Mary Lee wasn't around."

Hmmm. Although Christine appeared to be a couple of decades older than Dan, maybe the two were a clandestine couple. If they were in a relationship, maybe Mary Lee didn't like the idea, for some reason. She was a very controlling person. But did that give them enough reason to get rid of Mary Lee?

A loud buzzer rang, startling me and signaling the end of the visiting time. We both stood up slowly. I had started to reach for Dee when a guard yelled, "No contact!" I pulled my arms in and hugged myself instead. She gave a limp wave and shuffled toward the line of women at the door, her legs shackled. The sight of her in chains gave me a chill, and I had to fight to keep control over more tears. As she moved through the doorway, she gave me one last wave. I forced a smile and waved back, hoping she could read my mind: *I will get you out of here, if it is the last thing I ever do.*

Brad and my mother were still sitting at the table when I entered the room. Andrew had joined them, and looked like he was busy scrutinizing a bunch of papers. He tapped his pencil vigorously—nervously?—in between jotting down notes. When Brad stood up to greet me, Andrew hurriedly gathered his papers. In his haste, he dropped them on the floor. As he leaned over to retrieve them, he nearly fell off the bench.

I turned to Brad with a raised eyebrow.

"Andrew is a brilliant lawyer, Presley," he whispered. "Honestly, I wouldn't have hired him if I didn't believe he could help your friend."

I frowned skeptically but said nothing.

Andrew stood up, disheveled papers in hand, and placed them neatly in his open briefcase. He closed the case, snapped the locks at exactly the same time, and hugged the case as if it were filled with treasure.

"Do you have your own firm, Andrew?" I asked, trying to get acquainted.

"I work for Siegel and Associates, the largest law firm in the city," he said flatly, although his enunciation was perfect. "We have to go now, Bradley. I'm due back at the office by four o'clock. I can't be late."

Brad shot him a look. Something passed between them. Andrew turned to me and said, "Nice to meet you, Ms. Parker. Have a nice day."

Without offering his hand, he spun around and headed out the door.

I looked back at Brad, my eyes narrowed. "He seems very . . . precise," I said, almost at a loss for words. "He goes to the office on Sundays? He must be quite dedicated. Or he has no social life."

"Both," Brad said. "He works seven days a week—never misses a day. That's part of what makes him such a good attorney."

"He called you Bradley. Are you friends from school? Or is he always so formal?"

Brad met my eyes. "Andrew has Asperger's syndrome. And he's my brother."

Chapter 10

PARTY PLANNING TIP #10

Choose vivacious and outgoing people to play the various roles at your Murder Mystery Party. Avoid mumblers, party poopers, and people with irritating idiosyncrasies. There's nothing worse than a socially awkward suspect.

In spite of the fact that Brad had confirmed my hunch about Andrew, I was still surprised—not only that he had Asperger's, but that Brad had a brother! How little I knew about this intriguing man in the white Crime Scene Cleaners jumpsuit and Zips.

As for Andrew, he had many of the signs of the disorder. While Asperger's is a form of autism, it differs in degree for most people. Those with the disorder often function well in society, especially when they find their niche. Apparently Andrew had turned his obsession for organization and detail, plus his interest in solving crime puzzles, into a productive and useful career. It was a challenging accomplishment for anyone, but especially impressive for someone with Asperger's.

I wondered if all good lawyers fell somewhere along the spectrum of Asperger's.

Like others with the disorder, Andrew appeared to be intelligent (he'd passed the bar), articulate (his speech was clearly enunciated), and focused to a fault, as witness his intense concentration while compiling his notes. Plus, he hadn't been comfortable when he was introduced to me. Being socially awkward was another characteristic of Asperger's syndrome.

But would he really be a good attorney for Dee? I could only hope so.

"I gotta go," Brad said, interrupting my thoughts.

"Wait a minute. I never knew you had a brother . . ." I was interrupted by my cell phone. I checked the caller ID. Blocked. I said hello. No answer. I hung up.

"Who was that?" Brad asked.

"I don't know. Someone keeps calling and hanging up."

"That's not good," he said, frowning. "Look, I've got to take Andrew back to the office. But how about we meet later? I have something I want to talk about with you."

"Yeah, okay," I said. "Thanks again for getting Dee a lawyer. I just hope he's . . ." I let my thought drop.

"Good? He is. Don't worry." Brad squeezed my arm gently before following his brother out the door.

I pulled my mother away from her new BFF and herded her out of the building and to my MINI. As usual, I was alert to my surroundings, looking for nearby transients, drug dealers, and gang members who might be visiting relatives at the jail. The Hall of Justice area wasn't the best place to leave a car, but as I approached the MINI from a distance, I could see it still had all four tires. The windshield hadn't been smashed. And the convertible top hadn't been slashed. So far, so good.

My mother stopped abruptly as we reached the car. "What happened to your paint job?"

My heart leaped. "What do you mean?"

She pointed at the passenger side of my car.

I looked closely.

A long zigzagging line stretched from one end to the other.

My jaw dropped. "Oh no!"

I followed the mark around the trunk, and surveyed the driver's side. My darling little MINI had been totally keyed.

"Oh my God!" I said, glancing around the neighborhood as if I'd find the perp with a telltale weapon in his hand. The car would need a whole new paint job. This was going to cost me a fortune to fix. I cursed as quietly as I could so as not to disturb my mother.

But she wasn't listening to me. Her attention was focused down near her feet. "You know, honey, your tires look kind of flat too." She kicked the front tire daintily with the sharp toe of her alligator pumps. "I think you need air."

I looked down at the tires. Flat. I moved around the car. All four—flat as a bottle of day-old champagne.

I cursed loud enough for the inmates in the nearby jail to hear.

My mother blushed. "Presley, such language! In my day, ladies didn't use language like that. Now, call a tow truck and a cab, so we can be on our way. I have a scrapbooking class at four o'clock."

I muttered a few more F-bombs as I dialed Triple A and asked for a tow to the nearest MINI Cooper/BMW dealership. Next I called a cab, to first escort my mother home and then deliver me to my office.

While we waited, we reentered the Hall of Justice to file a useless complaint form.

"Any chance you'll catch whoever did this?" I asked the watch commander.

"Not likely," the uniformed African-American woman said. "We get a lot of auto vandalism around here. The perps are usually visitors upset that their 'innocent' loved ones are in jail, and they take their anger out on the nearest vehicle. It's a quiet crime, easy to pull off—even right in front of the building. Probably trying to send a message. Your insurance will cover it."

Insurance? Without the salary I'd once pulled down teaching at the university, I had taken the bare minimum in auto insurance—collision. And only because it was the law. If I didn't collect my fee from the de Young event, I'd be screwed in more ways than one.

I handed her the complaint form and waited outside with my mother, sulking, until my car was towed and the cab arrived. She chatted about her scrapbooking class on the drive back to her place, but I heard little she said, still pouting about my car. I made sure she got safely into her building.

When I returned to the cab, I gave the driver my office address on Treasure Island. He knew the island, but had no clue where the barracks were, so I directed him once we passed the main gate. After he dropped me off, I started up the barracks steps, then stopped, struck by an idea. I spun around on my heels and marched over to Dee's Smart Car, which had been idly collecting a thin layer of dust in the lot while Dee had been in jail.

I tried the driver's-side door. Locked up tight.

With my MINI in the shop, I needed a car. With Delicia in jail, she didn't.

All I had to do was find her key and hope she didn't put out an APB for a stolen vehicle—if you could call a Smart Car a vehicle.

I rushed into the barracks, passed Brad, who had returned from delivering his brother, and entered Dee's unlocked office. Nothing had been touched since Detective Melvin removed Dee's computer.

I pulled open each of the drawers in her desk and filing cabinet searching for her car keys. No sign of them.

Duh, I thought. Women don't keep their keys in desk drawers. They keep them in their purses.

So where was Dee's purse? Detective Melvin hadn't found it when he searched her office. I would have seen him with it. Had the cops taken it when she was arrested?

I visualized her arrest and was certain she hadn't had her purse when they handcuffed her.

The last place she would have put it was in the makeshift changing room adjacent to the crime scene room. It had to be there.

Brad appeared in Dee's office doorway.

"What are you doing?"

I smiled at him as seductively as I could. "I need a favor."

"You mean *another* favor."

"Whatever." I told him what had happened to my car at the Hall of Justice and my urgent need for wheels.

He made a face.

"No, not your truck," I said quickly. "I'm going to borrow Dee's Smart Car for a couple of days. Just until mine's fixed."

"So what do you want from me?"

"A ride."

"Where to?"

"The museum."

Brad's eyes narrowed. His frown deepened. "Presley, you realize you could be in serious danger if someone thinks you're sticking your nose into their business."

"You could join me," I suggested. "After I'm done, I'll buy you something at the museum café."

He sighed. "You're offering me a bribe?"

I knew I had him and gave him a warm smile. "Thanks, Brad."

"Okay, but don't complain to me when you get helmet hair."

Helmet hair?

I walked down the hall to the reception area and peered out the window. There was no sign of his Crime Scene Cleaners SUV. How had I missed that?

In its parking spot was a big black BMW bike.

Great. There's only one thing I fear more than seeing clowns, getting leprosy, drowning in quicksand, going to the dentist, dying of rabies, or being hypnotized.

Motorcycles.

I retreated into my office to wait for Brad to finish up whatever he was doing and sat down at my desk. Time for a shot of chocolate to fortify me for the windy ride over to the museum. I opened my chocolate drawer to retrieve some Ghirardelli squares and pulled out a couple of dark chocolate with raspberries. Ripping one open, I popped it into my mouth. As the smooth rich flavor melted over my tongue, I woke up my sleeping computer to check my e-mail. The screen flickered on, I pushed a key, and my screen saver—a picture of the San Francisco skyline—melted into what looked like an Internet search for "Presley Parker."

I leaned into the screen. Yep, that was me, all right, Googled, with links to all kinds of personal information— how long I'd taught at SFSU, what subject I taught, where I'd gotten my degree and credentials, who my mother was, what parties I'd given recently, and other details about my business, Killer Parties.

One of the sites even included my address and phone number.

A tingle of fear ran up my spine. I stood up and backed away from the machine as if it were possessed. Someone had been in my office and used my computer to find out information about me. Recently. I scanned the room for other signs that an intruder had been in my office. Nothing seemed stolen, disturbed, or broken. Nothing was out of place.

I glanced back at my desk more carefully this time, to see if my papers were still there.

Another rush of heat warmed my body.

The guest list from the museum party was missing, including my suspect list.

"Brad!" I called across the hall.

"Okay, okay. I'm ready," he answered, feigning exasperation. He appeared in my doorway and saw my face. "What's wrong?"

I pointed to my desk. "Did you take my guest list?"

"What guest list?"

"I left it here on my desk, and it's gone!"

"So?"

"So. Don't you get it? Someone was in my office."

"You're going too fast," I screamed at the back of Brad's helmet. We were practically flying across the Bay Bridge toward 101 South. Either he didn't hear me or he chose to ignore me, and may have, in fact, sped up just to taunt me. I grabbed him tightly around the waist and shut my eyes, missing the views along the way. No matter. I'd seen it all many times before. It wasn't until we'd passed Golden Gate Park's panhandle that I opened one eye.

Most of the things I'm afraid of, like quicksand, rabies, and clowns, came from watching movies. But I don't like motorcycles because I had a boyfriend in high school who skidded off the road and hit a tree. He died instantly. Another close friend in college was paralyzed when his bike was cut off by a truck. I swore I'd never ride on one—or date anyone who did. And here I was, on the back of a death machine. I prayed as we roared along that this would be my last motorcycle ride—by choice.

Brad, on the other hand, was in his element. He took the corners at an angle, whipped through traffic lanes as if the other cars were standing still, and occasionally revved the loud motor more than he really needed to.

"Show-off," I yelled, when we pulled into a parking space at the de Young, my ears still buzzing from the noise. I yanked off the bug-spattered helmet and tried to fluff my hair.

"You loved it," Brad said, ruffling his own hair, which fell into place perfectly. I unzipped the black jacket he'd lent me—a woman's jacket—and handed it to him. He stuffed it, along with his own, into a side compartment, locked them up, then secured the two helmets to the handlebars—if that's what you call them—with a bike lock.

"Lead the way," he said, gesturing toward the museum entrance.

I marched ahead, held open my purse, and passed through the security checkpoint easily, in spite of the bag of deflated balloons I always carried with me.

"So where do you think Delicia's purse is?" he asked, trailing my quick step.

"I'm hoping it's still in the changing room, off the mural room. That's where everyone stored their stuff during the play."

We stepped into the mural/crime scene room. Empty. I walked over to the far door that led to the small anteroom and tried the knob. The door opened. I stepped in, crossing my fingers Dee's purse would still be there.

That room was also empty.

I stepped out and looked at Brad, unable to hide the disappointment on my face.

"Try lost and found," he said.

I perked up. "Great idea." When he didn't follow me out of the mural room, I asked, "Aren't you coming?"

He shook his head. "I'll stay here and have another look around."

"For the weapon?"

"That too."

"If you're still trying to figure out how the killer got in, it had to be through that side door. And it was locked, remember? The killer had to have had a key."

"True, but it wasn't locked just now, when you went in to look for the purse."

He was right—that was odd.

"Okay, I'll be right back," I said. "Would you keep an eye on this?" I handed him my knockoff bag.

He frowned as he took it. "This really isn't my color," he said, holding it out as if it were filled with toxic waste.

I laughed, then headed for the front desk. The docent there directed me to the security office where they kept the lost and found articles, tucked downstairs in the basement.

"Can I get there without a passkey?"

"Oh yes. The security office is always accessible."

I rode the elevator to the basement and, when the doors opened, stepped out into a dimly lit hallway. The office was located directly across from the elevators. I rapped on the door and waited only seconds before it opened.

"Yes?" said the uniformed man. He was probably in his seventies, with salt-and-pepper hair and glasses. Surely this was a part-time, semiretirement job for him. His nametag read "Ed Pike."

"Uh, hi. I, uh, left my purse here last night, in that little room off the mural room. I wondered if you'd found it. The volunteer at the desk directed me here."

His chest puffed up, and he put on his hat, which he'd been holding in his hand. "What's it look like?"

I knew Dee's purse well. It was easy to describe in a nutshell. "It's beaded, about the size of a lunch pail, with Cinderella on the front."

He nodded, closed the door, and reappeared a few minutes later with a small bag covered in rhinestones, the Disney princess prominently featured. It fit Dee to a tee.

Thank God it hadn't been confiscated by the police.

I reached for it. He pulled it back.

"Got any ID?"

Think fast, Presley, I told myself. "Uh, my ID is in my purse." I pointed to the bag.

He opened the purse, pulled out Dee's wallet, and looked at the picture on her driver's license. "Don't look like you," he said, glancing back and forth between me and Dee's picture. We were both dark-haired, but that's where the resemblance ended.

"I know. I was so sick that day, and my hair was long back then, and I had colored contacts . . ." I rambled on. The frown deepened. I tried another tack. "Check my birthday. It's June seventeenth, 1980." As a party hostess, I knew a lot of my friends' birthdays, including Dee's. "And inside you'll find my car keys attached to Tinkerbelle."

He eyed me suspiciously; although I could see the keys in his hand, he wasn't going to relinquish the purse easily.

"Listen, is Sam Wo here? He knows me."

The guard turned around and yelled Sam's name. Seconds later, a familiar face appeared. He grinned when he recognized me. "Ms. Parker! Nice to see you again."

The other guard frowned at me. "I thought you said your name was—"

I cut him off. "Sam, my friend Delicia left her purse here last night. I was just trying to get it back for her. I thought—"

"Give it to her," he commanded Ed Pike.

To my surprise, Pike handed it over, although with a

protesting grunt. "Try not to lose it again," he grumbled, and disappeared inside.

"Thanks, Sam. Once again, you're a lifesaver."

His face flushed magenta, and he smiled sheepishly. "How's it going for your friend?"

I filled him in on the latest, which wasn't much. "Have you heard anything more?" I asked, figuring if anyone was in on the museum gossip, a security guard would be the one.

His bright smile fell. "Not really. Everyone here thinks your friend did it. They all heard about the big fight. And they knew about Ms. Miller's attempts to stop Corbin from seeing the girl."

"Was there anyone else having a problem with Mary Lee lately?"

His eyes narrowed. There was something Sam wasn't telling me.

"Sam?"

He looked at his watch. "I gotta get back to work. Maybe later?"

"Sure," I said, then thanked him for Dee's purse and headed back to the elevator. I pushed the button for the main floor and returned to the scene of the crime.

"I got it!" I said to Brad, holding up the princess bag.

He nodded distractedly, as if he hadn't heard me.

"Are you listening?"

"Look at this." Brad waved me over to the side door where he stood.

"What? I told you, that door was locked after Dee entered. She was the last one in here."

"But like you said, maybe someone had a key. Who else would have that type of key?"

"The security guards, I assume."

"And perhaps the staff? Including Mary Lee herself."

"I . . . suppose. Did they find a key on her . . . body? And what would that prove anyway?"

"That Delicia wasn't the only one who had access."

He was onto something. "Then we'll have to find out who among the staff also had access to this room," I said, stating the obvious. "That could be quite a list. Besides, someone could have just reached in and turned the lock before shutting the door."

He took my hand and pulled me over a few steps. "Stand here." He turned me around so I faced the interior of the room, with my back to the anteroom door.

"What?" I said.

He glanced up at the camera in the corner. A yellow light was lit up.

"It's motion activated," I said. "The security guard told me."

He smiled at me, waiting for me to read his mind.

Seconds later I did. "There must be videotapes!"

"Yep. Melvin's already reviewing them. I'll see if he saw anything, but with everyone in costume, that might be a problem."

"Brad, I have to see those tapes—"

The thud of heavy, running footsteps and shouts from outside the room cut me off. We dashed to the front entry. I spotted Sam Wo rushing past, with Ed Pike following him to the exit doors. Their faces were tight and earnest.

"Sam!" I yelled after him. "What's going on?"

He dashed out of sight.

I glanced at Brad, then ran after Sam, with Brad at my heels. Following the shouts and footfalls, I sped out the main entrance and around to the gardens to a circular frog pond. By the time we caught up, Sam, Ed, and a female guard were pulling at something heavy that was caught in a thicket of reeds in the middle of the pond.

It only took a second to realize what it was.

A human leg.

Chapter 11

PARTY PLANNING TIP # 11

*Make the refreshments easy to eat by serving finger
foods at your Murder Mystery Party. Not literally, of
course. Although snacks that look like fingers might
be a nice touch . . .*

Brad and I sat in the museum café sipping lattes—his as
stimulant, mine as sedative—waiting to talk with Detective
Melvin. At the moment, the detective sat at another table
talking with Sam Wo, Ed Pike, and another security guard,
the African-American woman I'd seen earlier. Apparently
she'd been the one who'd discovered the leg protruding from
the pond and called the others.

The leg was attached to a body.

Whose body remained a mystery.

After dismissing the two guards, Detective Melvin sauntered over, interrupting our attempts to come up with possible suspects. So far I'd listed Christine Lampe, Jason Cosetti,

and his son, Corbin, if I didn't count the two hundred plus party guests.

"I need a coffee. You two want anything?" Melvin said, being uncharacteristically thoughtful.

Brad shook his head; I held up my coffee mug to indicate I had plenty. The detective strolled over to the counter and returned with a coffee and a slice of chocolate cake. Brushing imaginary crumbs from the arty metallic chair, he sat down.

I shifted uncomfortably in my hard, cold chair.

"What's up?" Brad said to Melvin while I sipped my latte.

Detective Melvin leaned back and stretched his lanky legs under the table. Even during a murder investigation, he looked impeccable. "Dead man in a frog pond," he said simply.

"Wow, you cops are sharp," I said, hoping my voice dripped with sarcasm. I couldn't help myself.

He tossed me a smirky smile and took a big bite of the four-layer, triple-chocolate cake. I felt my mouth watering at the sight of the thick, rich icing.

"Any ID?" Brad asked.

"Nope. No wallet, nothing."

"Any idea when he died? Or how?"

Melvin shook his head. Not a hair moved. "Looks like he hadn't been in the water long. No blistering, skin slippage, that sort of thing."

Yuck.

Melvin continued. "ME thinks he drowned. Had a pretty deep contusion on the back of his head. He may have been knocked out, then dragged to the pond after the blow. We'll know more after the autopsy."

"So it's murder, right?" I tossed out.

Detective Melvin shot me a look, then stabbed another piece of his cake.

I pressed on. "Either that or he bumped the back of his head on something hard, then staggered over to the frog pond, jumped into the cattails, and drowned." Sarcasm and facetiousness are two of my best traits. Why waste them?

Brad put a hand on my wrist, like a parent shushing an errant child. I snatched my arm away and took another sip of my calming latte, hoping to stem my ire. Didn't help.

"No one around here recognized him?"

Melvin downed another bite of cake, then glanced up at me and licked his lips. He was torturing me with the cake, and he knew it. I only hoped I wasn't openly drooling.

"Not yet. Face was puffy, discolored."

On second thought, the idea of eating anything at this point made me want to upchuck.

"Think it's related to Mary Lee's murder?" Brad asked.

"I don't believe in coincidence," Melvin said.

I sat up. "What kind of shoes was he wearing?"

The detective's next forkful of cake froze midway to his mouth. "Shoes?"

"She's got some kind of shoe fetish," Brad explained, with a smirk.

I slapped his arm. "I do not! I have a master's degree in abnormal psychology, and I happen to know that shoes tell a lot about a person."

Detective Melvin stuck a foot out from under the table and wiggled it. "Yeah? So what do my shoes tell you?"

I raised an eyebrow at his large feet. "You sure you want to know?"

"Bring it on."

"Well, they're Rockports, so you have good taste." *You spend too much on shoes.* "You appreciate quality." *You're covering a slight inferiority complex.* "You hope to make police chief someday." *You think you're smarter than you are.*

"Huh." He grinned at my superficial analysis, apparently pleased, and clueless that I was holding back lots more. "Okay, the dead guy was wearing Birkenstocks."

Birks? That said artist, bohemian, or hippie.

"Authentic or knockoffs?"

"How would I know?"

"Sock or no socks?" I continued.

"No socks."

"Pedicure?"

He rolled his eyes.

I thought for a moment while both men watched me.

"So?" Detective Melvin finally prompted.

"So, he could have been a hippie—with money, if they were real Birks. They usually run over a hundred dollars. Or maybe he was an aspiring artist and affected the starving-artist look. Then again, maybe he just wanted to be comfortable rather than stylish and didn't care if they were brand name."

"Well, that should narrow it down," Melvin said, sticking his tongue in his cheek. He scooped up the last bite of cake, finished it off, and wiped his mouth. Slapping the table like a drummer, he stood up and brushed off his sleek pants. "Gotta run. See you at the Presidio course Saturday?" he asked Brad.

"Game on," Brad said. They bumped fists, and Detective Melvin sauntered out of the café.

"Jerk," I whispered into my cooling coffee.

"What?" Brad said.

"Nothing."

Brad rubbed my shoulder, apparently aware of the tension the detective had created in me. "Hey, he's just doing his job. Cut him some slack."

I wasn't going to disparage his friend—at the moment. There would be plenty of opportunities later, I was sure. I decided to change the subject before I said something I meant but didn't want Brad to know.

"So tell me more about your brother."

"Andrew?" He sighed. "Well, he's two years younger than me. He's got an IQ over 130. My mom homeschooled him after he was diagnosed, and I think that's why he's done so well, in spite of having Asperger's. She recognized his knack for solving logic problems. He was obsessed with all the legal shows on TV and always deduced the outcome long before the show ended. Unfortunately, he doesn't 'play that well with others.'" He added finger quotes to the pop psychology phrase.

I took a moment, trying to decide how to phrase my next question, then asked, "Do you think he can really . . ."

"What? Handle Delicia's case? I told you, I wouldn't have brought him in if I didn't."

I could feel myself blush. Shame on me. My prejudice was showing. I, of all people, knew that diagnostic tools couldn't reliably categorize a person. Disorders were on a continuum, a spectrum, and we all fell along that line— some further out than others. Like lots of other people, I shared some characteristics of Asperger's. I had my obsessions—coffee, chocolate, diagnosing people according to their shoes. I had a tendency to stay focused on a single element rather than look at the big picture. I sometimes had trouble with close relationships.

"It's getting late, and I better get back," I said abruptly, reaching for my knockoff bag and Delicia's princess purse. "I have a few things to do at the office, a few errands to run, now that I have access to Dee's car."

We headed back to Brad's bike, and I climbed on behind him, feeling that fear of motorcycles rear its ugly head again. I held on tight as he took me on a Mr. Toad's Wild Ride, up and down the hills of San Francisco to the flatlands of Treasure Island. I had a feeling he'd deliberately chosen the long way—was it really necessary to take twisty, touristy Lombard Street? Still, I had to admit, I liked seeing the city from the back of a bike. Everything seemed up close and personal, filled with a variety of sounds and smells.

And wrapping my arms around Brad hadn't hurt the experience either.

I just hoped we didn't die.

"Thanks for the ride," I said, returning his jacket and helmet after we pulled up in the barracks parking lot.

"My pleasure," he said with his signature half grin. In the dusky light, his brown eyes sparkled with a hint of gold.

I hesitated a second, then turned awkwardly and headed to my office. Brad followed me in and entered his own office. I sorted through a few party requests and returned a few phone calls. There were three more unidentified hang ups, which gave me pause. Someone was either trying to irritate me—or scare me. Why?

I picked up the two purses, mine and Dee's, locked my office door behind me, and waved at Brad, who seemed intent on his computer. He barely looked up from his glowing screen, and I found myself a little disappointed he hadn't asked me to have dinner with him.

Once in the parking lot, I pulled Dee's keys from her princess purse and pushed the UNLOCK button for her little yellow Smart Car.

This was going to be an interesting and no doubt bumpy ride.

I ducked my head and slowly slipped into the black leathery seat, concerned I wouldn't fit. I needn't have worried. Surprisingly, the inside felt larger than the interior of my MINI Cooper. Surrounded by oversized windows, I felt like a puffer fish in a goldfish bowl.

Although Dee had talked endlessly about her Smarty—"Shaq has one! And so does Dave Grohl from Foo Fighters!"—I was sure a single gust of wind coming off the bay would roll this yellow marble right into the water. The question was, would it float or sink?

I started the engine, searched for the clutch, and realized the car was some sort of word combination stick and automatic. I backed up jerkily, made a tight U-turn, and drove hesitantly down the quiet street toward the bridge. As I approached the incline that led to the bridge on-ramp, I felt sweat break out on my forehead. My shoulders were in knots.

Once I reached the entrance, I stopped, waiting for a break in the traffic. Watching the hundred-ton rigs lumbering by at top speed, I sensed it wouldn't take much of a hit to knock this Smarty into the bay. Or be squished like a little yellow bug.

As soon as I exited the bridge, I relaxed my death grip on

the steering wheel and tried to breathe normally. After a few blocks, I started to get the feel of the car.

Until I reached California Street, one of San Francisco's famous hills. Would the Little Engine That Could make good? Or would I go rolling back down the slippery slope like a roller-coaster car?

I reached the top, barely able to see over the steering wheel and into the abyss below. Either the car would make it over the steep hill—or launch into space like an airplane.

The car lurched as it automatically shifted into a higher gear, but by the time I was back on level ground again—and breathing normally—I was in love with the little thing. It was time to put it to the test—could I talk while driving? I punched in a number, illegally using my cell phone. Stupid law.

"Hello?" my mother's cultivated voice said.

"Mom?" I said.

"Yes, honey? Are you all right?"

She always asked me that. What was she expecting?

"Yeah, Mom, I'm fine. I wondered if you were in the mood for another outing and dinner afterward."

"With my favorite daughter? Sounds lovely. You'll have to see what I made in my scrappers class. It's a memory book of your big party last night! I think you'll love it."

Just what I wanted—a memento of my most recent disaster. "Sounds cool, Mom. Can't wait to see it."

"So where are we going?"

"How about Fisherman's Wharf? I have to research the Wax Museum for a party site, and I thought we could have a sidewalk crab cocktail and clam chowder in one of those sourdough bowls. Sound good?"

"Oh! I haven't been to the Wax Museum for years! I wonder if Scarlett O'Hara and Rhett Butler are still there. I used to have lavish garden parties like they had at Tara, with mint juleps and croquet and corseted gowns. Honey, *you* should have a *Gone With the Wind* party! I could help you!"

"Great idea, Mom. But right now, I've already got enough on my party platter. You remember Dan Tannacito, one of the museum assistants who was in the play? He wants to have his daughter's next birthday party there."

"How . . . unusual," my mother said, clucking. "So how shall I dress?"

"Oh, casual, Mom. We're just checking out the place. Then we'll have dinner with the tourists at Pier 39. Wear something warm and tacky. I'll be there in a few minutes."

"Tacky?" I heard her repeat before she hung up.

I reached her place fifteen minutes later, zipping around traffic in the smart little Smart Car. I felt a little naked without my MINI wrapped securely around me, especially with all the stares I got. The car certainly attracted attention.

"What is that?" my mother said, as when she spotted the car in front of her building. I'd parked it on the sidewalk, leaving plenty of room for pedestrians to maneuver around it.

"It's a Smart Car. Belongs to Delicia. I'm borrowing it, since mine's in the shop. What do you think?"

She pulled her fake-fur coat around her as if chilled. "That's not a car. It's more like an outfit. We can't *both* fit in there!"

"You'd be surprised. Hop in."

I opened the passenger door, and she grimaced as she maneuvered herself inside. "Put on your seat belt," I said before closing her door. It took me three steps to reach the driver's side. I got in, put on my belt, checked for pedestrians and cars, then pulled onto the street. Mother held on to the sides as if she were riding a rickety stagecoach.

On the way to the Wax Museum, we passed a dozen other Smart Cars in a rainbow of colors. This was apparently *the* car to have in the city. By the time we arrived intact at Fisherman's Wharf, Mother had visibly relaxed. I found a parking spot barely large enough to fit a bicycle and slid in easily.

Amazing.

I just hoped no one came along and lifted the tiny car onto the back of their truck.

As we headed to the Wax Museum in search of Frankenstein, Dracula, and the Wolfman, I was excited at the thought of seeing my childhood horror movie favorites again. A rotating wax figure of the president greeted guests as they passed by, enticing tourists to pay the admission and "see the stars."

I met briefly with the manager whom I'd called earlier, a friendly, thirtysomething blond woman named Colleen Casey, who proudly showed me around. Her father had owned the place, and passed it on to her. It had been her idea to rent out the museum for parties, everything from horror and sci-fi gigs to political and historical themes. As I followed her through the old building that had been there since my childhood and listened to her commentary, I grew nostalgic about the powerful political figures, brave war heroes, brilliant scientists, and glamorous Hollywood stars that were long gone, replaced by their waxen replicas.

It was all I could do to drag my mother along the tour. She

kept stopping at each figure, awestruck by Marilyn Monroe, tearful at John F. Kennedy, and swooning over Elvis, from whom she'd purloined my name.

My heart skipped a beat when we reached the infamous creatures in the Chamber of Horrors. There they were, baring their teeth, howling at the moon, and hiding in the bushes ready to scare the crap out of unsuspecting visitors.

"We clear this area," Colleen said, "so there's plenty of room to dance, while all the monsters look on." Clearly she enjoyed her work. I was sold. This was going to be a fun event after all.

As I turned to go, I realized my mother was no longer with me.

"Mother?" I called, then called again, louder, with more urgency. On a hunch, I backtracked and, sure enough, found her staring at Vivien Leigh. This had truly been a trip down memory lane for both of us, but in different ways.

"Is she still alive?" Mother asked, looking disoriented as she gazed at the beautiful woman in the hoop skirt and flowered hat.

"No, Mom, she's been gone a while." I wondered if this visit to the past had been a mistake for her. Befuddled, she stepped back and let me lead her back to the lobby.

After thanking Colleen, my mother and I were back on the street in search of San Francisco's iconic food. I bought a sidewalk shrimp cocktail from Alioto's, while Mom ordered clam chowder in a sourdough bowl. We sat on a bench and enjoyed the classic fare while watching the mass of tourists pass by. I listened to the attraction barkers compete with the sea lions for attention, and inhaled the fishy smell of the bay.

When we'd finished our meals, I collected the trash and headed for the nearest can. My cell phone rang just as I'd dumped the paper containers, and I pulled it out of my purse. "Number blocked" appeared on the screen.

"Hello?" I said.

Criminy. Not another hang up. The recent spate of crank calls was really beginning to get on my nerves.

I was about to hang up when I heard a low voice say, "Is your mother there?"

I laughed. I hadn't been mistaken for my mother for years. Must be a salesman.

"I'm sorry. I'm not interested." I hung up the phone, returned it to my purse, and headed back to the bench.

My mother was nowhere in sight.

Chapter 12

PARTY PLANNING TIP #12

Don't forget to take pictures at your Murder Mystery Party. You'll want to capture your guests as they investigate the crime scene, gather hidden clues, search for telltale evidence, or commit a party foul . . .

"Mom!" I screeched like a lost child into the crowd of tourists. Only she was the one who was lost. And with Alzheimer's, that could turn into a serious situation very quickly.

"Mom! Mother!"

With rising panic, I scanned the immediate vicinity for a woman in a fur coat, with a French twist and knockoff Coach handbag. The blur of people passing by made me dizzy as I tried to spot my mother's familiar face.

She couldn't have gotten far—could she?

I glanced over at the bay and saw a sprinkling of lights in the darkness—boats heading back to their docks. I shivered as I realized how close the water was. My skin broke out in goose bumps at the thought that she might have—

"Stop!" I said aloud, forbidding more morbid thoughts from taking over.

Find her! I commanded myself.

She hadn't just vanished into thin air.

The phone call! The one I'd received when I threw away the trash.

The caller had asked about my mother. And seconds later she was gone.

My heart pounding, I grabbed a man walking past. "Have you seen a woman . . ." I stopped. From the wide eyes and disturbed look, I guessed he didn't speak English.

I gave up and moved on, questioning half a dozen other tourists who either shrugged, shook their heads, or looked at me as if I were a crazy person. Beads of sweat broke out along my forehead and my armpits tingled.

Where the hell had she gone?

Out of the corner of my eye, I spotted a kiosk manned by a security guard and ran over.

"Can you help me?" I asked breathlessly through the opening in the glass window. "I've lost my mother . . . ," I panted. "She has Alzheimer's. Do you have some kind of PA system or some way to help me find her?"

The young man looked fresh out of security guard school. His mustache was sparse, his uniform ill-fitting, and his look eager. "You mean like a Code Adam?"

"What?"

"Code Adam. When a kid is lost, we radio-contact security guards and police in the area. Unfortunately, we can't seal the area, since it's outdoors, but—"

"Yes!" I said, cutting him off. "Please! Do a Code Adam

or whatever. My mother is about five eight, around a hundred and fifty pounds, wearing—"

"I want to report a crime!" came a strident voice, interrupting me from behind. I turned around, irritated at her rudeness, and caught my breath.

"Mother!"

"Presley!"

"Where *were* you? I've been looking all over for you! I thought you were—"

"I was robbed!" she said to me, then turned to the security guard. "Mugged! Violated! Purse snatched!"

"Calm down, lady," the guard said, resting his hands on his hips. "Can you describe the man?"

"Oh, it wasn't a man. It was a woman. I was sitting on the bench over there." She pointed to the spot where we'd had our chowders. "She came walking over, and all of a sudden she grabbed my purse and starting running—that way." She indicated the interior of the pier. The area was swarming with a multicultural crowd illuminated by old-fashioned streetlamps.

"I tried to chase her, Presley, but she was too fast. . . . I got a little turned around. . . ." Looking befuddled, Mom took my arm, her hands trembling. "I'm tired, honey. Could you take me home now?"

"Sure, Mom." I gave her a comforting hug.

"One last question, ma'am," the guard said. "Can you describe the mugger?"

"I only caught a quick look at her. Reddish hair, medium length, partly covered with a scarf that looked Egyptian. Dark, oversized sunglasses—not brand-name. She was wearing a black sweatshirt and matching pants, sort of like a jogger."

"Great job, Mom," I said, truly impressed with her short-term recall. By tomorrow she would have forgotten most of the details, but at the moment, her ability to remember so much was impressive.

"What kind of shoes was she wearing?" I asked.

Mother thought for a second. I could almost see the wheels turning as her green eyes gazed out the bay. "That's odd."

"What?"

"She wasn't wearing running shoes. They looked like just regular black dress shoes. But she ran so fast, I only got a glimpse." Mom looked down at her slender, empty hands. "I feel so naked without my pocketbook."

I left my contact number with the security guard on the chance Mom's purse was found, but I had a feeling it was a lost cause. By now it was in a Dumpster and the contents in the thief's pocket.

"It was a Coach bag. You gave me that purse, Presley."

"It was just a knockoff, Mom. I can get you another one—a real one, next time." I gave her a squeeze. "Did you have anything of value in it?"

"Of course. Everything. My identification, the keys to my building and my room, my cosmetics. Pictures of my old beaus. My pills. Address book. A letter from the mayor . . ." She continued to list the contents as we walked to Delicia's Smart Car. Nothing of any real monetary value, but those personal items were priceless to her. How she held all that stuff in one bag was a mystery to me. The items that really concerned me were her ID and keys.

On the drive to her building, I asked her more questions about the woman who had grabbed her bag. Pickpockets and purse-snatchers often frequented heavily touristed areas in the city, but this thief seemed odd. Rather than the expected young guy in baggy pants and a dark hoodie, this woman sounded more like one of the many joggers who ran along the Embarcadero.

Except for the scarf and the shoes.

"Did you notice anything else unusual about her, Mom?"

"Not really. I think she was short—shorter than me. Not very attractive, but she had beautiful red hair, very silky looking. I wondered what kind of conditioner she used. . . ."

"Did she say anything to you?"

"No, not a word. I thought she was going to join me on the bench, but instead she just walked up, grabbed my purse, and ran. It took me a minute to realize what had happened." She started to tear up.

"It's okay, Mom. It's just a purse. We can replace it, and most of the contents."

She dabbed at her eyes with her fingertips. "It's not that. It's . . . the way people are these days. You used to be able to leave your front door unlocked, even here in the city. Now you can't sit on a bench in a public place without worrying if someone is going to accost you. And a woman at that."

I'd been burgled a few times on Treasure Island and knew how she felt. Shocked. Vulnerable. Invaded. But this theft bothered me even more. The thief had her address and keys. I could only hope the perp was after what little cash my mother had, rather than her personal information.

I used my key to get her into her building, then explained to a staff member what had happened. I requested that the lock on her door be changed and she be issued a new key. There wasn't much I could do about the key to her building.

"'Bye, Mom," I said, seeing her to her room and using my copy of her door key to let her in. She moved slowly, and I could tell she was exhausted from the emotional strain. "Get some sleep. I'll call you in the morning."

I left the building with a sense of dread and glanced around the dark street for anyone who might look suspicious. After I'd entered the Smart Car and locked the doors, my iPhone chirped, alerting me to a new IM. I rarely used the messaging system—not many knew my IM address—but I pulled out the phone to read the words on the screen:

How do you like the picture?

A chill of fear ran through me.

Picture? What picture?

Another chirp, this one signaling a new e-mail. I tapped the envelope icon, and the message popped up, along with a photo. Staring me in the face was a photo of my mother and me enjoying our seafood meals on the bench just an hour ago.

I glanced at the address information, my hand trembling. It read:

Anon-To: KillerParties.com.
Sender: Remailer@mailtext.net.

Exhausted, I headed home to spend some quality time with my cats and catch up on my sleep.

The next morning, having overslept, I took a quick shower and had a quicker breakfast, then called my mom to see how she was doing. She didn't answer her phone, so I left a message, asking her to call me back.

I spent a couple of hours at my office, catching up on party requests, then searched the Internet for information on "How to send an anonymous e-mail." I found step-by-step directions from About.com. Although it sounded like an involved process, it must have been easy enough for any computer-savvy person to accomplish. According to the information, the anonymous sender uses a "remailer," which forwards the message to the recipient without a trace of the sender's return address.

Two hours later, there was no sign of Brad. Raj, Berk, and Rocco were in their offices working, but Delicia's and Brad's offices remained dark. I checked my watch. Ten o'clock. The museum would be open, and hopefully Christine would be at her desk.

I jumped into the Smart Car and made it to the de Young in record time, passing over a dozen other Smart Cars in a rainbow of colors along the way. Half of the other drivers waved at me, as if we were all in some secret club. Apparently this was *the* car to drive in the city. I parked easily, turned off the motor, and took several deep breaths to help me relax, nearly hyperventilating in the process. I locked the car and headed for the museum entrance. On my way I punched Brad's cell phone number. He answered just as I reached the security checkpoint.

"Hey, Presley." He knew it was me from his caller ID.

"Hold on," I said, as the guard searched my bag. She waved me on. "Brad, if someone sends an anonymous e-mail, is it airtight, or can it be traced?"

"You got a remailer?"

Why was I not surprised that he was familiar with an anonymous mailing program? "Yeah. At least, that's what the return address says. Is there any way to find out who it's from?"

"It's not easy, but a hacker could probably do it. If the sender uses two or three remailers, and sends the message in an encrypted form, it can be tough. You have to have a GnuPg, PGP keys, know the steps. But it's possible. What's up?"

"I'll explain later. Thanks."

"Wait! Presley, what's going on?"

"I can't talk now. I'm at the museum. I'll tell you everything when I get back. Any news on the dead guy?"

"Haven't heard back from Melvin yet. Listen, Presley . . ." He paused.

I waited. "Yeah?"

"Nothing. See you when you get back. Maybe we can grab a burger and beer at the Grill, talk about all this."

Was this a date? The Treasure Island Bar and Grill isn't the most romantic place on the island—it's the *only* place— but they serve great garlic fries, and the view of the yachts, Bay Bridge, and city skylines makes up for the limited menu.

And what was he not telling me?

"Brad, what aren't you telling me?"

"It can wait."

"Fine, but at least tell me how your brother's doing with Delicia's case."

"Like I said, we'll talk. I want to know more about this anonymous e-mail."

I hung up, puzzled at Brad's lack of candor and hesitant

manner. Something was up. Whatever this "date" was about, it would have to wait. I already had a date—with the elusive curator of the de Young museum. Only problem was, she didn't know it.

"I'm here to see Christine Lampe," I told the volunteer at the desk, deciding on another ruse.

"Do you have an appointment?" she asked, a thin smile crossing her well-worn face.

"Yes. Well, not exactly. But I'm Presley Parker. I hosted the event here the other night. Christine was in the play, and I have some museum things to return to her." Some of us with ADHD are quick on our feet when it came to making stuff up. I learned it in school when the teacher asked questions and I didn't have an answer. Great deflector.

"I'll have one of the security guards see you up. Please wait over there." She nodded for me to move over to the side of the large desk so paying patrons could slap down their money to view the latest art and artifacts. Five minutes later a security guard appeared.

"Sam!" I said, happy to see his pleasant face.

"Ms. Parker! You're back again? They're going to have to name a wing after you if you keep showing up. You're our most frequent visitor these days."

Sam nodded to the volunteer and gestured for me to follow him to the elevators. The doors opened, and I stepped in, followed by Sam. He passed his security card over the sensitive panel, then pushed number four.

"So, have you learned anything about the murders?" he said, after the doors closed.

"I was about to ask you the same thing. Not much. How about you?"

"Nothing. And we're under a lot of pressure here, as you can imagine. Especially me, since both happened on my watch. To tell you the truth, I read a lot of detective stories, but this mystery has got me stumped. I mean, why would anyone want to kill our most productive benefactor? Sure, she wasn't the most popular person in town, but she did so much good for the de Young, raising all that money when the city wouldn't come through."

"Any idea who the guy in the frog pond was?"

He shook his head. "So far he's a mystery man. There are a lot of homeless people in the park. Although . . ."

The elevator doors opened, and we stepped out. I paused outside and held the doors open. "Although what?"

He looked up and down the hallway, then leaned toward me and whispered, "Well, people are talking, you know?"

My eyes widened. "About what?"

"It's just gossip, but a lot of the staff are whispering about Mary Lee's 'friend,'" he said, adding finger quotes.

"What friend?" I said, puzzled. Then it dawned on me. "You mean, a lover?"

He peered around again, then nodded to a closed office door a few steps away.

I glanced at the name on the plate.

"Dan Tannacito? Christine's assistant? You're kidding. Isn't he a little—"

"Young for her?" Sam said. "Sure, but she's—she was—a powerful woman. Power and youth make a strong couple, don't you think?"

"I suppose so . . ."

"I hear she was his sugar mama, but," he added, "you didn't hear this from me." He zipped his lips with his fingers.

"I'm just telling you in case it helps you find who killed her."

I zipped mine. "Interesting," I said, forgetting my lips were supposed to be zipped. Had Dan "invested" in Mary Lee? Was she the "antiquity" that had recently paid off? Enough with the museum metaphors. "Do you think Dan might have had something to do with her death? A lover's quarrel, maybe? Maybe his bonus money had been cut off . . ."

"I'm not suggesting anything. I am, however, doing a little investigating of my own."

I nodded thoughtfully. "If we work together on this thing and share information, I'm sure we'll find the killer."

"Just as long as I don't lose my job," Sam added.

I shook his hand. Sam was a virtual gold mine of information. And much like a party planner, who would know more about what goes on behind the scenes than a security guard?

"Anything else?" I whispered, even though the hallway was empty.

"I heard from one of the docents that there may have been trouble in paradise."

Goose bumps rose on my arms. "What kind of trouble?"

"Apparently there were rumors of another woman. Of course, rumors abound in a place like this. But still . . . there's often some truth to such things. . . ."

I heard a door open and spun around, letting go of the elevator door. Dan Tannacito stepped out from his office and closed the door behind him. He blinked in surprise when he spotted me.

Had he overheard us talking?

"Ms. Parker! What a nice surprise. I assume you're here to talk about my daughter's party plans. Did you get to see the Wax Museum?"

I glanced back at the elevator. The doors were closed. Sam was gone.

"Uh, yes. I just wanted to let you know that it's all confirmed. No problem with hosting the party there."

"Wonderful! Snuffy will be thrilled. Or 'psyched,' as she would say. Do you need anything more from me at this point?"

I was having trouble looking at Dan, knowing what I knew about his relationship with Mary Lee. "No, I'm good."

"Are you headed down? Be glad to escort you. I'm on my way out."

"Actually, I stopped by to try and see Christine again. I haven't been able to connect with her."

"Cool. I'll let you go then. We'll talk more soon. Snuffy's really excited, as you can imagine. She already has her costume. She wants to dress up as the Bride of Chucky."

"Yes, I'll be in touch," I said as he stepped into the elevator. As soon as the doors closed, I walked down to Christine's office and rapped on the door. No answer. I opened it and peered in. A secretary's desk sat abandoned in the front part of the office. The door to the inner office was ajar. I was about to knock when I heard Christine's concerned voice. I paused and listened, waiting for an appropriate moment to interrupt her conversation.

"You're kidding!" Christine hissed.

Intrigued, I stepped closer. Silence. I guessed she was on the phone, listening to a response.

"Are you sure?" she said after a brief pause. "I see. Well, thanks for calling."

I heard her hang up the phone. I tapped on the door, then peeked inside.

"Excuse me, Christine. Sorry for the interruption, but I wanted to ask you a few questions. Is this a good time?"

Although I didn't know her well, I knew she didn't usually look this pale. The times I'd seen her at rehearsal she'd been poised, confident, and professional. At the moment, sitting at her desk, she didn't look any of these. Rather, she appeared a little confused, even drained.

I stepped inside. "Are you all right?"

She blinked rapidly, as if disoriented, then looked up from the phone she'd been staring at.

"That was the police," she said softly, her face tight.

Oh boy. "What did they want?"

She hesitated, as if searching for words, then said, "The body in the pond has been identified."

I broke out in goose bumps. "Who was it?"

She met my eyes. Hers were large, dark, and staring.

"Jason Cosetti. Mary Lee's ex-husband."

Oh my God.

Chapter 13

PARTY PLANNING TIP #13

While hosting a Murder Mystery Party, try not to slip and accidentally expose the murderer's identity. Not only does it ruin the party, but you might find yourself the next victim.

My first thought was: Delicia would be released! She couldn't have killed Mary Lee's ex-husband, because she'd been in jail.

"Do they know when he died?" I asked, easing into a chair across from Christine's desk. The surface of the desk was lined with small artifacts—a decorative bowl, a beaded necklace, a stone grinder, an arrowhead as long as my hand. The telephone sat in the middle.

She shook her head as she looked out a side window. "Not yet. He said it's not easy to pinpoint an exact time on a floater."

"A floater?"

"That's what he called it. He said it's affected by things

like water temperature, degree of decomposition . . ." She stopped, grimacing. Too much information.

I sagged in the chair. Even assuming both murders were committed by the same person—which I couldn't prove—Delicia wouldn't be off the hook until the police could determine that Jason Cosetti died *after* Mary Lee did—and *after* Dee's arrest. And even that didn't necessarily clear Delicia for Mary Lee's murder—there could be another killer. Meanwhile, my friend would remain in jail, with all the horrors that entailed—unless Andrew could get her released. Would she be eligible for bail?

I tried to return my focus to Jason Cosetti. Why had he been killed? Had someone disliked Mary Lee and Jason enough to want both of them dead? If so, what was the connection, other than they were once married—and had a son?

Corbin was the obvious link between them. Surely he wouldn't murder both of his parents. Yes, it happened now and then, but what did Corbin have to gain by their death? I guessed he would inherit a great deal of money from his wealthy mother, but his father had supposedly fallen on hard times and had even asked Mary Lee for help. That must have been humiliating.

"Christine," I said, interrupting her from her trance. She turned away from the window and met my eyes with little interest. "I'm came here to see if you could help me clear Delicia. She isn't the one who murdered Mary Lee—or Jason. Is there anything you can tell me that would help? Do you know anyone who might have wanted her dead?"

Christine folded her hands thoughtfully on her pristine desk and sighed. "All I know is Mary Lee wasn't well liked around here. She was always telling people what to do, as if she were Queen Nefertiti herself. A lot of people kissed her ass, but as soon as her back was turned, they wanted to kick it. She was a powerful woman, and everyone knew it. Any of us could have been out of a job if we got on her bad side."

"Were you on her bad side?" I asked, wondering if Christine had wanted to kick Mary Lee's ass.

She fiddled with one of the artifacts—the arrowhead—spinning the sharp-edged weapon around with her fingers. "No, of course not. I'm the curator here. She trusts—trusted—my judgment. And my background is impeccable." While Christine's words sounded determined, the woman kept her eyes on the spinning arrowhead, belying her confidence in them.

What was behind her conflicting behavior?

"So was there anyone at the de Young who might have had a reason to kill Mary Lee or her ex-husband? A disgruntled employee? A pressured donor? A person with a secret that Mary Lee—and Jason—might expose?"

Christine gave a small laugh. "Probably all of the above, if you're just talking about Mary Lee."

"No one in particular?"

Christine glanced out the window again.

"There was someone, wasn't there? Who?"

She set the arrowhead back in its spot along the edge of the desk, making sure it was perfectly aligned. "No one. I really have to get back to work. The loss of Mary Lee means more paperwork for—"

The door to Christine's office opened, and Dan Tannacito peeked in.

"Oh," Dan said, suddenly flushing. "Didn't know you were still here, Presley."

"Just trying to figure out who might have killed Mary Lee," I said to him, then glanced at Christine.

I caught a look passing between them I couldn't read.

"I'll leave you two alone. Talk to you later, Chris." He shut the door.

I turned back to Christine. Her jaw was set, and her dark eyes narrowed. Something was going on between the two of them, I was sure.

I stood up. "Thanks for your time, Christine." I reached over to shake her hand. She rose and met my hand with a cold, damp palm.

"Sorry I couldn't be of more help." She didn't look a bit sorry. The expression on her face was something else.

Like fear?

Brad was nowhere in sight when I returned to the office.

Standing me up?

In spite of my growling stomach, I went straight to the computer and keyed in the name Christine Lampe. There was plenty of recent information to read. In the past ten years she'd become a highly respected curator at the museum. But I could find little about her before the last decade. I tried searching for the name "Christine" and "Lampe" separately, along with the word "museum," and got several dozen links, but each led to a dead end—no connection to the Christine Lampe I was looking for.

I was about to give up when I had a thought. I typed in "classmates.com" and waited for the site to fill the screen. I did a search for the University of Oregon and typed in "Christine Lampe."

Nothing. There was no record of that name during the

years she was supposed to have attended. Had she lied about her credentials? If so, how had she gotten the job at the de Young Museum? Would Mary Lee have hired her without making sure she was legit?

I clicked the word "Yearbook" for 1970 and checked for a picture of Christine. Still nothing. I did a search for "Mary Lee Miller" and found her photo right where it should have been.

Christine and Mary Lee had supposedly been together at the U of O.

So where was Christine Lampe?

On a hunch, I began scanning the rest of the photos. My eyes were burning by the time I got to H. I almost missed the photo of "Judith Hofmann."

Judith Hofmann looked like a very young Christine Lampe.

I stared at it. It had to be her. Why had she changed her name?

I closed the site and typed in Judith Hofmann. Voilà. I found a Judith Hofmann employed at the Portland Museum as an assistant curator, soon after she'd matriculated from graduate school. I read the item and was impressed with the up-and-coming Judith Hofmann.

So what had happened to her?

I scrolled down the links and found a site that caught my eye. It read: *". . . museum curator Judith Hofmann was suspended after being suspected of acquiring questionable artifacts, a matter she denied at her hearing by the board of directors."*

She was quoted as blaming her staff for falsifying documents and framing her as the fall guy. In the end, she had left the museum with a healthy severance pay, and her where-abouts were "unknown."

The knock on my office door startled me.

"Hungry?" Brad stood in the doorway in his soft blue jeans, a red "Life Is Good" T-shirt stretched across his chest. A cartoon stick figure lying in a hammock was featured prominently on the front of the shirt. Naturally he wore his favorite shoes—cushy white New Balance Zips.

"Beyond hungry," I said, rubbing my tummy. I tagged the site, shut down the computer, and gathered my purse and notebook. Giving the office one last glance, I locked the door and headed for the parking lot. Brad was right behind me, his hand barely touching my back as if leading me out. It was a comforting—and sexy—gesture, and I suddenly felt self-conscious about this "date."

I hadn't been on a real date since I dumped my cheating boyfriend, an associate professor at the university. I'd caught him sleeping with one of his TAs—what a cliché. A thought jumped to mind. Had the look that passed between Christine and Dan been something romantic? If so, why had they looked guilty? Both were single, weren't they?

Or was I just horny and making a romance out of a friendship?

Brad and I walked the few blocks to the Treasure Island Bar and Grill, the only restaurant currently on the island. The fog had lifted, and although there was a chill in the air, the walk kept me warm. I filled Brad in on my computer sleuthing, and he told me more about the "floater," aka Jason Cosetti.

"Why do they call them floaters?" I asked, and then

wished I hadn't. It didn't make for a good prelunch conversation.

"Floaters are corpses found floating in water, and it's harder for the ME to determine their time of death. They decompose more slowly in water than on land."

My stomach lurched. I tried to think of another topic to change the subject. Brad apparently felt the need to share his knowledge.

"If the body is in there a long time, say a couple of weeks, first the body sinks. When it starts forming gas, it rises again. Jason hadn't been in that pond long enough for his body to swell much and the skin to separate."

"So they can't tell how many hours he'd been dead, only how many days?"

"Like I said, it slows down the process. But they'll figure out a ballpark figure."

By the time we reached the restaurant, I'd lost my appetite. But the smell of burgers and fries brought it back, and I led the way into the double-wide trailer. We sidled up to the bar, placed our orders, and carried a couple of beers onto the attached glass-enclosed patio to watch the colorful windsurfers.

"So Christine was married, divorced, and lost her job at another museum," Brad said, summarizing my latest information, his upper lip damp with beer.

"Which proves nothing, really." I took a deep pull from my own beer. "I feel like I take two steps forward and I fall back three. Either that, or I'm going around in circles."

He leaned back in the wicker chair. "You need a specific game plan."

"I have one," I countered. "Except it's a party plan."

He frowned, puzzled.

"I've been using one of my party planning sheets to try to solve this. Planning a party and solving a mystery have a lot in common. The problem is, I'm a newbie at this event planning career, and not even close to being a detective."

Brad sat up to welcome the burger plates from the waiter. He immediately decorated his bun with heavy dollops of catsup, mustard, and relish. When the waiter asked if we needed anything more, I almost suggested he bring Brad a hose, but instead I shook my head and dove into my own lightly seasoned burger.

"I know you're no detective," Brad said as soon as the first bite had cleared his mouth. "But like a detective, a party planner is a problem-solver."

Grabbing a napkin, I wiped away a drip that had made its way down my chin. I was sure I looked adorable with hamburger juice all over my face.

"A detective gathers details—clues—to discover whodunit," Brad continued after a swallow of beer. "The party planner—"

"Event planner," I corrected him.

"Event planner," he said, enunciating the words, "gathers details—props and stuff—to provide the perfect party. It's all in the details."

I set my burger down and wiped my greasy fingers on two napkins, then pulled out an annotated party-planning sheet from my purse. "Okay, here's what I have so far: the victim, Mary Lee, aka guest of honor, is dead. She was stabbed to death with a sharp instrument like a dagger, aka the theme. The weapon wasn't missing from the crime scene, aka the party venue. And one of the guests, aka my-primary-suspect-slash-her-ex-husband, is also dead. That's about it."

"Think about who had something to gain by killing Mary Lee," Brad said.

"Everyone?"

"That narrows it down," he said sarcastically. "Seriously, who?"

"Her ex, for one—before he got himself killed. I suppose her son, Corbin, but that seems like a long shot. I just don't think he has it in him to kill both parents. And now I think there's something going on between Christine and Dan. But I can't tell if it has to do with Mary Lee, or it's just personal."

"Okay, you now have three viable suspects. Who else?"

I took another bite of my burger and thought while I chewed. Was I overlooking someone? Someone at the party who had a hidden agenda? Someone in Mary Lee's social circle? Someone, someone . . .

"*Cherchez la femme,*" Brad said, interrupting my circling thoughts.

"What?" I asked.

"*Cherchez la femme,*" Brad repeated. "Only, instead of looking for the woman, how about looking at the woman's home? You learn a lot by studying the victim's home."

I took a sip of beer. "I doubt I can get into Mary Lee's house. Don't the cops have it secured?"

"Maybe not. It wasn't the crime scene. I'm sure they've been there looking for clues, but I'll bet you could get her son to let you in."

I sat up, suddenly energized, either by the burger or by the ideas Brad had suggested. "Good idea. And maybe I could get into his dad's place too. I'm sure there's a connection between the two murders."

We finished up our meals and drinks. Brad pulled out a few dollars for a tip from his leather wallet.

"You got the tab," I said, pulling my wallet from my purse. "I'll leave the tip."

"Next time," he said, standing up. He pulled out my chair.

The walk back to the office building was leisurely, no doubt due to our full stomachs. We strolled back in silence. I was pondering my options; I had no idea what Brad was thinking.

He stopped abruptly in the office parking lot and glanced at his motorcycle. "I'm got some errands to run."

I turned to face him, a little surprised he wasn't returning to his office. "Oh, sure. Uh . . . Actually, I meant to ask if you could take a look at that anonymous e-mail I got. Do you have a minute?"

Brad looked alarmed. "So that's why you were asking about the remailer? What did the e-mail say?"

"Not much. Whoever it was just sent a picture and asked how I liked it. It was a cell phone snapshot of my mother and me at Fisherman's Wharf." I filled him in on the purse-snatching and the fact that the snatcher now had my mother's address and room key.

The frown deepened. "Did you call Melvin?"

"I . . . meant to. I will. I figured it was a random purse-snatching, and there wasn't much they could do. Until I got the e-mail. So can it be traced?"

Brad followed me inside my office. I sat down and called up the e-mail. He leaned over my shoulder and read it. I could feel his chest brush against my back and smell his lime-scented aftershave.

"Like I said, a hacker could probably do it. And the police may be able to trace it, with probable cause. It's pretty easy these days to send this kind of stuff, with all the Web sites available. The sender can make the e-mail look like it came from any address he wants—if he knows what he's doing." He straightened up. "Call Melvin. Now. This is a credible threat."

I pushed back my desk chair. Brad extended his hand and pulled me to my feet, just inches from him in the crowded office space.

"I will. I promise. Thanks for lunch. And for your help."

He raised his hand and started to reach toward me.

I froze.

Oh God.

Was he going to kiss me?

He touched the side of my mouth. "You have a little something . . ."

I let out a breath, partly disappointed that he didn't kiss me, and completely mortified that I'd been wearing some kind of food on my face the whole way back to the office.

I reached up to wipe it away, but Brad caught my hand. "I'll get it," he said. "It's catsup. You'll smear it all over."

He placed his hand on my cheek, I assumed to steady my head while he removed the hideous red blob from my lip.

He leaned in—to get a better look?

And kissed the catsup right off my face.

Chapter 14

PARTY PLANNING TIP #14

Decorate the party room in keeping with your Murder Mystery Theme. Set the stage for a fake wake in a funeral home, a premature burial in a cemetery, or a surprise body in the parlor.

I sat in my office staring at a blank screen, unable to focus. I'd just been "cleaned" by a crime scene cleaner. And that kiss had sent an electric current from the tips of my toes to the ends of my hair.

Crap.

I tried to shake the feeling away, but it kept coming back. I really didn't need anything demanding more attention in my attention-deficit life. What did I really know about this man who'd moved into my life via the office across the hall? Only that there was something more to him than simple crime scene cleaning. I hadn't even known he'd had a brother until today.

Why did he have to go and kiss me like that?

"Enough!" I said aloud, slamming my hands down on my desk.

Raj Reddy appeared in my office doorway. "You okay, Ms. Presley?"

"I'm fine, Raj. Sorry about that."

"Enough working for today?" he said, his head bobbing side to side. "I'm down to that."

"I'm down *with* that," I said, breaking into a grin. I loved it when Raj tried to be hip with the English language. While well schooled in English, he'd only lived in the United States a few years and was trying hard to pick up the current slang. His malapropisms always cheered me up.

"It's a little early for quitting time," I said. "Been busy today?"

"Oh yes. Lots of tourists trying to sneak into the film set. Anytime Robin Williams is making a movie here, it's giving me a headache."

Raj was such a sweetheart. In fact, he reminded me of Sam Wo. Both men were conscientious, polite, and there to help out beyond the call of duty. They were almost father figures. I wouldn't have minded if my mother dated either one of them. At the moment, it looked like Sam was heading that way. He'd mentioned that his wife had recently left him. No doubt he was lonely, much like my mother. The thought of him becoming my next "father" was kind of weird, but if it made my mother happy, I could live with it.

I tried to work on party planning for the next couple of hours, then gave up. Brad hadn't returned, and I figured if he had more news, he'd let me know. Maybe I could focus better at home. I rose from my desk and gathered my things.

"'Bye, Raj," I called down the hall. "I'll see you tomorrow."

He peeked his head out. "Good-bye, Ms. Presley. Have a nice night. And please say hello to your kind mother for me."

Hmmm. Maybe Sam would have a little competition after all.

I drove the Smart Car the short distance to my condo and parked in the carport. I unlocked the front door and went inside to greet my cats. The place looked as if it had been vandalized, but then, it always looks like that. Makes it hard to know when I've actually had an intruder. Luckily, that had only happened once, a few weeks back, when I stuck my nose into the death of the mayor's unsuspecting bride-to-be. Since then I'd added a new lock, secured the windows, and tried to train my three cats to attack anything that moves— other than me. So far they preferred to ravage couch pillows, coffee table legs, and my feet.

I fed all three, filling their separate bowls, then snuggled up with Thursby and a glass of wine to watch the evening news. The de Young double murders were headliners, and Detective Melvin looked pretty hot during his interview, with his slicked-back hair and charming grin. The gorgeous female reporter was practically drooling for him.

Unfortunately, Melvin had nothing new to offer. He quickly fell back on the usual cop clichés—"We can't discuss an active investigation," "We have no further information at this time," blah, blah, blah. When the segment ended, I roamed the channels looking for something to take my mind off the endless whodunit loop playing in my head. I surfed past a romantic comedy on Lifetime, a romantic suspense on AMC, and a romance with zombies on Sci-Fi. When I realized I couldn't escape all the romance, I turned off the TV and went to bed.

Naturally I dreamed about a romantic crime scene cleaner.

Brad was just about to rescue me from a museum mummy who had come to life when my cat alarm went off. Cairo was kneading my stomach, digging in with his sharp little claws, while Fatman licked my cheek. Only Thursby slept in; he still lay across my ankles. Snoring. I knew cats purred, but I never knew they snored. Maybe he had a deviated septum. Maybe he needed rhinoplasty. Maybe I needed to get up.

I headed for the shower, my mind running random nonthoughts, until the warm water really woke me up and brought me back to more realistic concerns. Like getting Delicia out of jail. Or finding the real killer. Or dealing with that kiss . . .

Somewhere between the shampoo and conditioner I decided that I wanted to learn more about Mary Lee and Jason's relationship—and I needed Corbin's help. Like Brad had said—sometime before he kissed me—"*Cherchez la femme.*"

And Corbin was the only one with an all-access pass to their pasts.

I dressed in my usual black jeans and a T-shirt with a cat on it that read, "If you don't talk to your cats about catnip, who will?" After downing a triple latte and a cinnamon bagel, I pulled out my phone and tapped his number. After five rings, a lethargic-sounding voice answered, "Yeah?"

"Corbin, hi. It's Presley."

"Yeah, I know." Caller ID.

"You don't sound so good. Are you all right?"

"I'm great," he said, sarcasm lacing his tone. "My mother is killed, and now my father turns up dead. What could be wrong?"

"I'm so sorry, Corbin. That's why I need your help finding out who did this. Could we meet again?"

"What about Delicia?"

"Come on, Corbin, you know she didn't do it. She was in jail when your dad was killed. Don't you want to see the real killer caught?"

Silence on the other end. Then, "Whatever."

"You want to meet at the Bittersweet Café again?" The cafe was near Pacific Heights, where his mother lived. I had to convince him to let me see her home.

"I don't have a car . . ."

"Listen, I'll come pick you up. Where do you live?"

He gave me directions to his home in the arty district of Noe Valley, an expensive area filled with cute cafés, genre bookstores, trendy clothing boutiques, and eclectic shops. If you wanted to live there, you had to have enough money to pay the inflated rent. I had a feeling Corbin's mother had been subsidizing him. I doubted he could afford to live there otherwise.

Twenty minutes later I drove up to his house on a side street not far from the shopping district. The yard was unkempt, full of weeds and large rocks, a broken bicycle, and a rusty porch swing. I knocked on the heavily repainted door—it was currently red—and a few seconds later Corbin opened it. He waved me inside.

"Sorry about the mess," he said, running his paint-stained

hand through his tangled dark brown hair. He was wearing the same black T-shirt full of holes and kneeless jeans he'd worn the other day at our meeting. I couldn't tell if he'd affected the impoverished-artist look or he just hadn't bothered to change in the last few days. His bare feet looked dirty.

The living area was small, cluttered, and smelled of weed. He stepped over to a stained green velvet chair, swiped copies of underground comics onto the floor, and gestured for me to sit. I recognized several of the 'zines at my feet, by artists like Harvey Pekar, R. Crumb, and Art Spiegelman. Corbin cleared at space on the threadbare brocade couch across from me and plopped down, sinking into the sagging cushions. I spotted a mousetrap peeking out from under the side of the couch and shivered.

"You live here alone?" I asked, not knowing where to begin.

"Yeah. Had a roommate, but he joined the Peace Corps. I like my privacy."

I leaned forward, resting my elbows on my knees. "Corbin, I think we should take a look around your mother's house and see if we can find something that might help. Do you have keys to the place?"

"Yeah. I guess it would be okay. You'll have to drive. I don't have any wheels at the moment." Again he ran his fingers through his messy hair. Was this his look, or just a lack of interest in a shower and shampoo?

"No problem," I said, and stood up. "Shall we go?"

While he ducked into another room to retrieve his jacket, I noticed several canvases propped together against a wall. I meandered over and flipped through them. The subject matter was the same in every one—unfinished portraits of his mother. They weren't particularly good, but at least they weren't nudes. Still, was this evidence of the classic Oedipus complex? Or was he trying to please his mother by capturing her on canvas? That was the trouble with abnormal psychology— there were so many options for diagnosis. Now, if only he'd included her shoes in the paintings . . .

Corbin returned wearing a denim jacket and paint-stained sneakers, no socks. In his hand he dangled a key ring. Stepping over a pile of mail that had been slipped through the front door slot, I headed outside. Corbin followed, locking his door behind him. When he turned and saw Dee's Smart Car, he grinned.

"Cool car. You had it long?"

I stared at him, surprised at his lack of recognition. "It's Delicia's. Haven't you seen it before?"

His face clouded over as he opened the passenger door and slipped in.

I moved around to the driver's side, sat down, then turned to him.

"I thought you and Dee were, you know . . ."

He stared out the side window. "Yeah, well, that doesn't mean I know everything about her. We just met up a couple of times at the clubs. She never mentioned the car."

I raised an eyebrow. "Buckle up."

He snapped the belt around him and settled in. "It's bigger inside than I thought. How much does something like this run?"

"I think Dee paid around eighteen thousand for it. Give or take. I still can't believe you didn't know. Didn't you ever go anywhere in her car?"

"No. I borrowed my roommate's, mostly."

I started the engine. "Pacific Heights, right?"

"Yeah." He gave directions, weaving me through the varied city neighborhoods and streets. But entering Pacific Heights was like entering another world. The stately, landscaped mansions built within a parklike setting are home to some of the wealthiest city residents, like Dianne Feinstein, Danielle Steel, and Lars Ulrich from Metallica. The Academy of Art has a campus in the area, and there are several consulates and plenty of upscale shopping. *Mrs. Doubtfire*, *The Wedding Planner*, and *The Princess Diaries* are only a few of the many movies filmed here.

Driving through, I'd never seen so many turrets, towers, parapets, domes, cupolas, stained glass windows, and other architectural whimsies. The small but immaculate yards were festooned with all sorts of lawn ornaments—birdbaths, fountains, even a hooded saint and King Neptune rising out of the grass. I spotted fake ducks, turtles, deer, frogs, and penguins frozen to their spots. The only things missing were pink flamingoes and garden gnomes. Apparently they didn't belong in this neighborhood of professionally designed and tended yards.

"Wow," was all I could say as we pulled up to Mary Lee's mansion.

"Yeah," Corbin said. "Looks more like a museum than a home, doesn't it? Same guy who designed the de Young did it."

I parked the Smart Car in the driveway, and we got out. When I turned to lock it, Corbin shook his head.

"Don't bother. The car's safe here. Unless it gets towed for being 'a public nuisance.'" He added the finger quotes. It looked like a toy sitting there next to the ginormous mansion.

I followed Corbin to the massive front door and waited

for him to pull out a key. Instead, he slid open a small ceramic panel, revealing a series of numbers. He punched in a
code, slid the panel back, and pressed his thumb on the door
latch.

"Voilà," he said, ushering me inside.

Corbin was right about the house looking like a museum—
inside as well as out. Giant paintings covered the walls of the
high-ceilinged rooms, mostly modern abstract works of bold
colors. I recognized a Wayne Thiebaud cityscape, a dizzying
view of one of San Francisco's steep streets.

I followed Corbin into the front room, which was filled
with small statues on pedestals, mostly nudes. Two white
suede couches faced each other, looking as pristine as if
they'd never been used. Between them was a glass table mar-
bled with swirling colors. Indirect lighting lit up the artworks,
and a stained glass dome filtered in muted light from above.

"Is anyone living here now?" I whispered to Corbin, feeling I might be tossed out by a security guard if I made any
kind of disturbance.

"Nope. All the help leave at the end of the day. And most
of them haven't been around since she . . . died. She has a
bunch of guest bedrooms, but no one lives with her except
that dog of hers."

I glanced around for signs of the pooch. "Where is she?
The dog, I mean."

"No clue," he said simply, flopping onto one of the white
couches and spreading his arms on the back.

Hmmm. The dog had been at the murder mystery play
that night, tucked into its little purse-home at Mary Lee's
side. I thought I remembered Corbin holding it, right after he
discovered his mother's death. So where had it gone? To a

shelter? Surely someone would have taken in the animal. I'd have to check into that.

"Can I take a look around?" I asked Corbin.

"Knock yourself out."

Wow. Uncaring? Uncooperative? Or just upset by being in his mother's home?

"I'll be quick."

He laid his head back and closed his eyes. I moved into the next room, a formal dining area with a long dark wood table and enough seats to serve at least two dozen guests. Crystal chandeliers hung at either end of the table, and again the walls were covered with abstract and modern art. I moved past a dumbwaiter, through a spacious butler's pantry, and into a spotless kitchen, then on to a sitting room, library, several guest bathrooms, and an entertainment center with a massive plasma TV. Everything was immaculate—not a thing out of place, not even a dog hair. I headed up the curving staircase and checked out half a dozen guest bedrooms, each decorated in a different style—French country, Spanish hacienda, English cottage, and so on.

The master bedroom—Mary Lee's room—took my breath away. Everything was pink, from the canopied bed to the antique chaise longue next to the large stone fireplace. At the end of the massive bed sat a pink fur-lined dog bed, with the name Chou-Chou embroidered on one side.

There was no sign of the dog.

I checked the master bath, with the huge soaking tub and Jacuzzi, the spacious, glass-enclosed shower with its myriad jets and marble trim, and snooped in all the drawers and cabinets. No telltale signs that might indicate Mary Lee was a drug addict, pill popper, or had a medical condition. Not even a Valium lurked in her small cache of bottles. I did find lots and lots of Christian Dior, Lancôme, Elizabeth Arden, and Dior cosmetics on the shelves of her mirrored vanity, along with the usual antiaging concoctions. But nothing screamed, "I have secrets!"

Returning to her bedroom, I checked the walk-in (practically live-in) closet. It was filled with glittery gowns and designer duds. Her multitude of shoes occupied their own separate wall. I closed the doors, then noticed another door next to the fireplace.

I turned the knob and pushed the door open. Inside was a small office, outfitted with the latest electronic equipment—a computer, a laptop, two color printers, a scanner, a shredder, and two filing cabinets. I sat in the cushy desk chair and tried to log on to the computer, but it required a password. After a few failed attempts—"Corbin," "de Young," "Chou-Chou"—I gave up. I checked the shredder, filled with crisscross-cut confetti, and the filing cabinets, containing a couple hundred alphabetized files. I rifled through a few—"Adams Ceramics," "Anderson Arts & Antiquities," "A–Z Restoration"—then closed the drawer. It would take days to sift through all of the files in search of hidden clues.

I had a thought and returned to the A–G file drawer. Flipping through, I found the one I was looking for—"Employees"—wondering if she kept a record of disgruntled staff members who might have harbored a grudge against her. While I was in the A–G vicinity, I checked for a "de Young" file and found it between "Daniels and Daniels Designs" and "Dietz Cabinetry."

Inside I found a single sheet of paper with a number: 4-1-1-2-3.

Chapter 15

PARTY PLANNING TIP # 15

Hide clues related to the Murder Mystery Party around the room for the amateur sleuths to discover. Make sure the clues are visible so your more intoxicated guests have a chance to solve the crime, too.

Once we were back in the car, I asked Corbin, "How about your dad's place?"

"Whatever," Corbin said. I was getting worried about him. He was showing signs of depression—lack of interest, lethargy, lack of concern for himself. And why wouldn't he, with both his parents murdered? The only emotion missing was grief.

I pulled into light traffic and tried to chat him up on the drive to the marina docks. I asked about his relationship with Delicia, his art, his plans, but he was tight-lipped, giving one-word answers and shrugs. I gave up and concentrated on not wrecking Dee's car as I drove through the city streets.

Fifteen minutes later we pulled up in front of the East

Dock, where dozens of luxury yachts and colorful sailboats were berthed. I found a parking spot and guided the Smart Car effortlessly into the small space. We got out, and I followed Corbin to the gate, then waited for him to unlock it. Once inside, we headed for the boat at the end of the pier where it was moored.

"This is it," Corbin said, leaping onto the boat deck. I waited for him to offer me a hand, but he seemed oblivious to me. Squatting down, I held on to a metal bar and eased myself onto the deck.

I don't know much about boats, but this one was beautifully maintained. The wood was polished to a mirror shine, and the deck sparkled in the noon sun. It had to be expensive.

Corbin stepped over to the cabin door and opened it.

"It's not locked?" I asked, surprised.

"No need. Sailor's honor. If you have a key to your dock, that's all you need."

He ducked inside, and I followed him into the small, dimly lit interior. I gave the place a quick glance and spotted several built-ins—cabinets, seats, and a table. In contrast to the exterior, the inside was cluttered with a variety of artifacts—sculptures, objets d'art, totems, pottery, masks, ceremonial tools, and several dozen weapons. Jason Cosetti could have supplied an army with the number of scythes, swords, scabbards, spears, and stilettos he'd amassed. The treasures would have been impressive if they'd been mounted or framed, but most of them were jumbled together in a heap or stacked, one on top of another. The rest appeared to be in the half dozen cardboard boxes that were strewn on every surface and most of the floor.

"Wow. Did you know your father had all these things?" I asked Corbin, who had cleared off a built-in shelf and sat perched on it.

"Yeah, he never stopped trying to make a name for himself as an art dealer."

I picked up a random sword and felt the blade. Sharp enough to make a major dent in a human being. "Was he successful at all?"

"Not really. He kept trying to sell stuff to the de Young and other museums, but I don't think he had much luck. He couldn't even get Mom interested."

"How did he come by the boat?"

"Friend of his let him watch it while he's gone."

"I heard you're not allowed to live on the boats here."

"Yeah, well, Dad did a lot of things you're not supposed to do."

I couldn't help but wonder if Jason hated his ex-wife enough to kill her. She'd made a success of her life, while his seemed to go nowhere. Maybe it was revenge. Or maybe he had something to gain by her death. Was he mentioned in her will? Of course the point was moot, due to the fact that the suspect had also been murdered. So if he did kill Mary Lee, why did he end up dead?

I glanced at Corbin, who was dangling his feet like a bored schoolchild and staring down at his shoes as if they were fascinating. While he was in his trance, I looked around, in cupboards and boxes, hoping to find a telltale note, a cryptic phone number, a clue that would tell me something about his death. The place was such a mess, it would have been difficult to tell if someone had broken in and taken something of value. Hopefully the locked gate would keep intruders out. Except me.

"Are any of these things worth money?"

He looked up from his swinging shoes. "I dunno. Probably not. A few years ago Dad tried to sell something that turned out to be a fake. Kinda ruined his reputation in the business. He asked Mother to take a look at his stuff, but she blew him off."

I ducked into what looked like the bedroom. It housed two small built-in bunk beds, one covered with stacks of artifacts, the other with a rumpled sleeping bag. I peered inside a mini-closet that was built into the wall. A raincoat and several flannel shirts hung on wire hangers. Glancing down, I found a pair of well-worn work boots—Sears DieHards. I guessed they were secondhand. Next to the boots I spotted some wadded-up clothes and bent down to examine them. I lifted what looked like a gray houndstooth cape. Hidden underneath were a deerstalker cap and a meerschaum pipe.

Sherlock Holmes.

I picked up the costume parts and looked them over. In the pocket of the cape was a tiny magnifying glass—the kind I'd used to decorate for the Murder Mystery Party.

Jason Cosetti had been at that party. In disguise.

I returned to the main room, costume in hand. "Corbin, did you see your dad at the party?"

"Nah. He wouldn't come to a thing like that."

I held up the cape in one hand, the hat and pipe in the other. "I found this Sherlock Holmes costume in his closet. Any idea why he might have had it?"

Corbin's eyes narrowed. "Not a clue. Maybe it's not his."

"I found a party favor in the pocket. I'm pretty sure he was at the event. Do you remember seeing a Sherlock Holmes there?

"Yeah"—he snorted—"a bunch of them."

Corbin was right. Detective Holmes had been one of the most popular characters at the party. Note to self: View Berk's videotape of the party and see if I could tell which Sherlock Jason might have been. I glanced around for a recent photograph of Jason and found one of him with Corbin, posing on the deck of the boat.

"May I borrow this?" I asked Corbin.

He answered in his usual manner: with an automatic shrug.

"I think I'm done here. I'm going to hang on to the costume and see if I can match it to a costume in one of the party videotapes." If I could tie the costume to Jason, it would prove he'd been at the event—and could have murdered Mary Lee. Since the costume had been returned to his closet sometime after the party, he must have come home and changed. That meant he was killed sometime after Mary Lee died.

And that meant Delicia would be off the hook.

Corbin hopped off his perch and followed me out without a glance back at his father's nautical home. We exited the gate, which slammed shut behind us.

I tried the handle.

Locked up tight.

"Hey, would you mind swinging by the museum?" Corbin asked as I started the car. "I need some stuff from my locker. Taking the bus is a drag."

Surprised, I asked, "You have a locker at the de Young?"

"Yeah. Art supplies and junk like that. I don't think I'll be spending much time there anymore."

Lockers. At the de Young.

Maybe Mary Lee had a locker there too.

"Sure," I said, looking over my shoulder for a chance to merge into traffic.

We zipped along toward Golden Gate Park, me jabbering about whatever came to mind, Corbin saying very little. Once again I parked easily in the underground garage, and we headed into the museum.

"Where are the lockers?" I asked Corbin as he started for the elevators.

"Fifth floor."

"Don't you need a passkey for the elevator?"

He pulled out his wallet, opened it, retrieved a plastic card, and showed it to me.

"Your mother got it for you?" I said, stating the obvious. "Does she have a locker too?"

He nodded. "I'll be back in a few minutes."

Mary Lee did have a locker here! I thought about going with him, then decided I didn't want him to know that I planned to check it out.

I called after him, "If I'm not here, wait for me at the front desk."

He waved without looking back and disappeared.

I went over to the desk and asked them to page Sam Wo. He appeared five minutes later in his spiffy uniform.

"Back again, Ms. Parker? We'll have to get you a season pass." He laughed at his own joke. "I suppose you have more questions for me—"

"I do, but I don't have time right now. I wondered if you could do me a favor? I need you to open one of the lockers on the fifth floor."

Sam pulled me aside. "What? No way! You really do want to get me fired."

"Sam, Corbin said Mary Lee had a locker here at the museum. I need to see if there's anything important in it. Don't you have a master key?"

"Nope. They use combination locks, not keys. The only way to get in would be to cut it. And if the cops coming looking, they'd know someone broke in. Too risky."

I pulled a slip of paper from my purse. "I think I have the combination."

He looked at me, surprised. "Where did you get that?"

I ignored his question. "All you have to do is find out which locker is hers, then try the combination. No one will know."

Sam shook his head in defeat. "You're not going to stop until I'm on the unemployment line, are you."

I smiled devilishly at him. "By the way, my mother says hi. I think she's looking forward to hearing from you."

With a sigh, Sam said, "Follow me."

He led me to the elevators, but instead of riding up to the fifth floor, he punched the basement button.

"What are you doing?"

He said nothing as the doors opened and he stepped out. I followed him to the security office. He unlocked the door and went inside. "Come on," he said.

I stepped into what would have been a spacious office if it weren't for all the equipment. A guard sat at a computer console while another faced a wall of security cameras. The ambient light was dim, making the screens easier to monitor.

"Wait here," Sam said; then he entered his own office in the back and closed the door behind him.

"This is fascinating," I said, watching people move past the camera lenses in various rooms of the museum. "You can see everything from here."

"Just about," the man at the console said. "There are a couple of blind spots—hallways and the like—but we've got the important stuff covered."

One of the dark screens lit up as a young couple neared an exhibit. I remembered Sam telling me about the motion sensors. I glanced at the other screens, and one caught my eye. The dagger we'd copied for the mystery play. It was amazing how well the art department had replicated it.

Where was the missing blade that had been used on Mary Lee?

"Stay here," Sam said, holding a ring of keys. "I'll be right back."

"I can't go with you?" I whispered.

"Not a chance."

"Okay, but watch out for Corbin. He may be up there, and I don't want him to know I'm looting his mother's locker."

"Be right back, guys," he said to the two other guards. "Hold down the fort, will you? Don't let any art thieves steal my lunch." Sam seemed to have a natural camaraderie with nearly everyone.

Sam closed the door on his way out. I returned to the computer screens and watched the crowd shuffle by.

"Is there any way someone could sneak around without being caught on camera?" I asked the guard.

"Nope. Not unless the system broke down. And it never has."

"Could someone cut one of the wires?"

The guard turned to me with a grin. "I suppose that's possible, but the system is so protected, I can't even turn off a camera without it being documented. Why? You planning to steal something?"

I laughed, too loudly. The other surly guard shot me a concerned look. I recognized him from my attempt to get Delicia's purse. Ed something.

I sat down in a nearby chair and watched the screens, wondering how Sam was making out. He appeared ten minutes later, empty-handed. I couldn't hide the disappointment I felt. He waved me back to his private office and closed the door.

"Nothing?"

He opened his jacket, pulled out some papers, and set them on his desk.

I leaned over and flipped through them. There were five pages of alphabetized names with numbers alongside them.

I looked at Sam. "What do you think this is?"

"I don't know, but that's all that was in there, except for some makeup and dog treats. I have to return them, of course."

"Can you make copies?"

"I suppose." He stood up and set the papers on a copy machine. Seconds later I had copies of the five pages in my hand. "You think they're important?"

"I don't know. I need time to look them over. Thanks. I owe you."

"About that. I was thinking of asking your mother to dinner some night."

"I'm sure she would love that." Oh boy. There I went again, pimping out my mother for information.

Sam smiled, baring his crooked teeth. I think he may have even blushed. "Well, whatever you do, just keep me out of it. With those two murders, I'm not feeling particularly secure in this job."

I gave his shoulder a pat. "Don't worry. I'll protect my source, even if they send me to Alcatraz."

I rode the elevator back to the main floor and spotted Corbin waiting for me by the front desk. In his hand he held a backpack about the size of a turkey.

What was inside his locker—and now the bag—that he needed so badly?

And what was the significance of those papers from Mary Lee's locker?

Glancing in the reflective glass I passed on the way to the front desk, I caught myself frowning so intensely, I'd need Botox before my next birthday.

Chapter 16

PARTY PLANNING TIP #16

Give the guests at your Murder Mystery Party related favors to take home as memories of a good time, such as a mini–magnifying glass, some chocolate handcuffs, or clues to your next Murder Mystery Party . . .

I walked over to the front desk. "Sorry, Corbin. Hope you haven't been waiting long. Did you get your stuff?"

He pulled the cord on the bag and hoisted it over his shoulder.

"Yeah. Just some art junk. I figured with Mom gone, I might lose my access privileges. Art supplies aren't cheap, you know."

I headed for the doors with Corbin lagging behind. As we approached the museum gift shop, I turned to him. "Can you wait a second? I want to pick up something from the shop."

When he looked puzzled, I realized it was an odd request.

"I want to get a map of the place," I explained.

He nodded silently and sat down on a nearby bench to wait for me. He looked tired.

"I'll be right back." I went inside and walked directly to the cashier counter in the center of the room. "Do you have any—" I started to say to the woman, then stopped when I saw a familiar face among the store crowd. Brad's brother Andrew was flipping through one of the coffee-table-sized art books.

Abruptly I left the cashier, who stood waiting for me to finish my sentence.

"Andrew!"

He looked up slowly from the book and flushed. "Ms. Parker."

I reached my hand out to shake his, but he had a white-knuckled death grip on the big book. I dropped my hand.

"What are you doing here?"

He blinked rapidly and hugged the open book to his chest. "I wanted to learn more about the artifacts here."

I frowned, wondering why he was browsing through an art book instead of getting my friend out of jail. "Really? But what about Delicia? What about bail?"

"No bail," Andrew said simply, then returned to the page he'd been studying. "Judge said not in a murder case."

I stared at Andrew. This guy wasn't getting it. What had Brad been thinking when he gave him the job of representing Dee? After Andrew said nothing more, I asked, "What are you doing, Andrew?"

He lowered the open book for me to see and pointed to one of the artifacts on the page. I looked at it.

"Yes, it's a dagger," I said.

He bit the inside of his lip as he continued to examine the photograph.

And then it dawned on me. It was a picture of the dagger we'd replicated for the mystery event.

"I have to go," he said suddenly, closing the book and replacing it on a nearby table. Before I could say anything more, he sped out of the museum shop and vanished.

"Well, that was weird," I said aloud. A woman glanced at me, and I smiled at her to show her I wasn't entirely crazy. Returning to the cashier, I snapped up the detailed map of the de Young Museum, paid her, and went to join Corbin.

"Okay, let's go."

As I drove him home, Corbin gazed out the side window. I thought about Andrew's appearance at the museum and his odd interest in the dagger, and wondered what was going through his mind. People with Asperger's syndrome tend to notice details that others might not. Maybe the picture of the dagger was some kind of clue.

Corbin continued to look out the window. I tried a few conversation prompts, but again got little more than "Yeah," "Nah," and "Whatever." I pulled up to his place and turned to him. "Corbin, are you all right?"

He reached for the door handle. "Yeah."

"I know you're depressed. You've lost both your parents, and that's going to have a traumatic effect on you. Are you seeing anyone who can help you through this?"

"Nah. I'm okay."

No way was he okay. Clinical depression wasn't something he could control. I placed my hand on his arm. "Listen, if you want to talk about anything, I have a background in psychology . . ."

He opened the car door.

I tightened my grip on his arm. "Corbin . . ."

He turned back. "What?" he snapped. Instead of his usual blank look, his face grimaced in anger

I released my hold. "Um . . . just . . . be careful . . ."

Corbin got out of the car, grabbed his duffel, closed the door, and headed for his front door.

I waited until he was inside, then pulled into traffic, determined to find out more about the moody son of Mary Lee Miller. I had a gut feeling he was involved in this mystery—but how?

If he didn't have anything to do with the deaths of his parents, maybe he knew who did. Maybe he was being blackmailed?

Or maybe he was afraid he'd be next.

Back at my desk, I pulled out the papers Sam had found in Mary Lee's locker. Flipping through the five sheets, I tried to make sense of them—a list of names with numbers next to them. Surprisingly I recognized a few of the names, mostly well-known society people. But one name jumped out at me:

Christine Lampe.

Next to her name was the number 10,000.

Was it a sum of money? A donation? Why would Mary Lee have a separate—and hidden—list of donors and amounts?

Corbin had also retrieved something from his locker. What was in his backpack that was so important, he needed me to drive him to the museum?

I kept coming back to Corbin.

I typed the name Corbin Cosetti into my computer. The screen lit up with several links.

"Corbin Cosetti, son of philanthropist Mary Lee Miller . . ."

"Corbin Cosetti, a graduate of the San Francisco Art Academy . . ."

"Corbin Cosetti, up-and-coming artist . . ."

I scrolled down, looking for something beyond the routine announcements and brief mentions. My eye caught on the name "Christine Lampe" in one of the references.

Odd. Corbin's name linked to Christine's?

I pulled up the article from *ArtNews*, dated five years ago, and began reading.

"The de Young Museum is proud to announce the hiring of our new curator, Christine Lampe," said Mary Lee Miller, a primary fund-raiser for the de Young museum. "We're thrilled to have her and share her vision for our vibrant and growing museum.

"An alumnus of the University of Oregon, with a PhD in anthropology, Lampe held the position of assistant curator at the Portland Museum in Portland, Oregon," Miller continued.

"I'm honored to be a part of the city's most influential and progressive museum," Lampe said. "And I'm a longtime fan of Mary Lee. I'm godmother to her talented son, Corbin, an up-and-coming artist in his own right. Mary Lee's done great things for the city of San Francisco with her philanthropic efforts and I plan to take full advantage of her generosity to make this a world-class institution."

"Christine brings a unique perspective to the mu-

seum, with her longtime experience working and
studying in the Dogon region of Africa," Miller added.
"She'll be working closely with me on the design for
the remodeled museum, expected to be completed
within the next five years . . ."

I skimmed the rest of the article, which offered more
praise-singing and little fact-giving. But the article itself had
me wondering if Christine Lampe was in fact Christine
Lampe.

I did another search on Lampe, pairing up her name with
such words as "expedition," "Africa," and "Dogon," and
found no reference to any trips she was supposed to have
taken in the years between her position at the Portland museum and her hiring at the de Young. Had she really been
doing anthropological research among "lost civilizations"?
Or were those just "lost years"?

As for Christine's claim of being Corbin's godmother,
something didn't jibe. Corbin hadn't seemed especially
fond of Christine, and she hadn't paid particular attention
to him either, during the mystery rehearsals. In fact, I didn't
recall them exchanging two words, let alone a hug or a
smile.

Once again I kept coming back to Corbin. He had to be
the link in all of this—but I still had no idea how. I couldn't
accept the idea that he'd murdered both his parents. He was
depressed, not homicidal. And even if I bought the inheritance motive, he had no reason to kill his father.

Did he?

"Solve it yet?"

Brad stood in the doorway of my office, one hand behind

his back. His white jumpsuit had dirt on the knees and dark streaks down the front of the chest.

Blood?

"Yeah. Professor Plum did it. In the conservatory. With the candlestick." I nodded at his chest. "Got blood?"

He looked down at his jumpsuit.

"Chocolate. Spilled a mocha frap on my way here." He pulled out another from behind his back and handed it to me.

Grinning from the surprise, I took the drink. "You're a saint. This is just what I needed." The first sip sent a chill through my body. A brain freeze wouldn't be far behind. I set the frosty drink on my desk. "So, how's your brother doing on Delicia's case? Any progress on getting her out of jail? I can't stand the thought of her being in there with real criminals."

"Let me get out of this suit, and I'll fill you in." He slipped into his office, and I surreptitiously watched through the office window as he wriggled out of his jumpsuit, revealing a sky blue T-shirt and easy jeans. I had to stop myself from picturing the rest of the striptease.

Unfortunately, he caught me staring and grinned.

"Shoot," I whispered under my breath. Feeling my face fill with color, I turned back to my computer screen. I Googled "Asperger's syndrome" to find out the latest on the disorder and watched as the screen filled with links. Skimming the choices, I pulled up the official site and began to read. I was surprised at how much was now known about the disorder. For years it had been a little-known mystery, with little information beyond the fact that it was a mild form of autism under the category of Pervasive Developmental Disorders.

I read over updates in the *DSM-IV*.

In Asperger's Disorder, affected individuals are characterized by social isolation and eccentric behavior in childhood, with impairments in social interaction and nonverbal communication. . . .

As I read, I jotted down notes and thought about how each characteristic applied to Andrew.

Formalized speech. Andrew had used formal terms and enunciated clearly, his speech stilted.

Gross motor clumsiness. Andrew had tripped and spilled his papers in the brief time I'd seen him.

Special area of interest. While many people with Asperger's have a fixation on something like cars or meteorology or history, Andrew seemed to have channeled his obsession with the law into a career.

Less use of nonverbal behaviors—eye contact, facial expression, body language and gestures, formal pedantic language. Andrew'd had little eye contact with me, and lacked much facial expression. His body language had been more OC—obsessive-compulsive—than expressive.

Inability to develop peer relationships or share interests of others, read social cues. When Andrew was introduced to me, he'd responded as if he'd memorized the short reply.

Need for imposing routines. He said he needed to get back to the office.

I scrolled down to view the differences between Autism autism and Asperger's: Later onset. Less severe involvement. More positive outcome. Higher verbal IQ. Fewer neurological disorders.So that was it in a nutshell, I thought, and then regretted my choice of the word "nut." I heard Brad breathing behind me and spun around. He sat in a folding chair opposite me, his legs askew, hands at his crotch. Leaning forward on his knees, he said, "Reading up on Asperger's, huh?"

I closed the computer screen and tried to obscure the notes I had taken with a sheet of paper. "It's been a while since I've lectured on the subject. Thought I'd see what's new. Things change so quickly in this business, you know . . ."

"Learn anything?"

"Basically that Asperger's is still a puzzle."

He chuckled. "That's the organization's symbol—a puzzle piece."

"What was it like, growing up with him?" I said, studying Brad's face.

He gave a half shrug, but his flushed face countered the casual response. "You know. He was my kid brother—a pest, like any other kid brother. Sometimes he bugged me. Sometimes I felt sorry for him. And sometimes we just played like any other brothers."

"When did he become interested in the law?"

"As far back as I can remember. He was obsessed with shows like *Law and Order* and the old *Perry Mason*. He tried to predict the outcome, and he was usually right. But no one expected him to actually go to law school, let alone make it to college. He proved us all wrong. He was academically gifted and totally focused."

"Impressive. So, how's the case going?"

Brad stretched his legs out in front of him. His foot touched mine under the desk, and I got a tingle.

"He's working on it, but it's too soon to tell. He usually does research for the firm. This is something new for him."

I felt my neck tense up. "He hasn't done this before? What's his strategy?"

Brad sighed and glanced away. "I'm not sure. He said something about circumstantial evidence, but—"

"That's it?" I looked at him in disbelief. "That's all he's got?"

"Presley, calm down. He's a good lawyer and he'll do everything he can to help Delicia. Meanwhile—"

I stood up. "Meanwhile, the police are doing nothing to find the real murderer and Delicia is rotting in jail!"

"Pres, she's not exactly rotting—"

"You know what I mean!"

Brad took my hand. I jerked it away and turned my back on him. He stood up, took my arm, and spun me around. "Presley, we're going to find out the truth."

"When? And who's 'we'? Not your pal Melvin. He's convinced Dee did it. And Andrew's had little experience with this. He's only focused on the legal aspect. So tell me— who? Who's helping clear Delicia? Who's going to find her killer?"

"We are." He held my arms, then slid his hands down into mine. "You and I. Okay? We'll find out who's behind all this. And why."

He leaned in, possibly to kiss me. Like a fool, I burst into tears and tucked my head into his shoulder.

If Delicia was relying on me to get her out of jail, she was in big, big trouble.

Chapter 17

PARTY PLANNING TIP #17

Lubricate your party guests with alcohol during your Murder Mystery Party. Not only will the amateur sleuths have more fun—they'll overlook the minor gaps and inconsistencies in the plot.

"Sorry about that." I pulled back and blotted my tears on the bottom of my shirt. "I'm not usually a crybaby."

"Hey," Brad said, his voice low and comforting. "Don't apologize. You're under a lot of stress. And you feel frustrated. But we're going to figure this thing out."

I grabbed a tissue from my purse and blew my nose. "And just how are we going to do that?"

"Okay, now you're whining."

I gave him a soft punch on the arm.

"Let's start by reviewing everything we know so far, over a nice relaxing glass of wine and some food. I know just the place."

"Brad, I appreciate what you're trying to do, but—"

He gave my shoulder a gentle squeeze. "Get your purse. We're getting off this island. No argument. And no more whining."

I wanted to slap him and hug him at the same time. Mostly hug him. The idea of a glass of wine—or three—sounded beyond wonderful. And I was starving, now that I thought about it. I grabbed my purse and jacket and let him lead me out of the office.

Brad parked his van in the lot off Ellis Street and we jaywalked to John's Grill across the street. The restaurant is a landmark in the city, famous for being Dashiell Hammett's hangout while he wrote *The Maltese Falcon*. Sam Spade ordered chops there, in a scene from the movie.

"Are you here for the meeting?" a waitress asked as we entered.

I gave her a blank look.

"MWA. Mystery Writers of America. They're meeting upstairs."

Brad spoke up. "No, we just want a table for two."

The waitress led us to a spot near the window. It had been a while since I'd had a steak at John's Grill. I glanced around at all the fictional detective's paraphernalia, fighting for space with photos of famous diners. The dark wood walls, green leather booths, and white tablecloths captured the spirit of old San Francisco. I had a feeling not much had changed over the years, except for the prices.

While Brad scanned the wine list, I asked the waitress about the falcon itself. I'd heard it had been stolen some time back.

"It's back," she said, ready to write up our order. "Upstairs. Bolted down and in a glass case this time." Bet she answered that question several times a day.

To my surprise, Brad ordered a bottle of Tournesol cabernet from Napa Valley. I'd pegged him as strictly a beer drinker, but after hearing him ask the waitress some questions about the wine, I realized he knew a lot more about it than I did. I could tell red from white, and that was about it.

While we waited, I pulled out the papers Sam had found in Mary Lee's locker and copied for me. I unfolded them, pressed them flat, and turned them for Brad to see.

Before he could look them over, the waitress brought our wine. After Brad approved the wine and the waitress poured us each a glass, he said, "What's this?"

I took a sip before answering. The burgundy liquid felt like an anesthetic as it slid down my parched throat. I didn't know jack about "bouquet" or "woody" or "nosey," but this stuff was totally "drinkable."

I licked the purple from my lips and said, "I'm not sure. Sam found these in Mary Lee's locker at the museum and made copies for me."

"So?" Brad said, glancing at them. "Why would she keep a list of names with numbers next to them in a locker at the museum?"

Brad took another sip of wine, then studied the list.

"Some of the names are familiar," he said.

"I know. I suppose it could be a list of patrons and their donations."

Brad flipped through the five pages. When he reached the last page, he flipped it over, then looked up at me. "Where's the rest?"

"What do you mean?"

"The names stop at 'Watson.' There aren't any Xs, Ys, or Zs."

I thought a moment. "Maybe nobody named Young or Zachary made a contribution."

"Possible," he said. "But unlikely."

"So . . . you think there's a missing last page?"

The waitress appeared again to take our dinner orders. I hadn't yet opened the menu.

"You order for us," I said to Brad. "At this point, I'll eat anything. Except roasted falcon."

The waitress didn't laugh at my joke. Brad ordered two rib-eye steaks and baked potatoes, then glanced at me for my approval.

It was a lot for me, but I wasn't about to pass up a steak dinner. I nodded, then poured us both another glass of cabernet.

"I'm just saying, I think it's odd," Brad said when the waitress disappeared.

I took another sip of wine. At this rate, with no food in my stomach, I'd be wasted in a matter of minutes. Best to get my clear thinking done quickly.

"All right," I said, "suppose you're right. What do we know? Number one: Mary Lee apparently hid the list in her locker. Number two: The last page may be missing. Number three: The numbers next to the names may be donation amounts."

"But why hide the information if they're just donations?" Brad asked.

I glanced through the pages again. "They're obviously something incriminating," I announced, as if I had just solved the Da Vinci Code.

The waitress reappeared with our steaks. I was practically drooling when I took my first bite. Sleuthing seemed to make me ravenous.

"Delicious!" I said to Brad.

"It's one of my favorite places," he said.

I ate a few more bites of meat and potato, then set down my fork and took a sip of wine. "Brad, what if there's another set somewhere? Maybe the ones in Mary Lee's locker were copies too. I didn't really pay attention. If there's an original set, maybe it contains the last missing page."

Brad took another bite of steak.

I went on. "Where do they usually keep information about donations?"

"Accounting?" Brad offered.

I pulled out my Killer Parties pen and party-planning notebook and made a note to follow up on that possibility.

"I think you're going off track, Presley. This probably doesn't have anything to do with her murder."

I stared at Brad. Self-conscious, he wiped his mouth and chin. My eyes narrowed. It suddenly dawned on me—he looked different.

"What?"

"Your soul patch! It's gone." I tapped the space under my chin.

He scratched the spot. "Yeah, shaved it off a week ago. Saw one on Billy Ray Cyrus and decided mine had to go."

I liked his new look, although the patch had been sexy on him.

"You're still staring," he said. "Shall we get back to the problem at hand?"

Was he blushing?

"Sorry, ADHD. Where were we?"

He tapped my notebook.

"Oh yeah. I had another thought. Can you get Melvin to let you see the police tapes from the museum that night?"

"Already done." He signaled the waitress for the tab.

I sat up. "Really? Have you seen them?"

"Yep."

"And?"

"You can't see anything but the tops of people's heads."

I slumped in my seat. "You're kidding. Why? The camera should have captured the whole room and everyone who came in and out."

"Something must have knocked it crooked."

"What?"

Brad waited until the waitress cleared out dishes, then said, "It was aimed too high."

"So someone moved it? Obviously it was the killer! Can I see the tape?"

"Nope."

The waitress arrived with the bill, Brad glanced at it, then handed her his credit card.

"Why not?"

"Police evidence."

"What a crock. You're not a cop, but you get to see this stuff and I don't."

He grinned smugly.

"So what else did you see?"

"Like I said—tops of heads. Some hats—a few fedoras, police helmet, Sherlock Holmes caps . . ."

As he listed the hats, I jotted them down in my notebook, and tried to put a name next to the ones I remembered seeing.

Pink rhinestone hat—Mary Lee Miller as California Jones

Fedora—Corbin Cosetti as Sam Slayed

Pillbox—Christine Lampe as Agatha Mistry

Deerstalker cap—Dan Tannacito as Hemlock Bones

Cloche hat—Delicia Jackson as Nancy Prude

Beret—Raj Reddy as Hercules Parrot

Baseball cap—Berkeley Wong as Kutesy Millstone

Those were mainly the actors. Most of the audience members wore hats as well, many the same as my suspect/actors. Great. Now I had a bunch of hat-wearing suspects. But one hat in particular had stuck in my mind—the other deerstalker cap I'd found in Jason Cosetti's closet.

Shit, Sherlock, I thought, as I downed the dregs of my wine.

Brad drove me back to my condo with a promise we'd start fresh in the morning. Sitting next to him in his SUV, under the influence of wine and a long dry spell since my last relationship, I was mustering up the courage to invite him in to see my etchings. But before I could get the slightly slurred words out, he put a hand on my knee. His intimate touch shot a bolt of electricity through me. Maybe I wouldn't have to do the asking, I thought as he parked at my condo building.

"Listen, Presley," he said. "I'm sure the police are doing all they can to find out the truth. Melvin is—"

Uh-oh. He'd just pushed the wrong button.

I tried to keep my voice steady. "Your friend Melvin isn't doing anything, Brad. He's convinced Delicia is the murderer. You're blind when it comes to him—don't you get it?" I jerked open the door and put a leg out.

Brad gripped my arm.

"Presley. You can't do this yourself. Remember what happened last time when you took off on your own? You almost got yourself killed. I said I'd help you, and I meant it."

I shrugged out of his grip, got out of the car, and slammed the door. After fumbling with my keys for what seemed hours, I finally jammed the right one into the lock and went inside, slamming yet another door behind me. My three cats darted for safety at the loud sound.

A little overreaction, Presley, don't you think? Where had all that anger come from? Frustration at the thought of my friend spending another night in jail for something she didn't do? I couldn't imagine what she was going through. My mother had been arrested numerous times over the years, mostly for disturbing the peace, and I'd been to the jail plenty of times to bail her out. But she'd never spent a night there. And so far, neither had I.

Or was I upset that Brad sometimes treated me like a . . . a *girl*? And not the way I'd been fantasizing about lately.

Then again, it could have been your basic sexual frustration. In the back of my mind I'd been imagining a romantic end to the evening. And Brad had ruined it.

I threw my purse down and picked up the nearest cat—Thursby. I petted him so hard I was giving him rug burns.

To hell with Brad Matthews. Time to focus—and step it up. Even if it meant I'd be joining Dee at her new residence. Because what mattered now was freeing Delicia, and the only way to do that was to find out who'd killed Mary Lee and Jason.

Could be worse. I could end up where Mary Lee was headed—Colma, also known as Cemetery City. That's where many well-known San Francisco citizens ended up in permanent lockdown. Wacky Emperor Norton. Baseball legend Joe DiMaggio. Architect Julia Morgan. Lawman Wyatt Earp.

And Charles de Young.

I pushed the thought out of my mind. No distractions. I had a "mystery event" to solve. Only this time, I didn't know the ending.

Chapter 18

PARTY PLANNING TIP #18

If the guests have no idea whodunit after reviewing all the clues at your Murder Mystery Party, suggest they just choose someone with shifty eyes, a long facial scar, or a missing ear. That's what Nancy Drew would do.

The next morning, in a slightly better mood after dreaming about a giant marshmallow man, I dressed in black jeans, a Treasure Island Yacht Club T-shirt, and my black Doc Martens Mary Janes. I went by my office, hoping I wouldn't run into Brad. I was more confused about my feelings than annoyed, but didn't feel like psychoanalyzing myself at the moment.

I gave a sigh of relief—or was it disappointment?—when I saw no sign of his truck or bike in the parking lot. Entering my office, I sat at my desk, whirled around in my chair a couple of times, then left, locking the door behind me.

"Screw it," I said. I was about to leave the building when I had a thought. Spinning around in my tracks, I doubled back, bypassing my own office, and entered through Delicia's unlocked door.

Planting myself in her chair, I tried to channel Delicia. What had she seen in Corbin that she hadn't in all the other men who'd pursued her?

I glanced around at her walls, covered with theater bills from the local plays she'd been cast in—*Grease*, *Cats*, *Wicked*. She'd only had bit parts, and they were few and far between, but that didn't matter to Dee. She loved everything about the theater, from being onstage to working behind the scenes.

I got up and rifled through the boxes of mementos she'd saved from her various roles. I found a wand she'd snatched from *Wicked* and wished I could have waved it to get her out of this mess.

"Whatcha doing?" a familiar voice startled me from behind me. I whirled around to face Brad, feeling as if he'd caught me with my hand in the Ghirardelli chocolate store.

"Nothing," I said, placing the wand back on the shelf. "Just thinking about Dee."

"Listen, Presley. Sorry about last night." He hung his head. "I have no business telling you what you should or shouldn't do. You're a grown woman. I just have this thing . . . about wanting to take care of everything. You know, tidy up."

The ice around my heart melted a little. "It's okay. I know I can become obsessive about things."

He sat on the corner of Dee's desk. "Got some news."

"What?" My heart skipped a beat. "They found the killer? Is Delicia—"

He held up his hands. "No, no. Hold on. There you go jumping to conclusions again."

I glared at him and started for the door.

"Don't you want to hear what I've got?"

I turned to him, our faces less than a foot apart. I felt mine fill with color, being so close to him.

"I talked to Melvin. He talked to the ME."

"And?"

"The stab wound was almost a perfect match for the Styrofoam knife used for the play."

My jaw dropped. "You're kidding. That fake dagger wouldn't have penetrated her chest. It would have split, broken in half, or smashed the tip."

Brad had a wicked grin on his face.

I eyed him. "What are you not telling me?"

He kept grinning.

Annoyed, I thought for a moment. "Okay, so the wound was made by something the same size and shape as the fake dagger. . . ."

"Like . . ." he teased.

"Like . . . the real dagger!" I gasped. "But how? How could it have been used to kill Mary Lee? It was in a cabinet on the second floor, under the eye of the camera. Whoever took it would have been caught on videotape."

"Yep," Brad said simply. He was obviously enjoying this.

"We have to see those security tapes!"

"Been there. Done that."

"What? You went to the museum without me?"

"Nope. Saw them in Melvin's office."

My eyes widened. "Did they get it on tape—the person who took the real dagger from the case? That's got to be our killer."

Brad pressed his lips together, then said, "Yeah, about

that. First of all, they examined the dagger and found no prints or proof that it had been disturbed. Secondly, if someone did borrow it from the case, it wasn't caught on camera, which is triggered when there's movement."

"Maybe whoever it was figured out a way to outsmart the camera?" I thought aloud.

"It's possible. One of the security guards said someone could have sneaked along the wall to the camera, stood on something, and then covered the motion detector with something."

I felt my shoulders slump. "Crap. Back to square one."

Brad slid off Dee's desk. "Not really. Whoever did it knew the security guards would be distracted by the party that night, and used the opportunity to 'borrow' the real dagger. Then once he—or she—stabbed Mary Lee, he returned it to the case and removed whatever was covering the motion detector, with no one the wiser. He was so quick, the guards watching the screen would have just thought there was a brief glitch."

"But why?" I asked, walking slowly to my office. "Why go to all that risk and trouble to use *that* dagger?"

Brad followed. "Easy to hide the weapon, maybe? Or maybe it was some kind of symbolic statement."

I entered my office and sat down at my own desk. Brad stood in the doorway, his arms raised up to the doorjamb. God, he looked good in a simple T-shirt.

"What about Jason Cosetti?" I said, trying to get back on track. "He was killed by a blow to the head. But they didn't find the weapon."

"It was probably the same MO. Whoever did it may have taken a real statue, bonked him over the head, and returned it to its case."

"Meanwhile, we're no closer to knowing who did it, are we," I said.

I got out my iPhone and punched Corbin's number. He was the key to this, I was sure.

No answer.

I checked my watch and stood up.

"Where are you going?" Brad asked, dropping his arms from the doorjamb.

I bit my lip, then said, "Errands . . . I'm so far behind in my work. This mess has taken up most of my time."

"How about we meet for lunch? I may have more for you by then."

"Sure. I'll call you when I'm done."

As I headed for Dee's Smart Car, I could feel Brad watching me from the barracks doorway. I slid into the car, started the engine, and pulled out of the parking lot without a backward glance, eager to reach my destination.

It wasn't until just after I reached the peak of Macalla Road and began my descent onto the Bay Bridge on-ramp that I realized I had no brakes.

Chapter 19

PARTY PLANNING TIP #19

When hosting a Murder Mystery Party, be sure to throw in an occasional unexpected twist to stimulate the sleuths' little gray cells. There's nothing duller than a predictable solution to a puzzling crime.

"Holy crap!" I shouted, pumping the foot brake frantically as the car began picking up speed. The pedal offered no resistance. I stomped on it at least a dozen times before I accepted the inevitable.

Someone had tampered with the brakes.

With my heart thumping and my palms slick with sweat, I glanced at my rear and side mirrors, praying I wouldn't be hit by an oncoming car as I careened into the bridge traffic. I knew if I pulled the emergency brake, the car might come to a halt too quickly and roll or skid.

I braced myself as the car merged onto the far right lane of the bridge.

I'd learned by driving the Smart Car that it was a hybrid

of sorts—half automatic and half manual. Since the car was unfamiliar to me, I'd been using the automatic mode, but I quickly switched to manual mode and downshifted, hoping I wouldn't strip the gears. The engine whirred loudly. The car jerked, and then it began to slow a bit. Cars zipped around me as I tried to control the speed.

Frantic to get off the bridge, I strained my neck and eyes trying to spot the exit sign. I needed a ramp that wouldn't careen me downhill into the traffic like a disengaged roller-coaster car.

Gears screaming, the car reached the exit. I swerved onto the curving off-ramp, praying I wouldn't roll over. Shifting down to second, I guided the car down the ramp and made a wide turn onto the street, with only a little screeching of the tires. Hugging a yellow-painted curb, I waited until the car slowed enough for me to pull the emergency brake.

The car jerked, throwing my head against the steering wheel, then jumped the curb and came to a final rest on the sidewalk.

Gripping the wheel with two sweaty hands, I looked up. A handful of pedestrians stood gawking. A small crowd had gathered around my car. A homeless man in layers of tattered clothes shuffled over to the car window. He wore a knitted cap, fingerless gloves, and a filthy peacoat.

"Are you all right?" he asked. I could barely see his mouth for all the scraggly facial hair.

I rolled down the side window. "I think so. The brakes went out," I said breathily.

He scrunched up his face and scratched his bearded chin. "I can change a tire, but I don't do brakes. Better call Triple A."

I took a deep catch-up breath. "Will do. Thanks."

I pulled out my phone, and the man moved along. I pressed Brad's number and tried to slow my heartbeat with deep breaths while I waited for him to answer.

"Crime Scene Cleaners," Brad said.

I almost melted into tears when I heard his voice, but managed to stay under control. "Brad!"

"Presley?" he answered. "What's up? You sound breathless."

"I . . . the car . . . I think someone cut the brakes."

"Where are you?" he said firmly.

I glanced around for a street sign. "Uh . . . off Folsom and First. On the sidewalk, actually."

"You sure you're not injured?"

I felt my forehead where I'd bumped the steering wheel and winced at the pain. There was going to be an ugly bruise. "I'm okay."

"I'll be right there. Stay put," he commanded.

He hung up before I could argue—not that I would have. I didn't have a lot of options other than to wait for him. I glanced around at my surroundings. People passed by, hardly noticing the car parked on the sidewalk. Enticed by the aroma of coffee wafting from a nearby café, I got out of the car and headed over, my legs still shaky from what seemed like a possessed car.

I ordered my usual, then returned to the car to wait for Brad. Leaning against the front fender, I reflected on what had happened. The wait gave me time to think about what had happened. Had the been brakes cut, or did they just suddenly go out on their own? If they were cut, who had access to the car? And if someone did this on purpose, were they trying to kill me? Why? Or did they think Dee would be driving the car?

Brad parked, hopped out, and jogged over. Grasping my cold hands, he looked me over. Spotting the lump on my forehead, he reached up and was about to touch it. I winced and pulled back. "That's quite a bump," he said, dropping his hand.

"I'm okay, honestly." My shirt was still damp from sweat, and I shivered in the cold wind. I was just glad my pants weren't wet. It wouldn't have been sweat.

Brad took off his leather jacket and wrapped it around me. Then he turned his attention to the car, parked at an angle on the narrow sidewalk. "What the hell happened?"

"I don't know! I was driving up Macalla, heading for the bridge, and when I started downhill, I hit the brakes to enter the on-ramp and they were gone! If it weren't for Nancy Drew, I'd have been a goner too."

"Nancy Drew?"

"Yeah, someone tampered with her brakes in one of the books, but she kept her head and got away safely. I learned a lot from reading her mysteries."

Brad rolled his eyes at me as if I were crazy. With a shake of his head, he opened the side door of his SUV and retrieved a flashlight. Bending down, he shone the light under the car. When he straightened up, he didn't look happy.

"So, were they cut?" I asked.

"They were cut, all right."

"I knew it!"

"I wouldn't be so smug if I were you," Brad added. "You realize what that means, don't you?"

"Someone doesn't like Smart Cars?"

"Very funny. You're lucky to be alive, especially driving a toy like this in a roller-coaster city like San Francisco."

That sobered me up again. Someone was trying to kill me. But why? I had no idea who the killer was. Maybe, however, I was getting close.

"How hard is it to cut the brakes? I mean, doesn't it take some knowledge about cars or some kind of special tool?"

"Not really. All you need is a pipe cutter—seven bucks at Home Depot—and an Internet connection to look up the information."

"But wouldn't it take some strength to cut something like that?"

"Nah. You put the cutter on the brake line, tighten the knob, then spin it around the pipe a couple of times. If you keep doing that, eventually the line will break. Takes five minutes, tops."

"And you would know this, how?" I raised a suspicious eyebrow.

"Auto shop?" He grinned innocently.

"Yeah, just like I learned how to insert a knife between the fourth and fifth ribs in Home Ec."

He blinked, then said, "So you need a ride?"

I almost said "Duh," but changed my tone and replied, "Yes, please. I called Triple A. They'll tow the car to the shop. Meanwhile, I'm running out of cars."

The Triple A guy pulled up a few minutes later in a yellow tow truck. He laughed out loud when he saw the Smart Car. "What happened? Did the hamsters get tired?"

I forced a smile at his joke, then gave him my information. He hooked up the car with one hand—show-off—and drove off with it in tow.

"Hop in," Brad said when the tow truck driver was gone. He opened the passenger door of his SUV.

I stepped up, sat down, then leaned over the side of the seat to peek at the stuff Brad had stored in his vehicle.

Brad climbed in the driver's side. "Where to, m'lady?"

"Noe Valley?" I said in the form of a question.

"You got it." He started up the engine and pulled out into traffic.

I nodded toward the back of the SUV. "So what is all this stuff, anyway? Anything dangerous, like explosives or toxic chemicals?"

"You're safe. Don't worry." Brad winked. "As long as my brakes keep working and I don't crash into anything."

I glared at him. "Seriously."

He shrugged. "I have just about everything you need to clean up filth, debris, fecal matter, bodily fluids, expired food, moldy stuff, and hazardous materials." When he'd finished the list, he glanced at me to check my reaction.

I made a face. "Yuck."

"Plus I've got protective gear, latex gloves for bodily fluids, shoe covers, respirators, stuff like that."

"Bet you look cute in all that."

"Then there's the usual cleaning supplies," he continued, apparently on a roll. "Mops, buckets, spray bottles, sponges, brushes. And lots of chemicals and disinfectants to clean up blood and vomit."

He grinned as I squirmed. "Enzyme solvents to liquefy dried blood. Putty knives to scrape dried brain matter—that stuff dries like cement."

"I can imagine," I said flippantly, not daring to imagine.

He wouldn't let up. "Shovels, for large amounts of blood when it turns to Jell-O. You can just shovel it into bags."

I quit listening and focused on a couple of cameras I'd spotted on one of the shelves. When he was done trying to spook me, I asked, "Why cameras?"

"To take before-and-after shots—for insurance purposes."

I thought a moment. "So do you have pictures of Mary Lee's crime scene?"

"Yep. You can see them if you want, but I doubt they'll tell you anything."

"You never know," I said, facing forward. I was getting carsick, either from the motion or from listening to Brad's list of job supplies. "You like the work?"

"It pays the bills."

"Really?"

"I make about six hundred an hour."

My jaw dropped open. "Whoa, I'm in the wrong business. Need a partner?"

"Not sure you'd like it. It's not as fun as hosting a party."

I wrinkled my nose. "So what's the actual work like?"

Brad took a deep breath. "Okay, well, I'm called a secondary responder. I get there after the cops, techs, fire fighters, paramedics, and coroners are done. Most of the victims' families are surprised to learn they're responsible for cleaning up the scene. They figure the cops are going to do it. Not the case. That's when I come in. I do what's called CTS Decon—Crime and Trauma Scene Decontamination—which covers everything from cleaning up after a violent death—homicide, suicide—to decomp—a decomposing body—to meth labs, to anthrax exposure."

"Anthrax?" I shivered.

"There's not much of that. Mostly it's bodily fluids. They're considered biohazards—a potential source of infection. If there's blood, I have to make sure there's no trace to pass along HIV, hepatitis, herpes, and hantavirus."

Hantavirus? I'd heard about that. Rats carried it, didn't they? I wasn't sure I ever wanted to touch Brad again.

"How do you manage to do work that would cause most people to throw up?"

"Gotta have a strong stomach. Plus some emotional detachment mixed with a little sympathy."

"Sympathy?"

"For the grieving family members. They're often around when I'm cleaning."

There was a lot about Brad I didn't know. I tried to picture him cleaning up blood while consoling family members—not an easy task for anyone.

"You okay?" Brad asked.

"Yeah, sure," I said. "I just never realized how involved it all was. No wonder you have an SUV full of stuff."

"Couldn't do the job without it. This one's specially outfitted. Holds everything safely, including biohazardous stuff, like bodies."

A chill ran through me. "You mean, you haul . . . bodies in here?"

"Part of the job is disposal. Can't just put them in a Dumpster."

"Don't you burn out? I'd think all this gore would get to you eventually."

"Sure, there are days when I wonder why I do this. Especially since I'm on call twenty-four/seven. Some guys in the business suffer from stress, depression. You know, the kinds of things you're familiar with as an ab-psych instructor."

"So how do you cope?"

"Well, lately by getting involved in your problems. You've kept me pretty distracted." He shot me a look; there was a sparkle in his eyes

"Sorry about that," I said, sighing.

He patted my leg. "Look, the only thing you need to worry about right now is your own safety. Keep in mind— someone cut those brakes."

I had to admit he was right. And if I wasn't careful, I just might be his next Crime Scene Cleanup.

Chapter 20

PARTY PLANNING TIP #20

*To add atmosphere to your Murder Mystery Party,
assign each of the rooms with an intriguing label.
For example, instead of "The Multipurpose Room,"
"The Boys' Locker Room," or "The Powder Room," use
terms like "The Conservatory," "The Billiard Room,"
and "The Creepy Dark Basement."*

As we approached Noe Valley, I gave Brad Corbin's address.
Then, figuring that Brad's Crime Scene Cleaners SUV would
stick out like a bloody thumb in front of the home, I asked
him to park on a main street lined with bookstores, cafés,
and clothing boutiques. We walked the block and a half to
Corbin's place, stepped up on the porch, and I knocked on
the front door.

After a few minutes and no answer, Brad said, "Looks
like nobody's home." He shaded his eyes and peered into a
front window.

"Hard to say for sure," I said. "He doesn't have a car.
Could be asleep."

I knocked again. This time I heard a noise coming from behind the front door.

I whirled around to Brad. "Did you hear that?"

"Sounded like a dog barking."

I moved to the window, cleaned the dusty pane with my fist, and peeked in the slit between the tie-dyed curtains. "It's Chou-Chou, Mary Lee's dog!"

"Are you sure?"

"Yes! I'd know that irritating yap and unnatural pink fur anywhere."

"I thought you said Corbin didn't seem to like the dog."

"I did. He also said he had no idea where it was. So what's it doing here?"

Brad took a step back, straddling two steps. "He's taking care of it, obviously." He stepped off the porch.

Instead of following Brad, I said, "We've got to get inside."

"What? No way! Not without the owner present. That's unlawful trespass. I could lose my license."

"It's an emergency! The dog is inside . . . and it sounds . . . upset. What if it's hurt? Or what if Corbin's in trouble, and the dog is trying to alert us? I think that gives us just cause to go inside."

I glanced around the ground, spotted a large rock, and held it up, ready to pitch it through a window.

Brad grabbed my arm. "What are you doing? Are you crazy?"

"Got a better idea?" I asked.

He cursed under his breath. He knew I was determined to get inside, whether he helped me or not. "Wait here! Don't do anything. I'll be right back."

I reluctantly dropped the rock.

He pointed a finger at me, as if I were a disobedient child. "Just wait—you hear me?"

I crossed my arms and pouted like a disobedient child. "Okay, but hurry."

Brad jogged down the street and disappeared around the corner. I peered into the window I had almost broken. Other than the sound of yapping, there were no signs of life.

Minutes later I heard Brad's heavy footsteps racing up behind me. I turned around to meet him. In his hands he held a putty knife and a roll of duct tape.

"Duct tape?" I eyed him as if he were the crazy one now. "With all the stuff you have in your SUV, you brought duct tape?"

"Trick of the trade. You can use duct tape for just about anything."

"And the putty knife? Isn't that what you use to scrape up blood?"

"Among other things."

He glanced back and forth between the two front windows, pursed his lips, then moved around to the side of the house. I followed him behind the overgrown bushes that kept nosy neighbors from seeing much of Corbin's place. Brad scanned the area, found an old gallon container of paint in some weeds near a couple of trash cans, and picked it up. I watched as he placed the container underneath one of the small side windows. Stepping up onto the can, he wiped off the grimy pane with the side of his arm and peered through.

"See anything?" I whispered.

"No bodies," Brad said lightly. "Looks like a bedroom."

He pulled the duct tape from his wrist where he'd been

wearing it like a bracelet, and ripped off an arm's length, using his teeth to start the tear.

"What are you doing?" I asked.

He didn't answer. Instead, he looped the tape into a circle, sticky side out, stuck one end to the other, then pressed the tape onto the center of the window pane. He ripped off another length and placed that strip diagonally across the window pane, sticky side down, inserting it through the looped circle. Finally he placed a third strip crosswise, sticky side down, through the loop, forming an X on the glass.

I still had no idea what he was doing.

Pulling the putty knife from the pocket where'd he stuck it, he began chipping away at the aging trim that surrounded the window.

"Now what are you doing?"

He grunted, digging at the trim with the blade. "These windows are held in by this old beading. The new ones have the beading on the inside, so people like me can't do something like this. But this is an old house."

He stopped talking and kept chipping away at the strip around the window. In a few minutes I saw the pane loosen. He grasped the duct tape circle he'd made into a handle and pulled gently. The window came out into his hand without a crack.

"How did you learn to do that?" I asked.

He stepped down from the paint can. "You pick up all kinds of tricks in this business."

"Mmm-hmm," I said, knowing I wouldn't get much more information from him. So far I'd learned how to break into an old house without using a brick, how to cut a brake line with a pipe cutter from Home Depot, and how to open a lock when you don't have a key.

How sure was I that Brad Matthews was on the right side of the law?

"Well, you're certainly handy with duct tape."

"Couldn't do my job without it. If you're ever in hurricane country, make Xs on your windows to keep them from shattering."

"I'll remember that. Unfortunately, we live in earthquake country. Got a duct tape remedy for that?"

"Not yet. But I saw this show once where a girl made her prom dress out of different colors of duct tape. I imagine there's a use for it during a quake as well."

I looked up at the hole in the wall where the windowpane had been.

"Now what?"

Brad brushed his hands down the side of his jeans to clean them. "That's up to you."

I glared at him. "You don't expect me to climb through there, do you?"

He gave a half shrug and matching half smile. "*I* certainly won't fit." He was right about that, with those broad shoulders, wide chest, and muscular arms.

"Crap."

Wondering if I should rethink this, I stepped up on the paint can and put my arms through the opening. The bottom of the window came to my waist. There was no way I would be able to hoist myself through.

I felt a pair of hands on my butt.

I pulled my head out and glared down at Brad.

He withdrew his hands and raised them up like a criminal surrendering to the cops. "What? I'm just trying to help."

I narrowed my eyes, then stuck my head back in.

I felt hands on my butt again. This time they lifted the rest of me up and into the opening. As I headed over the windowsill, I reached forward to support myself on the cluttered desk beneath the window and slowly slid onto it.

It wasn't a pretty sight.

"I'm in!" I called.

"Quiet!" Brad hissed.

"Okay!" I hissed back.

A pink ball of frenzied fluff appeared in the doorway, yapping.

"Nice doggy," I whispered to it. Chou-Chou snarled and gave a guttural growl. "Pipe down, you pip-squeak. My cats would have you for a snack."

To my surprise, the dog sat down and wagged its tail.

"Good dog."

I slid off the desk and took a look around. "Corbin?" I called out. "It's Presley. Are you here?" I headed out of the room, trying not to step on the fur ball. Wasn't easy. The thing was right on my heels.

Within minutes I'd checked all the rooms in the house. No sign of Corbin. It was still a mess of art comics, pizza cartons, and paint-spattered clothing. Unopened mail lay on the floor under the front door flap. No sign of a body. Or blood. Or a murderer.

Where was Corbin?

I returned to Corbin's bedroom and found that the window had already been replaced. That was quick. I walked over to my landing desk, knelt down, and glanced through a few papers that had fallen during my entry. Nothing suspicious—just excerpts from articles printed from the Internet on DNA testing and genealogy.

I wondered how these topics tied into his art.

I stood up and pulled open the desk drawers and found them all empty—except the top drawer. Inside was a plain white envelope.

It was addressed to Corbin Cosetti.

The flap had been ripped open.

I lifted it and pulled out the single sheet of paper. It read:

STATE OF OREGON DEPARTMENT OF HEALTH SERVICES

Office of Vital Statistics— Certificate of Live Birth

Child's Name: Corbin Hofmann
Date of Birth: April 11, 1980
Sex: Male
City/County: Eugene/Lane
Place: Eugene Hospital
Mother's Name: Judith Hofmann
Year of Birth: 1950
Father's Name: Unk

Hardly believing my eyes, I reread the mother's name.

Judith Hofmann had given birth to a son named Corbin.

Before I had time to ponder this new development, I heard a tapping on the bedroom window. I peeked out.

"Presley!" Brad mouthed. After making my latest discovery, I'd almost forgotten about him. Brad gestured for me to come out. That's when I heard the sound of sirens in the distance. Not that that wasn't unusual in the city. But then I wasn't usually breaking and entering.

I nodded and darted out of the bedroom, into the living area, the yapping dog on my heels.

Chou-Chou!

My first thought was to leave it. Corbin was apparently taking care of it. A quick glance indicated differently. The dog's water and food bowls were empty. And Corbin had never really liked the dog. So what was it doing here?

I bent down to scoop up the little yapper and noticed a hand-addressed envelope visible under several bills and some junk mail, lying on the floor by the front door. I picked it up, turned it over—no return address. On a hunch, I stuffed it in my pocket, then snatched up the dog. Grabbing a black marker lying on the counter, I wrote a quick note on another envelope, asking Corbin to call me. Heading out, I pulled the door closed behind me and shoved my note under the door, with just a tiny corner peeking out.

I fled to the sidewalk where Brad waited.

The sirens grew louder. Brad took my arm and walked me hastily down the street toward his SUV. "I think a neighbor saw me standing around and probably called the cops. We gotta get outta here. I knew this was going to happen."

As we approached the corner, a cop car appeared, lights flashing, but no siren. Brad shoved me along, the dog in my arms, and I kept walking to the SUV, while we waited on the corner. He unlocked the door with his remote, and I hopped into the passenger side, closing the door behind me. I watched as the cruiser pulled up next to Brad. I rolled down the window a crack to hear.

"Hey, Matthews," one of the cops said. "You got a cleanup around here?"

"Not this time, Sarge. Just going for coffee. S'up?"

The cop nodded toward Corbin's house. "Got a call about a prowler. Male, Caucasian, over six feet, wearing a blue shirt, sort of like yours. Seen anyone who fits the description?"

"No," Brad said, "but then, I just got here. I'll keep an eye out, though."

While Brad chatted with the cop, I stroked the dog to keep it from yapping. At the moment it was giving my hand a tongue bath. As long as it stayed quiet, I'd have let it eat my hand off.

"Okay, see ya, Matthews." The cop tipped his hat at Brad and the car moved on down the road toward Corbin's place, sirens silent and lightbar dark.

Brad got into the SUV, turned to me. "What are you doing?"

"What do you mean?"

He nodded toward the dog, which was looking up at him with big glassy brown eyes.

"You're dognapping!"

"This isn't dognapping! I'm rescuing it. There was no sign of Corbin anywhere. The mail had piled up on the floor, and the dog had no food or water. I think something's happened to Corbin."

"He's probably staying with a friend or something. Meanwhile, you've stolen his only reminder of his mother—that dog!" He glared at Chou-Chou.

"Well, obviously it's starving. It tried to eat my hand

while you were chatting with your cop buddy. I'll keep trying Corbin's cell, but he hasn't been answering. I left a message at his place that I've got the dog."

Brad shook his head in frustration. "Where are you going to keep it? You have three cats."

I hadn't thought that far. "True. They'd use it as a chew toy. Maybe you can take it."

"No way! I'm not having that crazy mutt in my house. Not only is it incriminating evidence of dognapping, it's . . . pink!"

"Bigot," I said, lifting the dog onto my lap as we drove on toward the museum.

"You're impossible, Presley. You don't think things through. It's that ADD you keep saying you have."

"It's ADHD. Attention deficit hyperactivity disorder. So now you're making fun of my disability?"

"Disability? What a crock! You just toss that out to cover your impulsive decisions."

"That's what ADHD is, Brad. Impulsive decision-making, among other things. What about your brother? You wouldn't accuse him of having Asperger's so he can behave any way he wants?"

Brad was silent as we pulled up to the loading zone at the de Young Museum. "I'll wait here," he said, not looking at me. "Try not to steal any works of art. I don't think ADHD is a strong enough defense."

I set the dog down, got out of the car, and slammed the door shut. I heard yapping as I stomped toward the museum entrance. I only hoped I didn't return to find a bloody crime scene filled with pink fur in Brad's Crime Scene Cleaners van.

Chapter 21

PARTY PLANNING TIP #21

If you're sleuthing at a Murder Mystery Party, learn to eavesdrop. You may overhear an important clue that will help you undercover the murderer. Then again, perhaps the information will be useful for blackmailing purposes at a later date.

When I arrived at the front desk, I was informed that Sam Wo wasn't available. Great. Without him, I wouldn't be able to sneak upstairs and surprise Christine with a visit. I suspected Christine knew why Corbin had that birth certificate and wanted to confirm my hunch. I certainly couldn't ask his parents, and he seemed to be AWOL.

Nuts. How did they sneak into places on TV? By delivering pizzas? Flowers?

Balloons!

I slipped into the nearest restroom and pulled out from my purse the pack of balloons I always carry with me. It had become a habit ever since I started this business. Balloons came in handy at any party. And lying was coming easier and easier. What was up with that?

Light-headed from blowing up a dozen balloons, I tied them off with lengths of ribbon I kept just for this purpose and gathered them into a bouquet. Holding them slightly over my face, I returned to the main desk and told a different volunteer that I had a delivery for Christine Lampe.

"Sign here," she said, pushing a sign-in log at me. I scribbled "Nancy Drew" along the line, then asked where to go. She sighed, then led me to the elevator. Once I was inside, she waved her key card over the small square and punched "4" before ducking back out.

I held on to the balloons until the doors opened on the fourth floor. I stepped out and glanced up and down the hallway. No one in sight. I tucked the balloons behind a large fake plant, then headed for Christine's office to make my surprise appearance.

As I approached the closed door, I heard voices. Raised voices. I recognized Christine's strong, strident tone and paused outside the office door, straining to listen.

". . . how could you? I thought we had something . . ." Christine was saying.

A man's voice, much more soft-spoken, mumbled something I couldn't make out.

I leaned in to hear better. Christine was coming in loud and clear. Her partner in conversation, not so much.

". . . at the same time? . . ." Christine said.

Low, indecipherable mumbling followed.

". . . now she's dead . . . killed her!"

Her words startled me, and I bumped against the door.

Seconds later, the door swung open.

"May I help you?" Christine said, pulling the door wide. "Presley! What are you doing here?" Clearly she was surprised to see me.

Dan Tannacito stepped out from behind her.

"Dan!" I said, staring at the museum assistant.

"Presley?" Dan said, then looked at the museum curator.

I looked back and forth between them. They glanced at each other, red-faced, then looked down at the floor. It suddenly dawned on me why they were so embarrassed.

"You . . . and Dan?" I said, my eyes wide with surprise.

Christine crossed her arms and shook her head. "I . . . It's not . . ."

Dan laughed a little too loudly. "No, no. You've got this all wrong. We were just—"

Christine glared at him. "Shut up, Dan. It's too late. It's obvious she heard everything." She turned to me. "Didn't you, Presley. You nosy little snoop."

Whoa. Where had the venom come from?

She apparently assumed I knew more than I did.

She stepped around me and closed the door, blocking it with her body.

Trapped.

I glanced around in search of something to use as a weapon, in case I needed to defend myself. I spotted a sharp arrowhead on the desk, about the length of my hand. I rushed over and snatched it from its resting place, ready to stab anyone who lunged for me.

"What the hell are you doing?" Dan asked, no longer laughing.

"Have you lost your mind?" Christine said, reaching out a hand. "Give me that! It's priceless."

Neither one of them appeared frightened by my weapon. What was wrong with these museum people?

"If you're planning to murder us with that thing," Christine said, "you'll slice your fingers off first. Even the edges are sharp."

"Murder you?" I said, dumbfounded, and lowered the weapon. "Why would I murder you?"

Christine and Dan looked at each other.

"Isn't it obvious?" Christine said, nodding toward the arrowhead still in my hand.

I set the stupid thing back on the desk. "I'm not a murderer!" I said, exasperated by the whole scene. "What's going on around here?"

"Nothing!" they said in unison.

"Give me a break," I said. "You two are up to something. Tell me, or I'm calling the police."

Christine nodded toward Dan. "This jerk was—"

"Christine! Shut up!" Dan interrupted, his smooth exterior gone.

"—having an affair!" she finished.

"Yeah. With you!" Dan's voice boomed at her.

"And with half the women at the museum!" Christine screeched.

I blinked.

"Oh, don't look so surprised," Christine said. "Just because women work in a museum doesn't mean we're all relics."

I wasn't as shocked by the fact that they were coworkers having an affair as I was by their age differences. Like Mary

Lee, Christine was in her sixties, while Dan was only thirty-something.

"Apparently being Dan Tannacito doesn't preclude you from having affairs with multiple women at the same time," Christine spat.

Dan tried to hide a grin, but he looked more like a kid who'd hit a ball through a neighbor's window—sorry for the inconvenience, but proud of the hit.

"So that's what you were arguing about? Another woman?" I asked them.

Christine spoke up, her jaw set. "Not just another woman. How about my best friend?"

"Mary Lee?" My jaw nearly hit the floor at that revelation.

So Dan was seeing two cougars—who happened to be best friends—at the same time. What kind of player was this guy? Was he after money? Not in Christine's case, but possibly in Mary Lee's. Was he after a promotion, which Christine could probably grant him? Or maybe he just couldn't keep his priceless artifact in his khaki pants.

"Wow." It was a lot to take in. But what did it have to do with Mary Lee's death?

"I heard you say 'killed her' before you caught me listening. Were you accusing Dan of killing Mary Lee?" I asked Christine.

Dan interrupted. "I didn't kill Mary Lee. I had no reason. But *she* did." He thumbed Christine.

"I didn't kill her, you jerk! She was my best friend!"

Okay. Time to pull a rabbit out of my hat. I withdrew the birth certificate I'd found at Corbin's place, opened it, and held it up for her to see.

"What do you know about this?"

Christine's face lost all its color. "Where did you get that?" She reached over and tried to snatch it away from me.

I pulled it back. "I found it at Corbin's place," I said, returning the paper to the envelope. "I thought it was strange that it had his first name, but not his last name."

"I think it's time you leave." She crossed her arms and nodded toward the door.

"Not until you tell me the truth. Mary Lee may have been your best friend, but *my* best friend is in jail for a crime she didn't commit, and I'm not leaving until I find out how you two are involved. And what this birth certificate has to do with it."

"You found it at Corbin's?" Christine said, her voice trembling.

I nodded. "The date of birth coincides with his age, but like I said, it's not his last name."

I hadn't noticed until I stopped talking that tears had formed in Christine's eyes. It was then that I knew for certain what I had suspected.

"You're Corbin's birth mother," I said gently.

She squeezed her eyes together, sending the tears streaming down her face.

Chapter 22

PARTY PLANNING TIP # 22

If it turns out you're the murderer at the Murder Mystery Party, try to deflect suspicion by implicating another suspect. If you're convincing enough, he or she may even confess . . .

"You said Mary Lee was your best friend," I said. "You mentioned you two met at the University of Oregon and were in the same field of anthropology. You said you kept in touch after you graduated and went your similar but separate directions."

Dan's eyes widened at the news. Apparently he hadn't been aware of their longtime relationship. "Christine? You and Mary Lee were friends? I thought you hated her."

Christine grabbed a tissue from the box on her desk and dabbed at her eyes.

Dan went on. I could see the confusion in his face. "Corbin is your *son*? And he didn't *know*? What other secrets are you hiding?"

Tears welled up again in Christine's eyes. I plucked a tissue from the box and handed it to her.

"Yes, it's true. We both went to the U of O in Eugene, majored in anthropology, some forty years ago. I went on to get my master's, while Mary Lee went to San Francisco State for her degree in art history. That's where she met Jason, in fact. I stayed in Oregon and got my first job at the Portland Museum."

"That's where you got into some trouble, right, Christine?" I asked.

Christine sniffed. "Sounds like you've been doing a lot of snooping, Presley. Sure, I met this guy. The museum curator, actually. We worked together, and well, we became close . . ."

"Close enough to become pregnant?" I added.

Her voice turned bitter. "I was young and stupid. I thought he was in love with me . . ."

She blew her nose on the tissue. Dan opened his mouth to say something, but I shot him a "don't even think about it" look. He closed his mouth and retreated into the background, his face still full of wonder at Christine's confession.

"What did you do that got you fired?" I asked.

"I thought Mike would leave his wife—he was married, of course. But when I told him I was pregnant, he freaked. Needless to say, it wasn't the reaction I was expecting. Quite the opposite. And all of a sudden he wanted me out of there."

"He wanted you to quit your job?"

"Oh no. Not just quit. He falsified some provenance papers that made it look as if I'd bought questionable artifacts.

It blew up into a huge scandal—made the newspapers and local TV news. I was fired a few days later. And there was nothing I could do. I was out of a job and a relationship in a matter of a few days."

"You couldn't fight it?"

Christine sighed deeply. "I tried to reason with him, to get him to retract his allegations. When that didn't work, I threatened to expose our relationship—and my pregnancy. But he said no one would believe me—not with the ugly rumors he planned to spread."

"So you had the baby under your real name—Judith Hofmann—and gave him to Mary Lee to raise as her own. I assume she covered all your expenses, maybe more."

I waited for Christine's response. When she said nothing, I began making it up as I went along.

"Meanwhile Mary Lee created a fake birth certificate to show to Corbin, in case he asked for it. But when he sent for an official copy, there was no record of a Corbin Cosetti."

Christine bit her lip, then sighed. "That was back in the days before computers. We didn't anticipate that the records would be transferred to computer and available on the Internet."

"And that's when he found the name Corbin Hofmann— born the same day as he."

She nodded. "He put two and two together."

"He's a smart kid," I said.

She nodded silently.

"Why did you change your name to Christine Lampe?"

"After I lost my job, I couldn't use my real name anymore. I'd never get another one in my field, with the museum scandal hanging over my head. I had to change it to start over."

Dan stepped out of the shadows, disbelief written on his face. "How could you just hand your baby over to Mary Lee like that?"

Christine's face hardened, her eyes became slits. "You have no right to judge me. You don't have a clue what it was like. I had no husband, no job, no future, and my family wouldn't speak to me. When I called Mary Lee and told her everything, she called back the next day and said she wanted to adopt my baby. She offered to pay for everything, as long as I promised not to tell anyone it wasn't her biological child."

"Why would she do that?"

"You know Mary Lee. She wanted to acquire a child, much like she acquired art, but she didn't want to suffer through pregnancy and ruin her figure. Besides, she was having trouble with her marriage."

A light went on. "So she faked her pregnancy?"

Christine slowly nodded. "She and Jason were having marital problems. She hardly slept with him. Just enough to fool him and everyone else that she'd gotten pregnant. So she pretended to be pregnant, then conveniently went up to Oregon to visit her best friend—me—and came home with Corbin."

"And had that fake document made up," I added, "with her and Jason's names instead of yours."

A thought occurred to me that might give Christine a motive for murdering Mary Lee. "Was Mary Lee blackmailing you about the adoption?"

Christine looked puzzled. "No! Why would she do that? If you think about it, I could have done the same to her."

Maybe she did, I thought, then asked, "Maybe you wanted your son back after all these years?"

"That's ridiculous!" Christine barked. "What are you getting at? This was a mutual decision, and once we made it, we never spoke about it again. Truthfully, I have no regrets, other than the fact that I couldn't have any more children. The pregnancy was complicated . . ." Her voice drifted off.

I wasn't sure I bought everything Christine was saying. She sounded sincere, but giving up her baby to Mary Lee must have had emotional ramifications over the years. Mary Lee was wealthy, while Christine was not. Maybe Christine was jealous of all Mary Lee had and wanted her son back—or money to keep quiet. When she found out her lover, Dan, was cheating on her with her best friend, it must have been the final blow to her ego.

When did she learn about Dan's affair with Mary Lee? And was that motive enough to murder Mary Lee?

"Mary Lee got you the job at the de Young, right?"

Christine looked at me defensively. "She has a lot of clout, as you probably know."

"And she owed you. But maybe she regretted it after a while, and wanted you out of the picture?"

"Why would she? I was no threat to her."

"Dan?" I turned to Dan Tannacito, who was witnessing all this with wide eyes and an open mouth. "Did Mary Lee know about your relationship with Christine?"

He pressed his lips together, then said, "No . . ."

Christine whirled on him. "She did, didn't she! She knew! She'd been acting strangely—distant. Was she going to fire me too?"

Dan held his hands up, trying to keep up his innocent appearance. "No, no. I mean, yes, she found out about you and me. But I told her it was—"

"It was what?" Christine hissed.

Squirming, he said, "You know, just a fling. Nothing serious." I had to admire his nerve, but it was no match for his stupidity.

Christine closed her eyes. Her lips quivered, and her hands were trembling. I could practically read her mind. Betrayed again. This time not only by her lover Dan, but by her best friend Mary Lee.

"Get the hell out of my office!" Christine shrieked.

"Wait a minute, Christine," I said, holding up a hand. I turned to Dan. "What did Mary Lee do when she found out about you and Christine?"

"She was . . . upset, you know," Dan stammered. "But like I said, I calmed her down, reassured her." He turned to Christine. "Chris, I only saw her so I could influence her to get us more money for the museum. That was it. I didn't love her or anything. Not like I care for you." His eyes were pleading.

"You only cared for me because I was in a position to promote you to assistant curator," she snarled. "I'll bet you had plans to take over my job, too. You . . . you . . ." Out of names to call him, she picked up the antique arrowhead I'd recently threatened them with and threw it at Dan.

He covered his head with his arm and ducked.

The arrowhead flew by, narrowly missing him.

"Chrissy, darling, that's not what it was . . ."

Before Christine could respond, I shouted, "Quiet! Both of you! Christine, you had a motive to kill Mary Lee because she was two-timing you with Dan. And, Dan, you had a motive to kill Mary Lee because she threatened to get you fired when she found out about your affair with Christine. I'd say you both had a motive to murder Mary Lee. I think it's time to call Detective Melvin and let him figure out the details." I reached for the phone on Mary Lee's desk.

Dan stepped forward, his usually charming grin gone. He placed a hand over mine. "You don't want to do that."

I felt the hairs at the back of my neck tingle. "I don't? And why is that?"

"Because," he said, "none of this has anything to do with the murder of Mary Lee's ex-husband. Neither of us had reason to kill Jason."

I pulled my hand out from under his. "Maybe . . . maybe Jason thought you two killed Mary Lee, confronted you, threatened you . . . and you felt you had to silence him, too." It was a long shot—they had separate motives—but maybe I could shake something loose with my wild accusations.

"Give me a break, Presley," Christine said. "I can't speak for this two-timing jerk here"—she jerked a thumb at Dan— "but Mary Lee was my best friend and the mother to my child. Hardly motive enough to kill her, just because she fell for this gigolo."

"Well, I didn't kill her either," Dan said. "If things had worked out, I might have been the next Mr. Mary Lee Miller. With all the benefits that entailed." He shot Christine a "so there" look.

Christine's already blotching face filled with color. "Ha! I knew it!" She picked up another antique from her desk—a small stone statue—and hurled it at Dan.

It hit the wall behind him.

"Hey!" Dan shouted. "Knock it off! You were using her too, telling her what to buy, nagging her to raise more money, just so you could be the most prestigious curator in the country, if not the world."

That did it. Christine went after Dan, whitened teeth and polished nails. She beat on his chest and kicked his shins. Just when I thought she might bite him, I pulled her away before she really did commit murder.

"Christine, chill!" I pushed her into a chair. She slumped into the seat, sobbing into her hands. I passed her the box of tissues.

"You're both acting . . . inexcusably! Now shut up, before I call security and have you arrested for . . . for fraud or something."

My cell phone rang. Brad. I'd almost forgotten about him.

"Hi, Brad. Sorry. I got caught up in something," I said into the phone.

"Presley. Meet me at the tower." He sounded breathless.

"What's wrong?" I glanced at Christine and Dan and caught a look passing between them.

"Just hurry!"

He hung up, leaving me staring at the phone.

With a last look at Christine and Dan, I ducked out of the office and ran to the elevators. Brad had sounded upset. What had happened? Was the dog all right?

I punched the elevator button for the tower and heard a buzzing noise as the doors closed. The sound grew louder as the car reached the seventh floor.

Brad was waiting for me when the doors opened. He took my arm as I stepped out. The buzzing sound was even louder. "What's causing that noise?" I asked, grimacing.

He nodded toward a small crowd that had gathered at the

other elevator. I followed him as he shouldered through, and noticed that the elevator doors kept opening and closing partway. Something was blocking the doorway. Squeezing through a couple of onlookers, I glanced down to see what had jammed the doors and gathered such a gawking crowd.

There lay the body of a man.

He was facedown, had dark hair, and his cap was askew.

He wore a guard's uniform.

Goose bumps broke out all over my body.

Oh my God. "Sam!"

Chapter 23

PARTY PLANNING TIP # 23

To add atmosphere to your Murder Mystery Party, play sound effects or music in the background, such as the sound of wind howling or doors creaking, or the theme song from Murder, She Wrote.

"Can't you stop those damn doors?" I yelled at no one in particular as I stared helplessly at Sam.

Brad stepped inside the elevator and held down the DOOR OPEN button with one hand. With the other he made a call on his cell phone to Detective Melvin, whom I gathered was already en route. Once he finished the call, he pulled an on-looker into the car.

"Keep your finger there until we can get maintenance to shut it down," Brad told the man. Eyes wide, the man obeyed his orders. Brad knelt down and pressed two fingers on the side of Sam's neck, knocking his uniform cap to the floor in the process.

My stomach lurched at the bloody gash at the back of Sam's head.

The poor man. How had this happened?

The doors to the other elevator opened, and I turned my head to see if it was the police.

Out stepped another security guard.

Sam Wo.

"Sam! You're alive!" I squealed. I wanted to hug him, I was so relieved.

Sam blinked in confusion. "I just got here and heard there was some kind of accident. What happened?" He knelt down by the coworker I'd mistaken for him.

Sam rolled the body over. I recognized the short, dark-haired man who looked so much like Sam from behind. It was Ed Pike, the surly guard who had given me so much attitude. I felt a rush of guilt.

"Don't touch him!" Brad said, too late. "SFPD is on the way."

Although Pike resembled Sam in color and stature, I noticed now that he wore glasses. They were twisted and clinging to his face. They'd been obscured moments ago when he lay on his chest.

"Are you sure he's . . ." Sam's voice caught. He didn't finish the sentence.

Brad nodded. "What's his name?"

Sam looked down at the man, his face pale. "Pike. Ed Pike." He turned to me with anguished eyes. "What happened?"

"I . . . don't know, Sam," I stammered, and looked helplessly at Brad for a better answer. Brad said nothing.

Sam returned his attention to his deceased coworker.

Seconds later the police arrived via the second elevator. Detective Melvin stepped out and took in the scene. When he spotted me, he rolled his eyes as if I were somehow involved. He assigned one of the other cops to question me, while he huddled with the young clerk who had discovered the guard's body lying half in and half out of the elevator.

After my brief interrogation, I was left alone on a nearby bench to wait for news from Brad. Meanwhile, I interrogated myself. How had this happened? Had he fallen or been hit over the head? And who would want to kill him?

I'd been with Christine and Dan just before the body was discovered. They couldn't have killed him—or could they? I supposed it depended on when the guard had been killed.

Meanwhile, where was Corbin Cosetti?

Was he in hiding? If so, why? Had he run away? Or had something happened to him?

I watched as the paramedics took the body away. Had Ed Pike seen something, known something, that would expose the killer? Or did he have secrets of his own?

Tired of my own questions, I stood up and walked over to Brad, who was still engaged in conversation with Detective Melvin. "Brad, I have to get back to the office," I said, interrupting them.

Detective Melvin gave me one of his condescending smiles. "Got a party to go to, Ms. Parker?"

I ignored him. "I have some . . . paperwork . . . to do."

Brad frowned. "You mean reviewing the ones from the locker?"

"What papers?" Melvin asked, perking up. "Whose locker?"

Crap. Did Brad know nothing about subtlety!

"Just some papers from Mary Lee's locker . . ."

"How did you get into her locker?" Melvin pressed.

"I . . . uh . . ."

"Do you know what the term 'obstruction of justice' means, Parker?"

"I'm not obstructing justice, Detective Melvin," I snapped. "I'm trying to ensure it. May we go, Detective?"

Melvin raised an eyebrow at Brad. I thought I saw Brad wink. I'd slap him later, to avoid being arrested for assault at the moment. The two of them were thick as thieves, and I suspected Brad was supplying the detective with everything I'd discovered, while keeping Melvin's info to himself.

"I'm going to want to see those papers," the detective added.

I gave a barely perceptible nod. Brad took my arm, as if he were escorting a little old lady across the street, and led me into the second elevator—the one that hadn't contained the body.

It wasn't until we descended halfway that I suddenly remembered the dog.

"What did you do with little Puffy?"

"He's fine. He's in the SUV. I cracked the windows and filled an empty container with water. Left him a few snacks too."

I wrinkled an eyebrow. "What kind of snacks?"

"Some beef jerky. Had some in the glove compartment. For emergencies."

I smiled. "That was sweet of you."

"Yeah, I'm a sweet kinda guy." He winked.

"One more question. How did you know about the dead guy in the elevator?"

"Heard it on the police scanner. I was here, so I thought I'd check it out."

Brad really had a knack for right time, right place. I, on the other hand, would need an alarm clock and GPS to end up at the right time, in the right place.

My office door was locked when Brad and I returned, just the way I'd left it. But when I inserted the key, it didn't go in smoothly. I had to jiggle it to unlock the door. Once inside, I scanned the room. Everything looked normal—semichaotic with intermittent organization that only I would recognize.

I sat down at my desk and pulled open the top drawer, where I'd hidden the papers copied from the ones in Mary Lee's locker.

They were still there.

Only something was different about them. I'd thrown them in the drawer, and now they were neatly stacked, one on top of the other. It was as if someone with profound obsessive-compulsive disorder had been compelled to align the papers perfectly. My OCD was mild compared to most.

Someone had been in my office—and in my desk.

The hairs on the back of my neck stood at attention. "Raj?" I called out for the security down the hall. No answer.

I started to pull out my cell, then stopped. There was something odd about all this. The intruder had seen the papers, arranged them neatly, but hadn't taken them. Maybe those names and number meant nothing after all.

I dug in my purse for the birth certificate and found it, along with the envelope I'd picked up from the pile below Corbin's front door. The envelope was sealed, with no postage, no addressee or return address, only the words "Marina Yacht Club" embossed on the back. Someone had slipped it through the mail slot.

Jason?

If so, when? It had to have been sometime before he was killed.

Feeling a tinge of guilt about opening someone else's mail, I reminded myself that Corbin was missing, his father and mother were dead, and that precluded any hesitation on my part.

I slid my thumb under the flap and opened it. Inside were several sheets of paper stapled together. I withdrew them and spread them out in front of me.

I blinked. It was the same list of names as the ones from Mary Lee's locker

I crossed the hall to Brad's office. There was no sign of Mary Lee's dog.

"Where's Chou-Chou?"

Brad pointed under his desk. I leaned over and peeked. Sure enough. The curly-haired ball of fluff was curled up next to Brad's feet. My heart melted.

"Be careful you don't step on it," I said, grinning. What was it about big guys and little dogs?

Brad's cell phone rang.

"Could you come to my office when you're done?" I asked quickly.

He nodded as he answered the call.

I returned to my desk, sat down, and held up the two sets of papers—the copy of the ones from Mary Lee's locker, and the ones I'd found at Corbin's that appeared to have come from Jason Cosetti—and examined them. There had to be some significance to them.

I heard footsteps in the reception room and quickly shoved the papers back in my desk. Detective Melvin appeared at the entryway, looking more *GQ* than PD.

"Detective!" I sat up, surprised to see him again so soon after leaving the museum.

"Ms. Parker." He turned and nodded to Brad, who was still on the phone, then stepped into my office.

"What brings you here?" I asked nervously.

"You mentioned some papers you found in Ms. Miller's locker. I'd like to see them." He eyed me. "And I'd like to know how you got into her locker."

I didn't want to get Sam into trouble, so I lied. "I . . . uh . . . from Corbin," I stammered. With Corbin missing, I might get away with avoiding the truth. I pulled the top drawer open a couple of inches and withdrew one set of papers, leaving the second set in the drawer.

"Here they are." I handed them to the detective.

He looked them over for a few seconds. "Any idea what they mean?"

"No, but I haven't had a chance to really study them. I'm guessing your staff will have them analyzed in a matter of minutes."

"You got these from Corbin, you say?"

I nodded.

He shook his head. He knew I was lying.

I smiled sweetly at him.

He pressed his lips together, tucked the papers into an inside jacket pocket, and crossed over to Brad's office.

My heart beating like a hummingbird, I pulled open the drawer, slipped the second set of papers into my purse, and headed out of my office.

Detective Melvin leaned out. "Going somewhere, Ms. Parker?"

"The women's room, if that's all right with you, Detective."

I could feel his eyes follow me down the hall to the office restroom at the back of the barracks. Slipping into a stall, I locked the door, sat down on the toilet seat, and pulled out the duplicate set.

I glanced over the alphabetized names and their accompanying numbers for the umpteenth time. Like before, I recognized a few names—Christine Lampe, Dan Tannacito, a couple of San Francisco city supervisors, and some of the more well-known guests who'd attended the Murder Mystery Party. The rest were unfamiliar. Each name had a number by it—5,000, 10,000, 20,000 and more.

Were they just donations? Made at the party? Above and beyond the thousand-dollar-a-plate fee?

Then why had Mary Lee hidden them? And why had Jason dropped them off at Corbin's?

I returned to my desk with the papers stuffed deep into my purse and found Detective Melvin and Brad gone from the office.

Working quickly before the detective returned, I pulled out a file from the cabinet marked "de Young—Murder Mystery Party," sat at my desk, and flipped it open. Inside I found a note handwritten by Mary Lee. Placing it next to the list of names, I compared the handwriting. Her note was written in a delicate script with a light touch. The list had been noted with a heavy hand, bold script, with a slightly backward slant. A lefty? I was no graphologist, but these samples weren't written by the same person.

If not Mary Lee, then who? Jason? A secretary?

I'd need to get a few more handwriting samples to identify the writer, from Jason, Christine, Dan, and maybe everyone on that list.

Including Corbin.

I looked over the names and numbers again.

ANDERSON, Charles—5,000. *City supervisor*

BRIEN, Sansa and Dennis—20,000. *Well-known philanthropists. . . .*

I skimmed down the list, stopping when I spotted a familiar name.

GREEN, Davin—20,000. *Mayor of San Francisco . . .*

LAMPE, Christine—10,000. *Museum curator . . .*

TANNACITO, Dan—5,000. *Assistant curator . . .*

"Watson," I said aloud, reaching the last name on the list. Like Brad said, there were no names beginning with the letters X, Y, or Z. I turned the paper over in case there was something written on the back. Nothing there, except a tiny piece of paper stuck in back of the staple.

"Hey," Brad said, peeking his head in. "S'up?"

"Where's your BFF?"

"He took off." Brad stepped inside. "You wanted to talk

to me about something?" He pulled up a chair and sat down, leaned back, legs akimbo.

I held up the last page of the list of names and numbers for him to see. "Notice anything odd about this page?"

Brad looked at me quizzically. "Wait a minute. I thought you gave those papers to Melvin."

"I gave him a different copy."

"You have two copies?" He picked up the papers and gave them a quick glance, then shrugged.

I explained how I came by the second copy.

"But that's not the point. See the corner with the staple." I pointed to the tiny scrap of paper. "I think this proves there's another page."

"The last page was ripped off," Brad said, grinning as the light went on.

"Yes! But what's odd is, I think someone broke into my office and—"

He held up a hand to cut me off. "Wait a second. Someone broke into your office?"

"I think so."

He glanced around. "How can you tell? Looks okay to me."

"When I tried my key, it didn't fit easily. And then I opened the top drawer and found my papers all neatly stacked."

"Yeah, that's conclusive."

I wadded up a sticky note and threw it at him. "Anyway, whoever was in my office handled the papers I gave to Melvin."

"Well, just look for a neat freak then."

I stood up and crossed my arms. "I thought you were going to help me."

Brad laughed. "I am. I just don't see what a pile of neat papers has anything to do with anything."

I grabbed my purse and rushed past him to the door. He caught my wrist. "Hey, where are you going?"

"I . . . have a party to plan," I said haughtily.

"Am I invited?" He released my arm.

"Sorry. You're not on the guest list."

Chapter 24

PARTY PLANNING TIP # 24

Appropriate props add authenticity to your Murder Mystery Party, so don't overlook them. Park a vintage car in the driveway, hang a sparkly chandelier overhead, or install a secret doorway that leads to a hidden passageway.

Walking back to my condo, I tried to come up with a viable transportation plan. With two cars in the shop, I was running out of transportation. I didn't want to keep asking Brad to drive me around, but what options did I have? Raj drove a white Chevy SUV with the words "Treasure Island Security" printed on the sides. Berk had a VW, but he—and it—weren't around at the moment. I could try to get one of those share-cars so popular in the city—like a Zipcar or City CarShare.

But then I remembered Mother.

I'd nearly forgotten. She owned a car—an old Cadillac that one of her ex-husbands had given to her as part of a divorce settlement. She'd kept it as a souvenir rather than as transportation. Being a city girl, she'd rarely driven it, and now, with her illness, it was unlikely she'd ever drive again.

Mother had stored the monstrosity at a city parking garage, but when I moved to the island, she asked me to keep it there. I warned her that TI had a substantial auto burglary problem, but she insisted, so I had agreed to park it in one of the extra spots at the far end of the condo complex. I'd covered it with a car cover to keep it safe from the salt air and essentially forgotten about the thing.

Normally I wouldn't be caught dead driving the humongous, not-even-close-to-green machine. But I was desperate.

Would it still run? I wondered, as I unlocked the front door to the condo and greeted my cats. After feeding them a hearty meal and chatting briefly with them in kitty talk, I did a quick search of my junk drawer and found my mother's disco-ball key ring and keys. After kissing my kitties goodbye, promising them massages when I returned, I locked the door securely. I headed over to the car with one lingering question on my mind, the one that bothered me more than the missing last page.

Where was Corbin?

He'd virtually disappeared, leaving behind his mother's precious pup. And tracking down the answer to that question was enough to make me get inside my mother's boat of a car, start driving, and find out.

I could see dust collected on the car cover from several feet away as I approached. The thing hadn't been touched since I'd parked it there months ago. I peeled back the cover and stood for a moment, marveling at what was once an enviable status symbol, but now would be considered a gas-guzzling clunker. How dramatically the whims of automobile drivers had changed over the years.

Mother had selected this one because it was her favorite color—gold. One of her former husbands, a car buff, offered her a choice from his collection in the divorce settlement. Naturally she picked the most expensive one of the bunch. The car cover had done its job. The gold paint was as shiny as the day we'd driven here. It was hard to believe the car hadn't just come off the lot.

Unlocking the driver's side, I pulled open the squeaking door. The gold leather interior was pristine and the quilted seats luxurious as I slithered in. This wasn't a car. This was a coach meant for a king. A throne for royalty. A second home. What a contrast to the claustrophobic Smart Car! I snuggled into the seat, took in the scent of leather, then stuck the key in the ignition and twisted it.

Nothing. Absolutely dead.

"Nuts!" I said, and then sighed. There was only one thing I could do at this point, short of calling a cab. I got out my iPhone and tapped a familiar number.

Brad arrived in less than five minutes. As he drove up, I saw his mouth drop open, then lip-read the words, "Holy crap!" His SUV jerked to a stop next to me, and he hopped out, grinning like he'd found gold. And in a way, he had.

"Where did you get this?" he asked, practically drooling over my mother's Caddy. He'd never looked at me like that.

"It's my mother's. She doesn't drive anymore, so she asked me to keep it here."

Brad ignored me as he circled the car. "Whoa. This is a

1960 Coupe de Ville! Convertible! Look at those fins. Do you know how much this is worth?"

I couldn't care less about the value of the car at this point. I just needed it to get me from point A to points B, C, and D.

"Look at that grille! The chrome! This thing has 340 horsepower, with a V-8 engine. Must weigh two and a half tons . . ." He poked his head inside and gasped. "Gold carpeting. Gold dashboard. Pearlized steering wheel. Power windows, steering, brakes." He pulled his head out. "You know what this Mac Daddy Caddy sold for back then? Less than six thousand. This one, in such cherry condition, gotta be worth over forty."

"Is there anything you don't know?" I said crossing my arms.

Brad caressed the bumper. I got shivers.

"Guess I'm your basic renaissance man. I've been a car freak since I was sixteen and bought my first Mustang. Used. Ragtop. Raven black. I rebuilt the engine. Ran smooth as glass."

"Well, maybe you could take a look under the hood. I think the battery is dead. It's been sitting here for months."

Brad opened the door and scooted in. Before he even tried the key, he gripped the marbleized steering wheel and ran his hands lovingly around it.

What was it with guys and cars?

Brad turned the key in the ignition. Not surprisingly, nothing happened. He sat back in the seat as if pondering some kind of presidential decision.

"Dead battery, right?" I asked, bringing him back to the problem at hand.

Reluctantly he climbed out of the car. "Most likely. I've got jumper cables in my SUV."

While Brad spent the next several minutes doing battery stuff with a bunch of clips and cords, I went back to my condo and to get a thank-you beer for Brad. On the way back I called the museum and asked to speak to Sam. I was transferred to his voice mail and left a message for him to call me back. Brad was just wiping his hands with a disinfectant wipe when I handed over the beer.

"Did you fix it?"

"Hop in and give it a try."

I sat down and turned the key. The engine croaked, sputtered, and roared to life. "Great! I owe you one."

He tapped the top of the car. "How about a ride in this beauty?"

I pulled the driver's door closed, powered down the window, and smiled sweetly. "Sure. As soon as I get back." I backed the car out of the space, turned sharply onto the road, and took off, leaving Brad alone with his beer and the dusty car cover.

Like Brad said, the Caddy ran as smooth as glass. I felt like a kid playing in her parents' car as I drove the city streets. The thing was huge, and I was sure I was straddling both lanes of the road, about to sideswipe any car that tried to pass me.

The sun was setting quickly, shadows replacing the light. The temperature had cooled considerably by the time I pulled the Cadillac up in front of Corbin's place, my hand sweaty from the tension of flying this plane. Parking on the street would have been a challenge, so I drove into the oil-stained driveway. I hoped I wouldn't get a ticket—the tailfins stuck out beyond the sidewalk. But I didn't plan to be there long.

Several newspapers littered the front walk. No house lights were visible from the street. I stepped onto the porch and glanced down at the bottom of the front door. A corner of the note I'd left Corbin still stuck out from under the door. I knocked, listened for any sound inside, and gave up after a few minutes. I wasn't about to break in again. Besides, it was obvious he hadn't been back.

Disturbing thoughts ran through my head. Was he on the lam? In some kind of trouble? Or worse . . . ?

I knew from reading murder mysteries and listening to Brad that the answer to the whodunit question lay in MOM—method, opportunity, and motive. So far I had no idea what the real methods were, I wasn't sure about the opportunities, and I was still clueless about the motive or motives. But Brad had also recommended that I study the victims, the crime scenes, and the physical evidence if I wanted answers.

I sat in the car, locked the doors, pulled out my party-planning/crime-solving paper, and looked over the list of victims.

Victim number one: Mary Lee Miller, a wealthy socialite who'd raised a lot of money for the museum. Had she been skimming money off the donations? Blackmailing patrons for extra money? Or did it have to do with Christine and her biological son, Corbin?

Victim number two: Jason Cosetti, down-and-out ex-husband of Mary Lee's, still waiting for his ship to come in. Maybe he was blackmailing Mary Lee about some deep, dark secret? Did he have some kind of museum scheme going on? Or did it have to do with Corbin's recently discovered adoption?

Victim number three: Ed Pike, one of the security guards at the museum. What was his connection? Had he seen something he shouldn't have? Or did he have something on Mary Lee? And Jason?

I turned the paper over and wrote "Crime Scene."

All the murders had taken place at the de Young Museum. The first in the mural room off the main lobby. The second in or near the outdoor frog pond. And the third in the elevator.

Did someone have something against the museum? Was the killer trying to give the place a black eye? Or just get rid of key people?

Once again, I had more questions than answers. Underneath I wrote "Physical Evidence."

After hearing what the ME had reported about Mary Lee's wound—that the stab wound was almost a perfect match to the fake dagger—I had a hunch about the weapon, but it would take some snooping to find out if I was right. And it wouldn't be easy, considering all the security at the museum. In fact, it could even be dangerous, bearing in mind that whoever was behind the murders was most likely now after me. My MINI had been vandalized. My brakes had been cut. My office had been invaded. I'd been getting crank calls. And someone had mugged my mother.

I started up the engine. It purred like a kitten. Backing into the street, I thought about hosting one of those drawing room parties where the sleuth gathers all the suspects in one room. Then, after a lengthy cat-and-mouse game of misleading information, she reveals the killer to the crowd. I could make of Clue-style invitations, with caricatures of the suspects on the cover and intriguing party details inside. After snacks were served—little Clue-shaped weapons made out of chocolate—I'd announce whodunit to gasps of shock and surprise: "It was Mr. Green in the Museum with the Ceremonial Dagger!"

But how did the list of names and numbers tie in?

I pulled the list out of my purse and scanned the names. I'd missed it the first time, skimming it so fast, but there it was—Ed Pike, along with the number 1,000. If it was a contribution, it was small by comparison. But perhaps it was a lot on a security guard's salary.

There was something niggling at the back of my mind.

I entered the congested evening traffic on Fell Street and stepped on the gas. The car lunged forward.

It was time to return to the Scene of the Crime.

Chapter 25

PARTY PLANNING TIP # 25

Dim the lights at your Murder Mystery Party to put the amateur sleuths in an investigative mood. Plus, finding hidden clues is more challenging when the room is lit by candles or flashlights instead of chandeliers and fluorescents.

Golden Gate Park at twilight is another world. It's a magical place, a serene contrast to the urban chaos beyond its borders. Not only does it hold one of the world's foremost museums, but it's also home to dozens of recreational activities. Growing up in the city, I never had much of a backyard, so my mother took me to the park often. I'd ridden horses at the stables, rowed boats on Stow Lake, stood on the giant lily pads at the Conservatory of Flowers, listened to Mozart at the Music Concourse, visited the sharks at the Steinhart Aquarium, and been to outer space at the Morrison Planetarium more times than I can count. But my favorite place was, and still is, the Japanese Tea Garden, with its nearly vertical bridges, lush vegetation, and winding paths. It's got to be the most enchanting place on earth.

Each trip was accompanied by my mother's mini-lectures on the history of the park. By the time I'd heard all her stories about the past, I could have gotten a job as tour guide at the park.

"Presley, did you know that Golden Gate Park was once nothing but sand dunes sculpted by Pacific Ocean winds, and now it has over one million trees?"

"Presley, can you believe approximately seventy-five thousand people visit the park on an average weekend?"

"Presley, I'll bet you didn't realize that the park was deeded to the people in 1870, and developed by Scotsman John McLaren around 1890 . . ."

Yadda, yadda, blah, blah, blah. Back then I couldn't have cared less. Now I was glad those trivial facts were stuck in my head. I loved learning more about the history of the city, mainly because it came with a lot of fascinating stories of mayhem, muckraking, and of course murder.

I thought about one of my favorite stories on my way to the museum—the attempted murder of M. H. de Young, the museum's namesake. He and his brother Charles had founded the *Daily Dramatic Chronicle*, a predecessor to the *San Francisco Chronicle*, back in 1865. When Michael printed a less-than-flattering article about Adolph Spreckels, the sugar magnate, he was shot by Spreckels in 1884. Luckily he survived. However, Charles wasn't so lucky. A few months later, the son of a hellfire preacher running for mayor, unhappy with the newspaper's lack of support for his father during the election, shot Charles to death. A jury declared the son not guilty by reason of "justifiable homicide." In other words, the kid got away with murder.

That's why I love San Francisco and its colorful past. You can't make this stuff up.

I drove the Caddy alongside the park's panhandle and wound around the curving roads, past the archery field, basketball court, golf course, lawn bowling, and bocce ball court, the children's playground with the antique carousel. John F. Kennedy Drive, closed to cars on Sundays, was quiet as tourists and locals headed home from a day of biking, skating, running, bird-watching, playing Frisbee, or visiting the museums.

I passed a stone angel that reminded me of a game I used to play with my mother called Find the Statues. Horticulturist John McLaren hid several statues around the park, mainly because he didn't like them, so my mother and I used to try to find them. It was a little spooky playing the game at night—sort of like being lost in a forest without bread crumbs, certain there was a witch around the next tree ready to capture more ingredients for her next evil concoction. I shuddered at the memory. I'd had a big imagination back then.

As I pulled into the parking garage in my mother's big gold boat, I had that creepy feeling again—the one I used to get as a child. Of course, aside from an enchanted forest, there's nothing scarier than a nearly deserted parking garage.

I drove the Caddy to a spot close to the entrance, got out, and checked to see if I was within the lines of the space. Hardly. I checked my watch. Good thing it was about closing time. With that in mind, I hustled toward the doors. Hordes of art admirers were streaming out as I handed over my bag at the security checkpoint.

I spotted Sam down the hallway. "Sam!" I hurried to catch up with him.

"Presley," he said, looking surprised. He held his hat in his hand and was carrying a canvas satchel with a strap across his chest. "I was just on my way out. Done for the day. What are you doing here? It's almost closing."

"Sam, I need to talk to you for a minute."

Sam glanced at his watch. "Uh, okay. In my office?"

"That would be great." I was relieved that I'd caught him; I wouldn't be able to enact my plan if I'd missed him. I followed him to the basement, waited for him to unlock the door, and entered behind him. He led me to his small office in the back and sat down behind his perfectly neat and tidy desk. Like his meticulous uniform, there wasn't a proverbial hair out of place. No wonder he was good at his job.

I set my purse down, accidentally bumping my shoulder against the work schedule board on the wall next to me. It swung off kilter, then came to rest at an angle.

"Sorry!" I said, jumping up to fix it.

Sam beat me to it. "No problem." He had the board back on its hooks and perfectly squared in seconds.

I leaned down again, carefully this time, and opened my purse. Withdrawing a set of the mysterious papers, I placed them on Sam's desk. "Remember these?"

Sam's face flushed with color. "You didn't tell anyone I got them for you, did you?"

"No, no. Don't worry."

He visibly relaxed. "Did you find out what they mean?"

"Not yet. That's why I needed to talk to you. I think you're the only one who can help me figure this all out."

Sam handed the set back to me. "Uh-oh. I have a funny feeling you're going to ask me to do something I shouldn't—again."

I smiled sweetly.

"Presley, you're going to get me fired! I told you. This job is all I have now. . . ." Sam grew uncharacteristically quiet and began rubbing the spot on his finger where his wedding ring had been.

"I'm sorry, Sam. I don't want to put you in a compromising position. I'm just trying to keep my friend from spending the rest of her life in prison for a crime she didn't commit." I stood up. "But I understand your reluctance. You're right—I don't want you to lose your job." It was time to pull out the big emotional guns. "Neither would my mother. She's grown quite fond of you. I heard you two had coffee together this morning."

Sam sighed and finally waved me back into the chair. I sat stiffly.

"What do you want this time?"

I took a deep breath, fingers mentally crossed that he would help me again, in spite of the risks. After all, if I got caught, I'd be in big trouble too. And with what I had planned, it would be Big, Big Trouble.

"I need to get into Mary Lee's office again."

Sam sat back and rubbed his face. "Not that. Anything but that."

"I think we missed something the first time."

"And the police—you think they missed something too?"

I nodded.

"But they searched the place. If they found anything important, they probably took it with them. What good would it do to go in there now?"

"It's just a hunch . . ."

"Oh, a hunch." He stiffened. "Great. I'm supposed to risk my job for a hunch?"

I stood up again. "Okay, look. Mary Lee obviously liked to hide things, like the papers in her locker. I'll bet there's something hidden in her office that the cops didn't find. I know, it's a lot to ask."

Sam said nothing, just kept shaking his head.

I kicked it up a notch, playing on his interest in my mother. "Mother's been asking about you," I said. I was going straight to hell, using Mom like that.

"All right, all right. But this had better be the last time, Presley. Understand?" He stood up, grabbed the satchel he'd been carrying, and pulled a set of keys from another board. I followed him past the multiple computer screens, monitored by a female guard in a uniform similar to Sam's. I paused when I saw one screen light up with the image of the ceremonial dagger. An art lover had entered the room and triggered the camera before moving on. The monitor went black.

As expected, Mary Lee's office was locked. Sam inserted a key, opened the door, and gestured for me to enter.

"What are you hoping to find that wasn't found by the police?" Sam asked, standing by the desk as I scanned the room.

"Not really sure," I said. I headed for the filing cabinets against the far wall, pulled open each drawer, and hunted through the files, hoping a clue would jump out at me. Nothing did.

I heard Sam yanking at the top desk drawer behind me.

"It's stuck," he said.

Something hit the floor with a quiet thud. We looked at each other; then I bent down and looked under the desk.

A small leather-bound ledger lay on the carpet. I reached over, grabbed it, and stood up. "I knew it! She's probably got stuff hidden all over this museum."

"What's that?" Sam asked.

I flipped open the cover—and gasped. The small ledger contained the same handwritten list of names and numbers we'd found in Mary Lee's locker. Only this one appeared to be the original document.

I flipped to the last page. It, too, ended with the name Watson. I ran my finger down the inside of the spine and felt the jagged edges of paper.

The last page had been carefully torn out.

I closed the book. "Sam, is there an accounting department here?"

"Sure." He checked his watch. "But they may have all gone home. It's past six."

"Can you call and see? I need to ask them a question."

"Okay, but let's get out of here before we're caught." Sam led me out, locking the office behind him. He pulled out his cell and punched in a number. After a brief exchange with a voice on the other end, Sam hung up.

"Barbara's still there. She said she'd wait for us."

"Barbara, this is Presley Parker," Sam announced when we

arrived at the accounting department on the fourth floor. "She'd like to ask you something."

The accounting office looked nothing like most of the other rooms in the museum. Instead of artifacts, it was full of computers, faxes, printers, and a half dozen other office machines. What did I expect—artfully placed statues and priceless paintings?

I reached out my hand. "Hi, Barbara. Thanks for seeing me so late. I wondered if you could take a look at this ledger." I handed it to her.

Barbara smiled, releasing the twinkle in her eyes. Her curly graying brown hair seemed to be in constant motion. She took the ledger with freckled hands, slipped on her heart-decorated reading glasses, and opened it.

After flipping through it a few minutes and muttering several "Hmms," she removed her glasses. "Well, it's not one of our ledgers. But many of the names are familiar. Donors, museum members, and whatnot. The amounts—if that's what they are—seem to be unusually high. More like investment numbers rather than donations. But other than that . . ."

She started to hand the ledger back to me, but apparently misjudged the distance and fumbled it to the floor between us.

"I'm so sorry!" she said. We both knelt down to retrieve it, and as she picked it up, I noticed that the back of the ledger had broken loose. Odd for what looked like a newly purchased ledger. "Oh my heavens, I've cracked the spine. I'm so, so sorry!"

She was trying to close the dislodged back when a small

sheet of paper fluttered down. The three of us stared at it. It had obviously fallen loose when the spine was broken.

Had it been hidden inside the back cover? Why not? Mary Lee seemed to have an affinity for hiding things.

I flipped the back open and discovered a slit where the note must have been inserted. I bent down and picked up the mysterious note.

As I read over the handwritten note, Sam and Barbara waited, curious to see what it was.

I refolded the note.

"Just a grocery list," I said as I stuck it back into the ledger. I thanked Barbara for her help. To Sam I said, "Let's go, Sam," and headed for the door. He followed me into the hallway, closed the door behind him, and said, "That was no grocery note. What did it say?"

All I could say was, "Wow."

Chapter 26

PARTY PLANNING TIP # 26

Encourage your guests to use logic when solving the crime at your Murder Mystery Party. If the victim was supposedly poisoned, remind sleuths not to ignore the bloody gash on his head.

"What does it say?" Sam asked.

I read it aloud. " 'I know about our son. You've been lying to me all these years. And now you'll pay. $1,000,000 in cash. Or everyone will know what you did.' "

The note was unaddressed and unsigned, but it was obvious who it was meant for and who wrote it. "Jason was blackmailing Mary Lee."

"Sure looks that way," Sam said. "You going to turn that over to the police?"

I nodded absently, not sure what I was really going to do with the note. Something was bothering me about all this, but I couldn't put my finger on it. The handwriting could easily be verified by an expert, but I had a feeling it was authentic. And Jason's need for money—and revenge—were motives enough to blackmail his wealthy ex-wife.

But it didn't prove that he'd killed Mary Lee. In fact, he would have wanted her alive to get the blackmail money. It also didn't explain who killed him. Was it someone who knew about the scheme? Someone who wanted in on the deal? Like Ed Pike? And when Jason wouldn't share, Ed was killed? But then, who killed Ed?

What about Christine Lampe? With Mary Lee dead, Corbin's secret birth and adoption would be safe. And Dan Tannacito? Was his clandestine relationship with Mary Lee something more? Something that threatened his climb up the museum pyramid? Would he have killed anyone who got in his way—like Jason—or anyone who might have stumbled onto his secret—like Ed Pike?

As much as the idea troubled me, I had to admit that the one person who seemed to gain the most from all this was Corbin. He stood to inherit a fortune—unless someone proved he wasn't Mary Lee's biological child.

I took another look at the note, written in a different hand from the one used in the ledger.

How had it ended up in the ledger—a ledger that Mary Lee had obviously hidden under her desk?

Sam looked at his watch and said, "I've got to go," interrupting my thoughts. He started for the elevator. "It's mah-jongg night."

"Oh, Sam. Sorry. I'm so wrapped up in this, I forget other people have normal lives. You play mah-jongg?"

"Over in Jackson Square, with a bunch of old-timers like me. It's one of my few pleasures now. And it's free."

I felt for the man. We rode the elevator down to the main floor in an awkward silence.

"Thanks for everything, Sam. You've been beyond great."

He tipped his hat. "Keep me posted," he called as he stepped out and headed for the nearest exit.

I waved, then checked my watch. I had only minutes before the museum closed. Tucking the ledger under my arm, I climbed the stairs to the second floor, feeling like a salmon swimming upstream as visitors made their way down.

I hoped my hunch about the murder weapon would prove right. Neither the police nor Brad had found it in the crime scene room. That had got me thinking. How had it been smuggled out of the room? And where had it been hidden?

That's what I was hoping to find out.

I was so deep in thought, I tripped on the top stair step and dropped my purse and the ledger. Cursing under my breath, I gathered up the few items that had tumbled out of my purse—a handful of balloons (I never went anywhere without them), my Pinkerton Detective badge from the party, a couple of promotional "Killer Parties" pens.

Finally, I bent down to retrieve the ledger that had fallen open to the so-called last page. My eye caught on something as it lay in the indirect spotlight. Inside the back cover I could see soft indentations.

Whoever had written in the journal had pressed hard enough to leave impressions on the back page.

I dug in my purse for the only writing tool I had—a "Killer Parties" pen—and began to move the tip over the indentations as lightly as I could. Names began to appear—Wellesley. White. Wilson. Wo—

"The museum is now closed," a voice called over the PA system.

I cursed. I was out of time. I stuffed the pen in my purse, tucked the ledger under my arm, and hurried to the African exhibits. On my way, I pulled out my cell phone and called Brad.

No answer. I hung up and returned the phone to my purse.

The second-floor exhibits were now deserted. Alone in the dimly lit room, I felt a sudden chill and rubbed my arms. Glancing at the security camera, I saw the yellow light, indicating my presence. It gave me little comfort in the room filled with frightful masks, obscene statues, and deadly weapons.

A jumble of dark thoughts fought for attention as I headed for a specific exhibit. Had Jason figured a million in cash was enough and killed Mary Lee after she paid him to ensure her silence? Had Corbin discovered the truth and been so overwhelmed by the news, he'd killed his adoptive mother and father? Had the security guard discovered the motive or incriminating evidence and threatened to expose the killer? Or was he just an innocent bystander, caught up in someone's misguided plan?

And why had the last page been torn from the ledger and all the copies?

"The de Young Museum is now closed," came the announcement again. "Thank you for visiting. We look forward to seeing you again soon. The de Young Museum is now closed . . ." The message repeated several times, then went silent. The security guard on duty would soon be around to whoosh me out.

Time had run out.

I located the case that held the infamous dagger—the one that had been replicated for the murder mystery—and felt like I was right back where I started. Peering into the case, I was still amazed to see how closely the fabricated weapon resembled the authentic one.

Right down to the desiccated blood.

I heard a sound. Footfalls.

The security guard.

There was something odd in the step, a hesitation, and a shiver passed through me. The hairs at the back of my neck stood up like porcupine quills.

It sounded as if someone was trying *not* to make any sound. As if they were sneaking rather than simply walking into the room.

"Hello?" I called. If it was a security guard, surely he would answer.

I listened. The footfalls stopped.

I pulled out my cell phone and tried Brad's number again. No answer. I hung up and slid the phone back into my purse.

Another creak, barely audible. Coming my way and getting closer. The de Young is a maze of adjoining rooms. I tiptoed into the next room, trying not to squeak myself, and searched for a place to hide until the intruder passed. I only needed a few minutes to carry out my plan. And if I was right, my being caught after hours in the museum would not be an issue.

Spotting a camera high on the wall, I ducked behind a large case with a stone base and pulled myself into a tight ball. I held my breath. If the intruder was a security guard, explaining myself at this point, without actual evidence, would be awkward to say the least. And if it wasn't. . . .

I didn't want to think about that.

I listened to the footfalls move across the floor and into the next room. Letting out a breath, I tried to relax my tense muscles. I glanced at the camera. No light. So far, so good. But as soon as I moved, the camera would catch my presence. What did the thieves do in those heist movies? Cut the camera wires? Turn off the electricity? Tape a fake picture over the lens? I wished I'd done a little Internet research on "museum theft," but it was too late for that.

I'd just have to hurry before the security cameras caught me and sent a guard—or worse. I hustled back to the last room and over to the case that held the dagger, watching for cameras as I went.

Odd. The lights on both remained dark. The camera hadn't picked up my movement.

Was something wrong with the security system? Or did they shut the cameras down after hours?

Either way, I couldn't believe my luck.

As I reached the exhibit, I wrapped my arms around the Plexiglas case and tried to lift it. It wouldn't budge. I bent over to examine how it was secured and couldn't find anything obvious, like clamps or bolts or screws. Was it Super-Glued onto the pedestal? Sam had mentioned that the museum wasn't overly concerned about thefts.

I glanced back at the camera. Still dark.

Sweat beaded on my forehead, and I wiped it off with the back of my hand. If I messed up, I'd not only be in trouble, I'd lose all credibility with Detective Melvin. And this was a long shot. Praying I didn't get caught, I pulled out a "Killer Parties" pen from my purse.

I stabbed the pen into the base of the case and tried to pry it open. No luck. I moved around to the other side and noticed a small lock.

Now all I needed was a key, and I'd be able to prove my hunch right—that whoever killed Mary Lee somehow got ahold of the antique weapon, stabbed her with it, and then replaced it with no one the wiser.

Only a handful of people would have had that kind of access. And the name I recognized on the last page was one of them.

"Looking for this?" a voice came from behind.

I spun around and slapped a hand on my chest. "Sam! You scared the crap out of me!"

Sam, still in uniform, dangled a ring of keys in one hand. In the other hand he held some kind of small statue.

My voice grew hoarse as I tried to speak. "I'm so glad to see you! I thought you were gone, playing mah-jongg."

"I figured you might come here," Sam said evenly as he offered his charming smile.

I had to come up with something fast. "You're amazing, Sam. You always seem to know when I need you."

"I have my job to thank for that. I get the run of the place while practically being invisible. Too bad the pay is so low."

I frowned at Sam's words. He sounded friendly, but there was a false note behind his tone. "Are you all right, Sam?"

"I'm fine, Presley." He stuffed the keys in his pocket and lifted the two-foot statue. He slapped it into his other hand, like a cop with a threatening billy club. Only this was no ordinary statue. I immediately recognized the Dogon figure— the grotesque half-man, half-woman artifact he'd shown me when I'd first met him.

He slapped the statue in his palm again, illustrating its obvious heft.

I had to find a way to distract him. "Is that the real statue?"

"The real thing." He exposed a cold smile, and a chill ran down my back.

"Where . . . where did you get it?"

He leaned his head in the direction of an exhibit behind me. The Plexiglas case that held it had been removed and set on the floor.

"What are you doing with it, Sam?" I began backing up until I was stopped by the sharp edge of an exhibit case poking against my spine.

In the flash of an eye, Sam raised the statue and swung it at me.

The corner grazed my temple. The glancing blow knocked me flying.

Blood from the gash in my head ran into my eyes, blinding me.

The room spun around like the Golden Gate Park carousel as I hit the floor.

Chapter 27

PARTY PLANNING TIP #27

If you're trying to uncover the killer at your Murder Mystery Party, strike up a conversation with a suspect, such as "Where were you when the victim was killed?" Or "What's your sign?" You'll gain valuable information that may lead to the truth—or a date.

With the side of my face pressed against the cold marble floor, I forced my eyes open and saw blurred shapes fading in and out of darkness. Nauseated, I pushed myself up to sitting and felt my pounding forehead. My hand touched a slick, sticky gash. The coppery smell of blood stung my nostrils and I gasped for breath.

It took me a second to realize where I was.

And how I got there.

I looked up at a shadowy figure looming over me. He held a heavy-looking object in his hand.

I wiped the blood from my eyes. As my vision cleared, the object came into view.

The Dogon statue.

I almost wet my pants from fear.

"S-Sam . . . ?" I stammered, still not absorbing the truth in front of me.

"Don't get up," he said, almost politely. Underneath his even tone, I sensed a bitter, controlled anger. His eyes glinted in the dim light.

Understanding flooded through me, temporarily blowing away the pain. Sam had just tried to kill me.

"What . . . what are you doing?" I said, half demanding, half pleading. I pressed my hand against my bloody head wound.

"What do you think I'm doing?" he snorted. He slapped the statue into the palm of his other hand.

I had to keep him talking. "Seriously, Sam! Why did you hit me? I thought we were friends." Still woozy, I felt blood trickle from between my fingers and into my eye. I wiped it out with the back of my bloody hand.

"I had to, Presley. Things have already gone too far."

I didn't like the way he said my name. He had always referred to me formally, as Ms. Parker or ma'am.

"Sam, what are you talking about?" I started to push myself up to standing, but Sam kicked my arm out from under me, and I fell back down on my side.

I looked up at him incredulously. It was as if Santa had just turned into Satan.

"First I'm going to finish what I started." He held up the statue. "Then I'm going to return the Dogon to its exhibit case, turn the cameras back on, and wait for one of the other guards to find your body." He spoke evenly, no sign of emotion.

So I was right—the murder weapon was the real dagger.

When Mary Lee had been murdered, Sam must have removed it from its case, used it to stab Mary Lee, then replaced it. He'd no doubt done similar things to Jason and Ed Pike. He'd "borrowed" real artifacts from the exhibits—like the heavy statue he held in his hand?—used them as weapons, and returned them to their proper places, hidden in plain sight, right under our noses.

Sam Wo, the friendly, unassuming head of security at the museum, had murdered three people. Why? At the moment it didn't matter, because it looked like I was next.

Still groggy from the bludgeoning, my head splitting, I tried to think of a way to keep him from finishing the job. Sam was a talker. If I could get him to share his reasoning, it might give me time to think of a way to escape.

I glanced at the cameras. No help there. Sam had obviously disabled them, making sure I wouldn't be rescued by the other security guards. Unless they got suspicious and figured out the cameras had been turned off.

The museum was now closed to the public.

And no one—not even Brad—knew I was here.

Think fast, Presley. This is just like a party foul. Solve the problem.

"So what happened, Sam? Did Mary Lee plan to fire you? You talked about losing everything. Were you about to lose your job?"

"It wasn't you in the beginning, Presley. It was Mary Lee. At least, I thought it was. See, I thought I was making an investment in a sure thing when I invested in Mary Lee's financial plan. She promised my money back tenfold, guaranteed. And knowing Mary Lee's ability to turn stone into gold, I bought into it. It would have been all I needed to retire, take a trip with my wife, pay for my kids' college."

So that was the significance of the names and numbers in that ledger. Mary Lee was keeping a secret account of the money in some kind of investment scheme.

Sam sighed before continuing. "Instead I lost everything. My nest egg. My home. My wife left me. My kids won't speak to me. Hell, I've been sleeping here at the museum for the past few months and eating leftovers from the cafeteria, just to get by." His eyes filled with tears.

"That's awful," I said, trying to sound sympathetic while stalling for time.

"Yeah, well, it gets worse," Sam said, blinking back the tears. "When I found out there was no money coming to me, I confronted the Queen of the Museum. She claimed it wasn't her idea—that her ex-husband had blackmailed her into doing it. I asked Jason about it, and he said she was lying, that she was the mastermind behind it all."

"So you killed her?" I said gently, hoping I didn't trigger an impulse to do the same to me.

He sniffed. "When I found out the investment was bogus and I wouldn't be getting my money back, I wanted revenge, but I didn't have any evidence. So I killed her while she was alone—after everyone had been in but Delicia—and made it look like Delicia'd done it. Made sense, after that fight they had and her wishing Mary Lee was dead. I figured with Mary Lee gone, the scam would be discovered, and then the museum would reimburse me. If not, maybe Corbin would when he inherited everything."

"Why did you kill Jason, then, if Mary Lee was the one who duped you?"

"Because after she was dead, I went through her stuff, hoping to find some of the money. That's when I found the ledger. Trouble was, it wasn't her handwriting. That's when I knew someone else was the real mastermind."

"Jason," I said, breathlessly.

"Jason," he repeated. "He really had been blackmailing her—something having to do with their son is all I knew. When I figured it out from the handwriting, I went to Jason and told him I'd expose him to the cops if I didn't get my money back—or worse, that I'd kill him like I did Mary Lee. But he threatened to tell the police that I'd murdered her—and that he could prove it." Sam gave a short, barking laugh.

"How?" I asked.

"He was at that mystery party you gave the other night. Came dressed in a Sherlock Holmes costume and wore a mask so I wouldn't recognize him. See, I'd made a few threatening calls to Mary Lee about getting my money back, so she told him to come to the party and keep an eye out."

I glanced around surreptitiously as he told his story. I had to find some way to escape this maniac. My leg ached, and my head was throbbing. If I tried to run, I doubted I'd make it very far before he caught up and hit me again. The only thing I spotted that wasn't tied down was my purse, which had gone flying when Sam slugged me. Its contents were strewn all over the floor—and just out of reach.

"But you managed to kill her anyway."

He shrugged, as if killing someone was no big deal. "I had it all planned for that night. I knew about the play and her part in it from seeing the rehearsals. I'd tilted the camera up so it wouldn't record what happened. Then I sneaked into the mural room through the side door, right before your friend Delicia entered."

"With the dagger you'd stolen from its case . . ."

"Yeah, like I said, that one was planned. I disabled the cameras up there, unscrewed the case, removed the dagger, used it on Mary Lee, then replaced it—simple as that. I'd overheard Delicia arguing with Mary Lee and figured she'd be blamed for Mary Lee's death."

I tried to keep a clear head, in spite of my throbbing forehead and the still-trickling blood. Time, I knew, was running out. I had to keep him talking and figure out how to save myself.

"So when you realized you killed the wrong person, you bashed Jason over the head . . ."

Sam slapped the statue into his hand again. "I had to, since he was the one who really masterminded the scheme. I tried to get my money back from him, but he said he'd spent it all. Then he threatened to expose me to the cops. So I called him, told him I had the ledger with all his notations, and told him to meet me in the museum garden later that night—and bring cash. I came up behind him while he stood there, hit him with the Dogon statue, and dragged him to the pond. Once he'd been discovered, it was easy to replace the statue during all the commotion."

"Then why did you give me that list from Mary Lee's locker and let me search her office?"

"I wanted you to think one of the names in the ledger was the murderer—like Tannacito. My name was on the last page, which I removed. And when you wanted to go back to Mary Lee's office, I brought along the ledger and stuck it under the desk while you were searching the filing cabinet. I wanted you to find it. I just didn't figure you'd trace the in-dentations written on the inside cover. And when you did, well. . . ."

The deserted museum suddenly felt like a mausoleum, slowly entombing me. Ghostly shadows from the nearby arti-facts and exhibits sent home the message that I was alone with a calculating murderer. I glanced at a nearby camera, praying it would magically turn on, but the unlit sensor spoke volumes.

Nobody was watching.

I spotted my cell phone a few inches away and tried to reach it with my foot while he rambled on.

Sam caught me looking and kicked the phone away. "Oh no, you don't," he said. "It's time to end this, before you do something really stupid." He raised the statue.

Still lying sideways on the floor, I began to push myself backward and bumped into the base of another exhibit.

Trapped.

Sweat broke out on my forehead.

Reaching down, I pulled off one of my Doc Martens Mary Janes and threw it at him. Those suckers weight a ton.

The shoe bounced off his chin.

Unhurt but startled, Sam blinked. In that split second, ignoring the pain, I scrambled up and made a run for it. Be-fore I could get more than a couple of feet away, he lunged and tackled me. Hard. I slammed back onto the floor, knock-ing the breath out of me.

Sam lay on top of my back. I lifted my head, gasping like a fish out of water, and spotted a few more items from my purse within reach. I grunted, trying to get my breath and get Sam off of me, but his weight kept my lungs from expanding. Finally he pushed himself up, and I sucked in a big breath of air.

I rolled to the side, moaning. Out of the corner of my eye I saw Sam searching around the floor. The statue he'd been holding lay a couple of feet away. He must have dropped it when he tackled me.

As he reached for it, I grabbed the closest thing I could.

My "Killer Parties" promo pen.

Chapter 28

PARTY TIP # 28

If you've been tapped as the murderer at a Murder Mystery Party, try not to look too guilty. Instead, enjoy this opportunity to display your evil side without incurring the consequences.

Sam reared above me. He held the solid statue in both hands, high above his head. His face was a mask of determination, his eyes wide with anticipation, his mouth a grimace. I knew instantly that if he landed the projected blow, it would kill me.

As he began to bring the heavy artifact down, I rolled up to a sitting position, gripped the ballpoint pen in both hands, and clicked the button. With all the strength I had left in me, plus a little adrenaline, I jammed the sharp end into his thigh.

Sam screamed, his howl of pain echoing through the empty room. Doubled over in pain, he released the statue from his grip. I rolled over, just missing being clobbered.

Pushing myself up, the gash in my head thundering and my leg pounding, I stood, using a display case as a crutch. I glanced back to see Sam in a crumpled heap on the floor, gripping his wounded leg. Blood had feathered out on his khaki pant leg around the embedded pen.

My cell phone. In no shape to run, I had to find it and call for help. There was no telling what a desperate, hurting Sam might try next—even with a pen sticking out of his leg. Scanning the floor, I spotted the phone a few feet away and limped over to get it. I pushed the phone icon to reach Brad—his was the last number I'd called—but before I could tap the screen, two uniformed guards appeared out of nowhere.

"Thank God!" I whispered, too exhausted to speak any louder. Feeling dizzy, achy and near collapse, I stuffed my cell phone in my pocket and slumped down on the floor, waiting for the guards to take action.

"What's going on in here?" the tall black woman said, looking back and forth between the two of us.

The other guard, short, Asian, rushed to Sam's side. He gasped when he saw the protruding pen.

Before I could get a word out, Sam yelled, "She stabbed me! The bitch is crazy! She was trying to steal that statue over there!" He pointed to the dropped Dogon he'd used to nearly kill me.

The woman ran over to me. But instead of helping me up, she pulled out a plastic strip that looked like a garbage bag fastener, jerked my hands behind my back, and secured them together with the fastener.

"He's lying!" I croaked in a weak, hoarse voice. "He tried to—"

"Don't listen to her!" Sam screamed. "I caught her breaking into the exhibit. She took that statue and tried to get away." He pointed, then winced in pain.

"No, I wasn't—"

He cut me off. "When I tried to stop her, she stabbed me in the leg. If you two hadn't come when you did, I'd probably be dead. Murdered. Like she murdered Ms. Miller and Ed." He was gasping between words.

"That's not true!" I cried out, as the puzzled guards looked back and forth between us. "He killed Mary Lee. And Jason. And the security guard. If you don't believe me, call Detective Melvin at SFPD. He'll vouch for me." At least, I hoped he would.

"She'll say anything to save herself," Sam said, giving me a sly glance. "Susan, she may have an accomplice. Check the other floors. Then call the police. Mike, help me get this thing out of my leg."

After checking my wrist restraints to be sure they were secure, Susan left the room. I watched helplessly as Mike knelt down to assist Sam. As he leaned over Sam's leg to examine the wound, Sam grabbed the Dogon statue he'd dropped.

"Watch out!" I screamed as Sam swung it at the side of Mike's head.

The guard sagged to the floor. He never knew what hit him.

"Look what you've done," Sam said, puffing. "You've killed another one of my guards. Even tied up like that, you're a murdering menace. You have to be stopped . . ."

Sitting on the floor, my hands tied behind me, I scooted backward.

"Sam, it's too late. They'll never believe I killed him. You're just getting yourself in deeper and deeper."

He inched forward, dragging his wounded leg. His breathing was labored. "Oh, no, Presley. You're the one in too deep. I warned you to stop with my phone calls and messages. I even tried to scare you off through your mother. But instead of planning your next party, you had to snoop around. You planned your own death."

I struggled with the bonds; they cut into my wrists. I knew I didn't have a lot of options, even with an essentially one-legged Sam. With his hands free, he could still kill me before I could get away.

Flight was not an option.

But I still had fight left in me.

Sam pushed himself up using an exhibit for support and limped the few feet that separated us, grimacing with each step. The bloodstain on his pants had spread. In his hand he held the bloody statue.

It would only take one last blow.

And there'd be no one to tell the cops what had happened. Except Sam.

He closed in. I scrambled back until I hit a wall.

Trapped again.

Sam raised the heavy, lethal weapon.

Leaning with my back against the wall, my hands behind me, I waited until he was about to bring the statue down on my head. Then I rolled to one side, kicking out at Sam's wounded leg with my remaining Mary Jane as I turned.

Through my shoe, I could feel the pen dig deeper into his thigh, until it hit bone.

His scream was deafening. He grabbed his leg and crumpled onto the floor.

"Freeze!" a voice called from across the room.

Someone stood in the entryway, shining a flashlight on me. For a moment the light blinded me. I could only tell that there were several others. Reinforcements? The beam swung away, toward Sam. I blinked, clearing my vision, and saw Susan, the security guard. She was flanked by Detective Melvin and Brad Matthews.

Two uniformed cops entered the room, guns drawn.

Susan turned her flashlight back at me and pointed. "That's her! She's the one who killed Ed and the others." She started over toward Sam, lying a few feet away and moaning, but Melvin held her back.

"Stay put," he ordered.

"But—"

"I said, stay put!" Susan stepped back.

Brad rushed over to me while Detective Melvin got on his phone and called for an ambulance.

"Presley!" Brad said, kneeling down beside me. He eased me up to sitting and propped me gently against the wall. Pulling out a pocket knife, he leaned behind me, cut the plastic fastener, and freed my hands.

I rubbed my wrists where the plastic had cut into them. Brad took my arm and helped me stand.

"Are you all right?" He carefully pushed my hair out of my face, revealing the head wound.

"My head hurts," I said. "And my leg."

"We need to get that gash taken care of." He pulled off his T-shirt, folded it, and pressed it against the wound. I held it in place.

"How did you know I was here? Did that security guard call you?" I nodded toward Susan, who stood wide-eyed as she watched the two officers take charge of the scene.

"Nope. Got a pocket call."

"A what?" Feeling dizzy, I thought I misunderstood him.

"Pocket call. Haven't you ever gotten a call on your cell, and when you answer it, you can hear someone talking but they don't seem to be speaking to you? That means they bumped the phone and it dialed the last number automatically."

"You're kidding."

"As a matter of fact, I've gotten several from you."

I blushed. What had he inadvertently heard? The rush of blood to my head made it throb harder. I decided I didn't want to know.

"Yep. At first I thought you had your TV on. But then I recognized your voice. I heard the whole encounter between you and Sam. I called Melvin, and here we are."

Chapter 29

PARTY PLANNING TIP # 29

If you've been selected to play the victim, you may spend most of the evening lying on the floor in an awkward position. Be sure to wear clean underwear and feel free to nod off during the slower parts of the play.

Brad followed the ambulance to the hospital. I'd protested against going—I was sure I was fine—but he and Detective Melvin insisted, and I was too exhausted to argue. If I wanted to fight with these two, I had to be on my game.

Once the ER doctor had checked me, done some tests, stitched and bandaged my head, and given me a bunch of drugs, he gave me permission to leave. Brad waited for me the entire time, and drove me back to my condo. Once inside my home, he made me lie on the couch while he fed the cats (after taking his allergy pills), brewed a latte (for taking my own pills), and whipped up an omelet with whatever he found in my neglected fridge (three eggs, a few wilted spinach leaves, some slightly moldy feta cheese, and a jar of artichoke hearts). It was the best I'd ever tasted in my life.

"So," he said, after clearing the plates and returning with a beer. He lifted my feet, clearing a spot for himself on the couch, and sat down. Gently lifting my legs, he placed them on his lap. "That was another fine mess you got yourself into," he said, misquoting Oliver Hardy.

"Very funny," I said. "What did your brother say about Delicia?"

"He said she's good. Melvin and Andrew got her released while you were in the ER. She's at home, writing her memoirs, no doubt. She's called a couple of times—she wants to see you in the morning. I think she wants to thank you. Or maybe ask what you did with her car."

I grinned and let out a sigh of relief. Thank goodness Dee was free at last. I hoped a few days in the slammer hadn't changed her too much. "Thank your brother for me, will you? You know, I ran into him at the museum gift shop. He was looking at pictures of the artifacts. I thought he was just wasting his time, but I later realized he was onto something—the real dagger—which got me thinking. Anyway, I'd like to thank him in person. Maybe we could all meet for dinner next week?"

"You, me, Andrew and Delicia? You mean, like a double date?"

"Hardly. I have a feeling Dee won't be dating anyone soon. Not after the way Corbin treated her, dropping her like she was Jennifer Aniston. Jerk. He just dated her to irritate his mother. Who turned out not to be his biological mother."

"Poor guy. He was already screwed up. And then to find out after all these years that he's adopted, that his mother's best friend is his real mother . . ."

"I know. No wonder he took off and disappeared for a while, hiding on his dad's boat instead of staying at his own house. I guess he just wanted some time to himself and figured no one would come looking for him there."

"How did they find him?"

"Just good police work. Melvin's no dummy, even though you might not like him. He said the place was a mess of pizza boxes and beer cans. He arranged to have Corbin go to a fancy clinic to get some counseling. Figured he could afford it, since Corbin will inherit Mary Lee's money. Andrew said he's the sole beneficiary."

"I'm just glad he finally turned up. And glad he's getting some help."

Brad took a swig of beer and gently rested the cold bottle on my bruise, soothing the pain. "So how did you figure the murderer was Sam the security guard?"

"Like security guards, party planners spend most of their time behind the scenes, so they often see things others don't," I said, using what I thought was a mysterious Gypsy-like voice.

Brad rolled his eyes.

"Okay, well, first of all, he talked about his financial troubles a lot. Second, he was in the vicinity of all the murders. Third, he knew about the ongoing investigation—"

"Thanks to you, I might add. You told him everything the police were doing."

I made a face. "I thought he could help me if I shared my

information. That's why I told him so much. After all, he was on the inside of the museum and had keys to places I needed to go."

"Loose lips . . . ," he said, then licked the beer off his own loose lips.

I suddenly had an urge to kiss those lips.

"But it was when I finally started to figure out what was on that missing last page and saw his name—Wo—that things started to come together. At first I thought it was the beginning of a name. But when I saw Sam, it all fell into place. Up until then, I didn't even think of connecting him to the murders. But after I thought about it, I realized he had motive, opportunity, and method."

"So he made the phone calls and stole your mom's purse?"

"Yep—apparently wearing a red wig—all to try and intimidate me."

"He slashed your tires on the MINI and cut the brakes in the Smart Car?"

"Apparently, he's quite handy. He also disabled the cameras upstairs, opened the exhibit case, took the weapon, sneaked into the crime scene room, stabbed Mary Lee with the dagger, and then replaced it in the case. He figured it was the perfect place to hide the murder weapon. No wonder the police couldn't find it."

Brad rubbed his chin thoughtfully. I still missed the soul patch. "Obviously he had a key to the side door. He must have locked it after Delicia went in to leave her fake dagger. She was the perfect foil because he'd overheard her say she wished Mary Lee was dead."

Cairo jumped up on my lap, begging for attention. I

smoothed his fur while I pondered the loose ends. "Sam killed Mary Lee because he thought she'd conned him out of all his money. When he realized Jason was the mastermind, he bludgeoned him to death."

Brad downed the rest of his beer and set it on the end table. "And he killed the security guard . . ."

". . . Ed Pike, because Ed must have found out something incriminating," I said, finishing his sentence. "Maybe he saw Sam fooling around with an exhibit case on the monitors or found that last page of the ledger."

"I'm not sure we'll ever know. What I do know is, you were going to be his next victim."

That shut me up for a moment. Brad was right. Sam Wo wanted me out of the way because I was getting too close. And he probably would have killed anyone else who threatened his freedom. Typical of those with extreme OCD who want everything orderly and perfect. But suspecting him of murder wasn't exactly something I could tell from observing his black shoes.

"How did you find the last page of that list?" Brad asked.

"I asked Sam to let me into Mary Lee's office again, figuring since she hid photocopies of the papers in her locker, she might have hid the original somewhere else. But it was Sam who hid the ledger under her desk. He must have done it while I was checking the filing cabinet. He tore out the last page, then planted that note inside about Jason finding out about the adoption so I'd discover it. What Sam didn't realize was, Jason had pressed so hard when he wrote the last page of names that he left an indentation in the cover. An indentation that I traced onto paper."

"How did Sam get hold of the original ledger?"

"He had access to every nook and cranny in the museum. I suppose he went snooping through Mary Lee's stuff when he realized he wasn't getting his money back. He must have found it."

I thought about the chain of events and wondered what was going to happen to Sam after he got out of the hospital. In spite of everything, I felt sorry for him. He'd been pushed to the brink, losing nearly everything dear to him. But I also felt sorry for Corbin, who'd lost his adoptive mother and father. Which reminded me—there was still one piece missing.

"How's the dog?"

"Butch?"

"You're kidding! You can't call him Butch. Mary Lee would roll over in her grave."

"I can't call it Chou-Chou! Yaps all the time. Thinks it can sleep on my bed. Pees every time I walk in the door."

"That means he's excited to see you."

"Yeah, well, like I said. He's a pest."

"So are you going to keep him?"

"Hell, no. I'm going to give it back to Corbin when he gets out of rehab. If he doesn't want it . . ."

"You can't take it to the pound!"

"What, you want it?"

"With my three cats? It wouldn't survive the night. Although maybe we could set up a playdate . . ."

"Yeah, right."

"Actually, I know someone who might take it, if Corbin doesn't."

"Your mom?"

"She can't have pets at the care facility. I was thinking Delicia. It would make a good watchdog, don't you think?"

My cell phone rang. I pulled it out of my purse and answered it.

"Hi, Mom," I said, wondering how much she knew about what had happened. I hesitated to fill her in, but she had a way of finding out stuff through her network of friends.

"Presley, glad I caught you. You know that party you hosted the other night?"

"The mystery event at the museum?"

"Yes. Did you ever find out who murdered Mary Lee?"

"Yes, Mom. . . ." I decided not to give her the full story over the phone. I'd tell her about Sam Wo in person. "Uh, the police have the killer in custody."

"Oh, thank goodness. I was worried they might blame you for it again. Is your friend Denisha out of jail now?"

"It's Delicia, and yes, she's out, thanks to Brad's brother."

"Good. Well, listen. I met a man at that party you hosted— a security guard, I forget his name. Anyway, he's not my type, you know? I wondered if you could let him down easy for me. He seems to be a friend of yours."

"Sure, Mom. I'll take care of it."

"Oh, good, because I met someone else, here at the center, and it turns out his son is looking for a party planner to set up an event for his big high-tech corporation."

Speaking of parties, I needed to call Dan and see if he still wanted me to host his daughter's party at the Wax Museum. I didn't particularly want to work with Dan, but I didn't want to disappoint his daughter. She seemed like she could use some fun.

"That's . . . great, Mom, although I have a couple of other events to prepare . . ."

Ignoring me, she continued excitedly. "And guess what. He wants a séance theme!" The excitement in her voice was palpable. "And you'll never guess where."

Oh boy.

"Where, Mom?"

"The Winchester Mystery House! Won't that be fun? I gave him your card to give to his son and told him you'd be happy to do it. Don't worry—I'll help you out. And we'll think of some good cause to donate part of the profits to. Maybe Save the Pacific Heights Mansions or Bring Back the Sutro Baths."

"Sounds . . . great, Mom. Can we talk about it later? I have a bit of a headache tonight."

"Sure, sweetheart. Get a good night's sleep. We'll start planning tomorrow. I can't wait for you to meet Ramesh. *Namaste!*"

I hung up and sighed. I'd escaped being murdered by Sam Wo, but my mother would be the death of me yet. A séance party at the 160-room Victorian mansion would certainly be a challenge. Every schoolkid in the Bay Area, including my scout troop, had visited the Winchester Mystery House. Rifle heiress—and extremely superstitious—Sarah Winchester had kept construction going for thirty-eight years. At her death, the house held forty bedrooms, forty-seven fireplaces, six kitchens, and dozens of stairs that led nowhere.

Of course it was haunted. By the ghost of Sarah Winchester.

"Was that your mom?" Brad asked, massaging my sore

leg gently with his large hand. His touch felt soothing and exciting at the same time.

I smiled at him.

He stopped, moved my legs off his lap, and stood up.

"I'm taking you to bed," he said, setting down his beer.

"Why? I'm really not that sleepy."

His eyes sparkled, and he gave his infectious half smile. "I know."

How to Host a
Killer Murder Mystery

Party #1: Get a Clue Party

Remember when Mrs. Peacock got caught holding a candlestick in the conservatory? Bring back your favorite childhood mystery game with a Get a Clue Party. Just pull out your magnifying glasses, don your trench coats, and put your heads together to solve an intriguing—and entertaining—mystery based on the board game Clue!

Invitations

Make mysterious invitations by cutting out letters from magazines or using your computer to create a Ransom Note with a fancy font. Add specific details from the board game, such as pictures of the weapons, names of the rooms, and so on (see below for examples). Assign each guest a suspect role, either someone from the Clue game, or a new suspect you've created for the game, set perhaps at Clueless High School, Clueless Corporation, Clueless Hospital, or other site. (See suggestions below.)

What to Wear

After you assign the guests their roles, make costume suggestions for each one. For example, if you set the game at Clueless High School, the characters and costumes might include:

Cafeteria Lady White, dressed in white, with an apron and hairnet

Custodian Green, in a green T-shirt and overalls, sporting a janitor's cap

Coach Mustard, wearing a yellow sports logo shirt, a baseball cap, and a stopwatch

PE Teacher Peacock, dressed in a blue logo T-shirt, short shorts, and a whistle

Principal Plum, in a purple shirt, with glasses and a purple pen

Secretary Scarlett, sporting a red blouse or dress, necklace with a red stone, and red polish

If you have more guests than you have roles, ask the rest to come dressed as detectives or as characters from Clueless High.

Decorations

Cordon off areas in the house or party room and label them like the board game: the Library, Study, Conservatory, Kitchen, Dining Room, Lounge, Billiards Room, Ballroom,

Hall. Or create rooms from your theme, such as a Clueless High School Cafeteria, Principal's Office, Detention Hall, PE Locker Room, Science Lab, Gymnasium, Custodial Closet, and Swimming Pool. Lay out the "body" using a taped body outline and place the weapons on a table in the center of the room. You can use the traditional weapons from the game—a knife, candlestick, revolver, rope, lead pipe, and wrench—or use weapons that work with your Clue theme, such as high-school-related objects:

A Bunsen burner (use a cigarette lighter) for Coach Mustard

A whistle (big plastic one) for PE Teacher Peacock

A cafeteria knife (a plastic knife) for Cafeteria Lady White

A ruler (a large heavy one) for Principal Plum

A (toy) PA mic for Secretary Scarlett

Meat Loaf Surprise (a Play-Doh mixture) for Custodian Green

Games and Activities

Unraveling clues and solving the crime are your jobs as detectives, so put on your game face and see if you can guess whodunit!

Set Up the Crime

First decide who's the victim, such as the Crabby School Bus

Driver, Smart Aleck Student, Pompous Jock, Slutty Cheer-leader, Weird Science Teacher, Dorky Vice Principal, Slacker Crossing Guard, Zealous Narc, and so on. Select enough black cards from a deck of cards to equal the number of players, then replace one of the black cards with a red card, and mix them up. Pass out the cards. The player who gets the red card is the murderer. Tell her to keep this secret. Have each player make up three reasons why they could be guilty and include the motive, the weapon, and the opportunity. For example, the Cafeteria Lady might be guilty because:

1) she's sick and tired of cooking mounds of mashed potatoes (motive)
2) she's always packing a sharp knife (weapon)
3) she has a lot of free time while the potatoes are boiling (opportunity)

Then write down an alibi that prevents her from being the murderer—if she's innocent—such as "I was having an affair with the principal at the time of the murder." Make up one or two clues that help prove your guilt or innocence, such as flirting with the principal in front of the others, then write them on sticky notes and hide them in plain sight in the room.

The Accusations Fly

Give each suspect the weapon that goes with her character. Start introducing yourselves in character, state how you knew the victim, and why you're innocent. If you're the murder, you can stretch the truth but you cannot lie. Have the other guests and detectives ask questions—except they cannot ask directly, "Are you the murderer?" At the end of a timed session, have detectives try to guess whodunit, along with motive, weapon, and opportunity, based on what they've garnered from the statements of the suspects. If no one guesses correctly, continue the game until someone identifies the guilty party.

Refreshments

Serve colorful foods that represent each character and give them a creative name. For example, you might prepare Plum's Plum Jam 'n' Toast, Peacock's Blue Hurricane Blast, Mustard's Mustard Green Salad, Green's Green Beans, White's Mashed Potatoes, and Scarlett's Strawberry dessert.

Favors, Prizes, and Gifts

Send everyone home with a Clue board game, a murder mystery novel (*How to Host a Killer Party*), a copy of *Murder By Death* or *Clue* DVD, a magnifying glass, or a flashlight.

Party Plus

Buy an already prepared mystery game instead of writing your own—although it won't be as much fun! Or order one of my scripted "Library Mysteries" at www.pennywarner. com.

Read on for a sneak preview of
Penny Warner's next Party-Planning Mystery,

HOW TO SURVIVE A KILLER SÉANCE

Coming from Obsidian in March 2011

PARTY PLANNING TIP

*When hosting a Séance Party, be sure to contact an
agreeable spirit who's willing to communicate with
you. There's nothing more frustrating than a tight-
lipped ghost who only mumbles, grunts, or rattles
chains.*

"Condemned!"

I stared at the orange sign that had recently been posted
on the front door of my office barracks on Treasure Island
and skimmed the printed words.

"City of San Francisco . . . Barracks B . . . hereby condemned . . . dilapidated and unsafe, due to contamination
with asbestos, plutonium, radium, and other substances . . .
vacated by the end of the week . . ."

I glanced around looking for the jokester who had graffitied my place of business. Spotting no one, I ripped the
bright orange paper from its staples and got out my key.

That was when I noticed the padlock.

"You're freaking kidding me," I yelled into the early-

morning breeze that swept across the man-made island an-
chored in the San Francisco Bay, once home to the 1938–39
Golden Gate International Exposition, the Pan Am "Flying"
Clipper Ships, and the U.S. Navy. Decades later, when the
Navy had abandoned the island, they left behind crumbling
barracks, empty hangars, and toxic soil. But a few of the fair's
Art Deco buildings remained, along with breathtaking panoramic views of the city and low-rent housing that suited my
budget perfectly. Apparently my yell had frightened a low-
flying seagull passing overheard; he dropped a load of chalky
white poop at my feet, narrowly missing my red Mary Janes.

Where was a crime scene cleaner when you needed one?

Or a breaking-and-entering expert, for that matter?

I heard the screech of tires and spun around. Speak of the
devil. Brad Matthews had just pulled up in his SUV. Brad
and I had officially met when he moved into an empty office
in the barracks building. At the time, I'd thought he was a
burglar, and he'd suspected me of being under the influence
of alcohol. Since that auspicious beginning, we'd become . . .
friends. He saw me standing on the porch and waved. I
waved the orange placard at him.

He sauntered over, looking incredible in his black leather
jacket and black T-shirt with the red embroidered Crime
Scene Cleaners logo and catchphrase: "Our days begins
when yours ends." His hands were stuffed into the pockets of
his well-worn jeans, and there were no bloodstains on his
New Balance Zips. I wished I looked as good in the white
"Easily Distracted by Shiny Objects" T-shirt and jeans I was
wearing. Of course, he looked even better without anything
on. Okay, so we'd become more than "just friends." But I
wasn't ready to call him my "boyfriend" yet.

"Someone pop your balloon this morning?" he asked, obviously noticing my scowl.

I handed over the sign I'd snagged from the barracks door.

As he read it, his smile drooped.

"You're freaking kidding me," he said, only he didn't use the word "freaking."

"That's what I said. How are we supposed to get inside? All my stuff is in there."

Brad gave the notice back to me and sighed. "Well, I'm not too surprised. These barracks should have been condemned a long time ago. They're falling apart—that's why they're so cheap to rent. And they light up like a month-old Christmas tree when there's a match within a mile of the place. Remember that fire we had in the old building?"

How could I forget? I had almost been trapped in it. "But the low rent is the reason I took this place. Where am I going to go now? My Killer Party business isn't exactly turning a profit yet."

"I hear there are a few openings in Building One." Brad glanced in the direction of the Administration Building, also known as Building One. The curved Streamline Moderne–style Art Deco building, erected for the Golden Gate Exposition of 1939, was one of a handful of original structures remaining on the island. Intended as an airport terminal, the building now housed a number of eclectic small businesses, including the Treasure Island Museum, Treasure Island Wines, and the Treasure Island Development Authority.

"I can't afford the rent there! And, besides, how is that place any safer? One big earthquake, and the ground beneath it will liquefy like Jell-O. The whole island is built on landfill, and none of the old buildings was constructed to handle a major jolt."

"That might be a good negotiating point," Brad said. He was taking this condemnation awfully well. "Plus, I know one of the administrators—Marianne. Considering the circumstances, she'll probably give us a deal."

I checked my watch. "Meanwhile, I can't get to my stuff, and I'm late to meet my mother for breakfast. She called this morning saying she had something 'urgent' to talk about."

"She all right?" Brad asked. He and my mother had seemed to hit it off immediately when they first met. I think they talked about me behind my back.

"I hope so. She wouldn't say more. But if she sees something she wants on the shopping network or doesn't like the dessert they're serving at the care center, she calls that 'urgent.'"

"Do you need anything from your office right now?"

"I guess not, but I will soon. And so will Delicia and Berk and Raj and Rocco. . . ." I listed the other corenters, who ran their own small businesses and shared the barracks building with me. They often helped me out with some of my bigger events. Dee dressed up in theme-fitting costumes, Berk videotaped the parties, Raj provided extra security when I need it, and I used Rocco as my caterer.

"I'll get ahold of the housing inspector and see what I can do about getting our stuff. And I'll talk to Marianne. I'm sure she'll give us a deal you can afford. You've been doing well in your party-planning business lately—"

"Event planning," I said, correcting him.

He grinned at my insistence on calling my new career "event planning." I thought it sounded a little less frivolous, especially with a name like Killer Parties.

"Whatever. You must have made some heavy change with that last event you hosted at the museum."

It was true. I'd recently had some high-paying jobs—the mayor's interrupted wedding, the de Young Museum mystery party. Unfortunately, both had become victims of party fouls, which had not only been traumatic for everybody involved, but had nearly cost me my life in both cases. Still, in spite of the sensational headlines in the *San Francisco Chronicle*, people continued to call me for their parties. Apparently guests like a little drama with their bubbly and balloons.

"I have to run," I said to Brad, who already had his cell phone out, ready to call the powers that condemn buildings. "If you get inside, will you let me know? I've got half a dozen requests for events that I have to answer. I'm going to need them to pay my ever-increasing bills."

Brad said, "Hold on," to the person on the other end of the phone, then covered the mouthpiece and nodded toward the paper in my hand. "That's a misdemeanor, you know," he whispered.

"What?" I asked.

"Removing the sign. See the fine print at the bottom?"

Penalty for removal:
$700.00 and or 90 days in jail.

I wadded up the stiff paper and threw it at him, snowball-style. Missed by a mile.

"And that's littering," he called out as I headed for my car. "A hundred-dollar fine and a week of roadside clean-up!"

Ignoring him, I hopped into my red MINI Cooper. When I looked back, Brad was at the barracks door, holding the padlock in his hands. Knowing him, I was sure he wouldn't wait for any official to unlock the building. He'd MacGyver it open himself.

I drove along Avenue of the Palms, up Macalla to the Bay Bridge entrance. It was getting tougher to merge onto the bridge these days, thanks to generally increased traffic and bridge retrofitting. Finally I was able to squeeze in front of a slow-moving truck. I plugged earphones into my iPhone and listened to songs from my mother's day: Frankie Valli, Little Richard, Jerry Lee Lewis, and of course Elvis Presley. Thanks to her, I loved the music of the fifties. By the end of "The Great Pretender" by the Platters, I had arrived in front of the assisted-living facility off Van Ness where my mother currently resided. I parked the MINI in the loading zone and headed for the front door.

Using my passkey, I entered the building and found my mother waiting for me in an upright wing chair by the fireplace. She'd dressed more for a tea party than for breakfast, in a coral sweater set and a floral skirt. Still somewhat old school San Francisco, she never went anywhere without her hair and makeup done. At least she didn't insist on wearing gloves and a hat, like her mother had.

A handful of other residents sat around the "Social Room" at tables or in groups, watching TV, doing crafts and handiwork, playing cards and board games, or idly watching the others from their wheelchairs. Mother was talking animatedly to a handsome silver-haired man in a suit who sat opposite her. She touched his hand every now and then as she made her point, and she laughed flirtatiously after he spoke. Luckily I couldn't hear what they were discussing. Sex, no doubt, knowing my mother. Mother had been something of a party queen in her day, and early-stage Alzheimer's disease hadn't hindered her ability to charm men. She seemed to have a new beau every few weeks.

Mother spotted me and waved; the gentleman stood up and pulled at his suit jacket with one hand, the other falling to his side.

"Presley! You're here!" Mother reached out and pulled me down into a chair next to her. "I want you to meet Stephen Ellington! He's new here, and we're already great friends."

I'll bet, I wanted to say. Instead, I took the high road. "It's nice to meet you, Mr. Ellington." I clasped his cool, papery hand with mine and shook it. One of his blue eyes squinted as he gave a half smile.

"Stephen, this is my daughter, Presley. She's a party planner, just like her mother!"

"Event planner," I corrected her; then by way of explanation, I began rambling. "I used to teach at the university—abnormal psychology—until I was downsized—"

Mother cut me off. "Stephen is joining us for breakfast, dear. I hope you don't mind."

I eyed my mother. She was up to something.

"You said you had something urgent to talk about?" I forced a cordial smile in her direction. "Wouldn't you rather just the two of us—"

She interrupted me again. "Oh no! Stephen is the reason I wanted to see you. We have a very important matter to discuss with you—something I mentioned a few weeks ago, after your party at the museum. Remember?"

Not really, I thought. But I remembered that that party had turned out to be a disaster. "Sure," I said as I headed for the desk in the lobby and signed us out. Stephen held the door as we made our way to the street. "That's my car there," I said to Stephen, pointing to my illegally parked MINI. Sizing up Stephen's tall, lanky frame, I pressed my lips together, then said, "It's going to be tight."

"Dear, why don't you let Stephen drive? Then you can sit in the backseat. You're shorter than he is." I'm five ten, and there was no way I was going to scrunch myself into that tiny backseat. Besides, the old guy probably didn't have a license, and I wasn't about to let some stranger drive my car. Granted, in spite of his age—I guessed him to be in his seventies—and a slight droop on the left side of his mouth when he smiled, his cheeks were a robust color and his eyes twinkled devilishly. I wondered why he was living at the care home.

"I have an idea," I said. "Let's walk. Mel's Drive-In serves breakfast, and it's only a few blocks away."

Mother looked at Stephen, and he nodded.

"Let me move my car so it doesn't get towed," I said.

Mother and Stephen chatted in front of the building while I drove up the street in search of a legal parking place. I managed to squeeze in between a Smart Car and a VW bug; then I locked the car and headed down the hill. Stephen was just closing his cell phone as I approached.

"Shall we?" I said, leading the way to the drive-in turned chain diner. The fifties decor, popular with tourists, featured wall-mounted push-button mini-jukeboxes that I'd loved as a kid. Mother came for the freshly squeezed orange juice, the silver-dollar pancakes, and the crispy bacon. Why the woman didn't have high cholesterol was a mystery to me.

We nestled into a cozy padded booth, me on one side, Mother and her "date" on the other. I ordered a blueberry muffin and strawberries and passed on the coffee—no lattes at Mel's. Mother gave her usual order and Stephen had a three-egg omelet called Herb Caen's Favorite—ham and cheese—and black coffee.

Silence settled over the three of us for a brief moment after the waitress left. It didn't last long, not with my mother. She placed a hand on Stephen's hand, which rested on the table, and looked at me. "So, Presley, we have a job for you! Remember when I mentioned I'd met someone at the center and his son was interested in having a big party?"

Ever since I'd started Killer Parties, my mother had been booking me for parties at the care center. I'd already hosted a Red Hat Party and a Hot Flash Fiesta for her lady friends, but I had put her off when she suggested a Mardi Gras Mixer. Knowing Mother, I had a feeling there would be boob-flashing beads involved.

"Not really?" I said truthfully. "Things were kind of a blur after that party."

"Well, Stephen's son, Jonathan, is president of his own computer company, and he's about to announce an amazing new product. Stephen wants to help Jon promote it by organizing a party for him. Apparently the product is something that could revolutionize the movie business, so the guests would include a bunch of special-effects bigwigs like George Lucas, Phil Tippett, and that guy from CeeGee Studios."

The details sounded vaguely familiar. I looked at Stephen. "Does your son know about your plans?" A few months earlier, I'd hosted a "surprise" wedding event for the mayor, which had backfired because the bride wasn't in on the planning. I didn't relish doing any more surprise parties like that in the near future.

"Oh yes," Stephen said, glancing at my mother, his eyes sparkling. "In fact, he's looking forward to meeting you."

I blinked. This party sounded like it had started without me.

Mother's red-lipsticked smile went into overdrive. "Presley, don't you remember? He wants a séance party!"

"A séance party . . . ," I repeated. Suddenly it was all coming back to me.

"Yes! And he wants to hold it at the Winchester Mystery House!"

Oh God, I thought, feeling a chill run down my back. I thought I'd dreamed that part. I'd visited the hundred-plus-roomed house on a Scouting trip when I was in sixth grade. The mansion, built by Sarah Winchester to appease spirits she suspected of haunting her, was filled with secret passageways, winding hallways, stairs that went nowhere, and rampant ghost sightings. It had scared the crap out of me back then. "I remember," I said, "but why there?"

Mother glanced at Stephen; they both looked like giddy teenagers. "Because Jonathan wants to bring Sarah Winchester back from the dead!"

ALSO AVAILABLE

How to Host a Killer Party
A Party-Planning Mystery

Penny Warner

Presley Parker was just happy to get her party planning business off the ground. Now she's gotten the gig of the year, planning Mayor Davin Green's sumptuous "surprise" wedding for his socialite fiancée, to be held on Alcatraz.

But when the bride is found floating in the bay and the original party planner is found murdered, Presley becomes the prime suspect. If the attractive crime scene cleaner, Brad Matthews, doesn't help her tidy her reputation, she'll be exchanging her formal wear for prison stripes...

Available wherever books are sold or at
penguin.com

S0114